This is a work of fiction. Similarities to real people, places, or events are entirely coincidental.

EMERALD SILVERLOCK: A CRUISE TO ADVENTURE

First edition. July 28, 2024.

Copyright © 2024 Scott Tatt.

ISBN: 979-8227450319

Written by Scott Tatt.

A Cruise To Adventure

By Scott Tatt

Special thanks to everyone who purchased and read my first book. Your support has made this follow-up possible. XXX

Chapter 1: Pure Of Heart

There was nothing on earth that held the kind of beauty of the Norwegian fjords. There were forests of green stretching all around and very few man-made structures to be seen anywhere. The water flowing through the fjords was crystal clear and an example of nature at its finest with so much of it untouched by man. If it weren't for the odd village or town that could be seen here and there, it would be impossible to imagine that any humans actually lived in the fjords. Their pure beauty made them a common tourist attraction for anyone visiting Norway. Cruises through the fjords were especially popular with hundreds of passengers sailing on these giant ships just to experience the sight of the fjords and the gentle pleasure of slowly sailing through them. But there was a group of people in the fjords right now, and they were NOT tourists. They weren't interested in the natural beauty of the fjords or taking holiday pictures. They had other plans.

Barley drove one of the green troll cars that were used to take tourists up to Briksdalsbreen. His squad followed behind him, also in troll cars. They shouldn't have been allowed to do this as tourists weren't allowed to drive the cars. The staff would drive them up the winding pathways that led up into the mountains where the glacier was located. Also the tour was closed for the day, but Barley and his men had generously tipped the workers to look the other way and pretend they hadn't seen them. They were free to go. Three troll cars travelled up the road towards the glacier. They were small, squat looking vehicles with open roofs and yellow wheels. Because of their stocky proportions and small size, they looked more like oversized toys than proper vehicles. Barley and his team felt slightly ridiculous driving or riding in them but they had to do it. They looked like a part of the work force and if anyone happened to ask what they were doing, they'd just say they were taking the cars for a test drive to make sure they were still in good working order ready for tomorrow's tours. As the cars travelled around the bends and climbed up the road, the team were treated to breath-taking views of the lush green forest, low hanging clouds that cast shadows over the trees and stunning waterfalls that roared down the mountainside. However, Barley and his men barely even noticed the beautiful views as he concentrated on their mission ahead. The weather was cold and grey, typical of Norway, and it only got colder the further up the troll cars went. Barley didn't care. He and his team were suited up warmly enough so they barely felt the cold.

The ride was slow and it took them a while to reach their destination. But eventually, the team arrived at the end of the road and left the cars. Barley had eleven men with him and they followed as he led the way to the glacier. The cars only went so far and after reaching their stop, the tourists had to make the rest of their way on foot. They walked up the pathway leading to the glacier, their pace brisk as if to make up for the time they'd lost on their slow ride in the troll cars. They arrived at the famous glacier. Barley's face curled up into a grin of pleasure as he saw the huge mountain up ahead, topped with a layer of snow and ice that had a long white trail snaking down to the bottom. It was like a layer of icing on top of a cake and some of it was dripping down the side. This was Briksdalsbreen, one of the most famous glaciers in the world. Every year, the glacier attracted thousands of tourists who came to see yet another example of Norway's natural beauty. A small glacial lake spread out at the bottom and the water was so clear that every single stone or rock lying in the lake could be seen. It was strange to see the place look so empty for usually hundreds of tourists would be here right now staring at the beautiful glacier and taking photographs of the scenery around them. But the tours were over for today so nobody should be around to bother the squad, essential as they didn't need any nosy tourist poking in on their business. Barley led the team up to the glacier and all twelve men took out some mountain climbing equipment. Using axes and spiked boots, they climbed up the rocks and made their way up the glacier. The team was thankful they were doing this during a summer month as it would've been dark by now had it been any other time of year. It was a hard climb but after a long hour, they made it to their destination. Barley pulled himself up onto a ledge and looked ahead. He grinned with pleasure.

"There you are...just as our tip-off said." the ginger-haired man purred, "Looks like our little hike will be more worthwhile than I thought."

Ahead of him was a huge rusted iron door with ancient symbols decorating the edges of it. A large bird was sculpted into the middle of the door. Barley and his team approached the door and he grabbed the bird sculpture's head. Then with a mighty push, he pulled the head down and the rusty door groaned into life as it suddenly slid open. As the doors slid aside, the bird split in half. A loud rumble shook the men's bones. How long had it been since the door had last opened up? It looked as if nobody had been here in centuries. The entrance lead them into a cave and they found themselves approaching another door. This door was even more rusted than the one outside and there was a huge statue of an angel-like figure guarding the way. It had once been gold, but time and the elements had caused the beautiful colour to become faded, leaving very little of the gold left. It was just as rusty and corroded as the door behind it. Barley nodded. The tip-off had said they would come across this so he wasn't surprised. He turned on the earpiece he wore and spoke into it.

"Draven, this is Barley. We've found the treasure cove our tip-off informed us about." he informed, "We're preparing to go in now."

"Excellent work Barley." came the familiar deep voice of his boss, **"Exercise great caution. There's no telling if the cave might have any unpleasant surprises."**

Barley nodded. Experience had taught him and the hunters to always be careful when entering old caves full of treasure like this.

The hunters were an organization devoted to the protection of mankind. Their idea of protecting mankind meant extermination of any lifeform they perceived as abnormal. Anything that wasn't human or a part of the natural wildlife was considered a danger and had to be killed immediately, even if the creatures themselves might actually be harmless. Recently, the organization had taken quite a blow to their reputation. Draven, the cyborg leader of the hunters, had almost been killed in their last mission and their target, a Luminoid, had evaded their grasp. What was even worse was the fact that it had been a **child** that had nearly killed Draven. He had to be more careful following last time. The fact a mere teenager nearly killed him both angered and frightened him. Although Alice had saved his life and he'd long since recovered from the near fatal injury, an occasional pain in his chest served as a humiliating reminder of how close he'd come to death at a child's hands. Rimor had threatened to spill the beans on the circumstances of his near death if he dared to make another attempt on Ruby's life. Draven was undeterred, still vowing to kill Ruby for the sake of keeping mankind safe. If Rimor tried to tell the truth, he would find some way to spin it in a way that wouldn't sound as humiliating to his superiors. But as luck would have it, he may have found a way to deal with Ruby without needing to kill her at all.

The hunters had many contacts around the world and one of them had managed to find information of some kind of treasure hidden away in the Briksdal glacier. The treasure was said to be some kind of magical item that could grant the user's greatest wish. The Staff of Wishes, it was said to be called. It was supposed to have been used by angels, though Draven doubted that part of the story was true. He already knew what wish he would be making. With the staff in his hands, he could eradicate every supernatural being off the face of the earth and the hunters will have finally succeeded in keeping mankind safe from all supernatural threats. Draven would also make sure to wish that all traces of magic were gone too. Would it make Ruby disappear or would it simply get rid of her protection spell and she'd be normal? Either way suited him just fine.

Draven stood by for further updates as Barley approached the angel statue. The stocky man put a hand to his chin in thought.

"OK...so how do we get past that thing then?" he pondered.

Just as he said that, the angel statue suddenly sprang into life. Its eyes lit up with blood red orbs that glowered down at the hunters. Barley's team flinched and scrambled for their guns. Barley held up a hand, warning them not to fire. He shushed everyone and ordered them to standby. He looked up at the eyes of the angel statue. The eyes stared back into him.

"REVEAL THYSELF." the statue boomed.

A low, rumbling voice echoed all around the cave but the statue's mouth didn't actually move when it spoke.

Barley was unnerved by it, but he kept his cool. The hunters had faced more surreal threats than this.

"My name is Barley and I demand that you allow us into the cave!" he announced, sounding as grand and imposing as he could, "We seek the treasure inside!"

The statue didn't move.

"YOU ARE IMPURE." it boomed again, its voice like a judgemental god.

"Impure?" Barley asked incredulously.

"ONLY THE PURE OF HEART MAY ACCESS THE TREASURE I PROTECT." the statue informed, "NEITHER OF YOU ARE PURE OF HEART. LEAVE THE CAVE NOW OR FACE PUNISHMENT FOR YOUR DISOBEDIENCE."

Draven heard everything and he was astounded. There was a catch to the whole thing?! Why hadn't his informant warned him of this?! He should've known that information on the whereabouts of some hidden treasure was too good to be true! The fact his men were considered "impure" also shook him to his very core. His own men weren't considered pure of heart? And after all the good they'd done for mankind?! Did killing dangerous monsters and evil creatures not mean anything to the statue?! They fought for a noble cause, so how were they impure? If his men weren't pure of heart…then what did that make of him? Draven stepped away from the control console for a minute, stunned silent by the statue's words. Barley waited for Draven to give them orders but none came. He called to him but his boss didn't respond. Draven was deaf to everything around him. Barley huffed to himself. Looks like he would have to handle this! But what should his men do? They couldn't try and blow their way in as they'd only cause an avalanche and get themselves buried alive or killed by a cave-in. Digging their way in was not an option either. But they still had their axes. Maybe they could knock the statue down with them.

"Come on men!" Barley cried defiantly, "We didn't come all this way just to give up at the last minute! If this statue won't move, then we'll MAKE it move! Men, rip that thing off the door!"

He grabbed a pickaxe from his backpack and swung it at the angel statue. Some of his men followed his lead, their axes making a loud clanging sound as they hit the statue. Seconds later, they shattered to pieces. It was as if they'd just turned to glass right there in their hands. The squadron stared in horror at their useless axes. The statue wasn't even dented or scratched. The statue's eyes glowed brighter, becoming pools of fire blazing away in its eye sockets.

"INFIDELS!!!!" it roared, "YOU WERE WARNED AND YOU DEFIED ME ANYWAY! NOW NONE OF YOU WILL LEAVE THIS CAVE ALIVE!"

The very thing that snapped Draven back to reality were the sounds of hideous, bloodcurdling screams from his men as they were disintegrated by searing hot beams of energy that blasted out of the angel's eyes. None of them stood a chance. They were killed before they even had a chance to reach for their guns. The screams eventually died down and everything fell silent. The only noise was the sound of static from his deceased men. Draven switched off his comlink and stepped back in despair. Horror gripped him by the throat. Twelve lives just snuffed out in an instant and he was too slow to respond. He could've saved them! But he'd allowed the statue's words to get to him. Draven shook his head solemnly.

"We'll have to abort the mission. The Staff of Wishes will forever remain beyond our grasp." the cyborg sighed heavily, **"It's hopeless. Where on Earth would we ever find someone who is pure of heart? If even we aren't considered as such, what chance has anyone else got? Even someone who might seem kind and morally sound might have a dark side to them. We'll just have to continue our original mission, do this the hard way as they say..."**

He pressed a button on the control panel and gave the announcement. The mission for the Staff of Wishes was to be aborted immediately and they would be going back to their original plan. It was a terrible shame that a promising tip-off had led to nothing in the end, but Draven knew that that was one of the important rules of life: you never knew unless you tried. And in this case, they'd tried and failed. So it was better to just forget about the staff and continue the mission to kill the abnormal creatures of the world.

After all, how would it even be possible to find someone who was truly pure of heart, especially when the human race was full of selfish, greedy and bigoted people? Nobody was truly pure of heart. Or so Draven believed...

Chapter 2: Life in the Countryside

Emerald Silverlock was enjoying life in her new countryside home. Of the entire Silverlock family, she had become accustomed to the change in scenery and new lifestyle the quickest. It was in her nature to remain sunny and optimistic no matter what changes occurred in life. She even found herself genuinely preferring her new surroundings.

Ever since the incident with the hunters, Rimor had relocated the Silverlock family for their own safety. As far as they knew, Ruby had killed their boss and was going to be their number one target from now on. Rimor had managed to get the hunters to back off by threatening to spread the word on Draven's death, but it was a threat that wasn't guaranteed to work forever, so it was safer to relocate them. Their new home was a large two-storey countryside house that was the width of two houses put together. It was almost like a mansion with the size and amount of rooms it had. There were four bedrooms, one for Annie and Michael and one each for their daughters, a large hall with beautifully polished wooden floors, a kitchen with a nostalgic, rustic interior, a bathroom with a bath big enough for the whole family to sit in and a large garden with plenty of space for the family dog, Wilson, to run around and play in. The garden also held the Silverlock family's favourite thing about moving to the house, a Jacuzzi. They all enjoyed a good soak in there after a busy day, chatting or just relaxing and looking at the stars above. The house was the only sign of civilization for miles. Everywhere else was nothing but countryside, with Galarsfield only faintly visible in the distance. It only took twenty minutes to drive there if they needed to go into town for any reason. Idris had promised the family a comfortable new lifestyle and he'd delivered.

Emerald had made it part of a new routine she'd fallen into ever since moving to the countryside. After breakfast, she would take a basket of apples and seeds with her and feed the local wildlife. Emerald loved animals and being so close to them was one of the main reasons why she was enjoying her new life here so much. She hummed a merry tune to herself as she walked down to a nearby field with the basket hooked around her right arm. Emerald was twelve years old and the definition of innocence. She had a very sunny outlook on life and wanted to be everyone's friend. Her family loved her for her sweet personality and optimistic nature and because she was such a kind and gentle person, it was very hard for anyone to have anything bad to say about her. She was dressed in her usual green tam-o-shanter, hoodie, striped shirt and jogging trousers. The tam-o-shanter was the one item of clothing Emerald was rarely seen without. Ever since she'd gotten it for Christmas from one of her cousins up in Scotland, she'd never stopped wearing it. It had become something of a comfort item for the young girl. She readjusted it, making sure it was perfectly centred on her head as she walked to the field. Just as Emerald had hoped, her regular customers were there again.

Grazing in the field up ahead were two beautiful black horses. They had long manes that blew in the gentle breeze. The horses belonged to someone and were often grazing in this field. It had been easy for Emerald to make friends with them. The first time she'd met the horses, she'd fed them an apple each and since then, she made sure to feed them at least once a week. Of course, she'd needed permission from the owner and he'd agreed, provided Emerald didn't feed them daily, once a week was fine. The horses noticed her coming, their eyes twinkling with excitement. Emerald approached the horses with a sweet smile across her face. The graceful animals trotted up to Emerald. The young girl giggled and held up a hand.

"Whoa, easy there boys! No need to rush me!" she giggled, "I'm here now and I've got you a special treat again."

She tipped the basket and dropped all the apples onto the grass. The horses gobbled them all up greedily. Emerald beamed with pleasure. She'd never get tired of hearing the sounds of horses crunching up apples. One of the horses whinnied in thanks. Emerald patted the horse on the muzzle and then reached up to tickle it behind the ear. The horse nudged her gently.

"You're such a big, beautiful boy! Yes you are!" Emerald simpered, "Ooooh, I wish I could keep you both for myself! But we'd have nowhere to keep you! Besides, you're probably happier out here as you are."

The horse nickered. Emerald stroked its mane and then went over to give the other horse a pat.

"I hope you two are happy as you are." she said softly, "Me and Sapph are doing just fine...but my big sister Ruby, she's still troubled." Emerald lamented softly, "She's started having nightmares again. I wish there was some way I could help her."

The horse nickered as if offering its sympathy to her. Emerald stroked its mane and smiled softly at the animal.

"I'm sure you do want to help you big sweetheart." she said graciously, "But I don't think there's anything you can do, I'm afraid. Still, I appreciate the gesture. Thank you very much. Now I best leave you two be. Do have a good day!"

She waved to the horses and headed on back for home with her basket. As part of her routine, after feeding the horses, she would feed the birds next on her way back. There were plenty of birds that lived in this area and Emerald had made friends with many of them from robins to blue tits to blackbirds and more. She already saw a couple of starlings flying about up ahead. The brunette girl took out a bag of seeds she had also been carrying in the basket and reached in. She grabbed a handful of seeds and scattered them across the forest floor. The starlings heard the scattering seeds and turned around to see what it was. They flew down and immediately pecked up the seeds. Emerald threw some more seeds out.

"Morning little birds! Do enjoy the seeds!" she called out to them.

As she kept scattering seeds everywhere, more and more birds came flying in to peck at them. Soon there were flocks of birds gobbling up as much seeds as they could. Emerald watched the lovely scene with her eyes twinkling with awe. She wanted to spend the rest of her life with mornings like this. Nothing could be a better start to the day then getting to visit and feed the local wildlife.

"At least this is one good thing that came out of what happened back then. I couldn't do this back at the old home." Emerald said brightly.

She watched the birds for ten minutes before walking off again. As she made her way back, she passed a stream and got the pleasure of seeing a family of ducks waddling towards it. Emerald knew the ducks well. She saw them every day and they'd recently hatched a nest of ducklings. She saw the fluffy ducklings waddling after their parents. Emerald was tempted to squeal out loud but she kept herself calm so as not to frighten them. She took her phone out and snapped some pictures instead.

"They are adorable!" Emerald cried to herself, "They're so small and fluffy and...argh, I'm gonna burst if I watch them any longer!"

She watched the ducks go into the stream and swim away before continuing back to the house. Emerald walked in and greeted her mother, father and sister. Annie was sowing a hole in a shirt, Michael was setting up a vase of flowers on the coffee table and Sapphire was reading quietly on the sofa. Wilson was napping in his basket. Sapphire was the middle child and two years older than Emerald. She had blue dyed hair and dressed in a blue hoodie, striped t-shirt and jeans. Sapphire liked to read and ever since moving to the new house, she'd made the sofa her favourite reading spot. The book she was reading was all about Galarsfield history. Emerald had seen her reading it a lot since she'd bought the book last week. Maybe it would tell them something interesting they or their friends at Rimor could research as they continued their supernatural explorations. Annie, Michael and Sapphire looked to Emerald and smiled brightly.

"Hey kiddo, you're back!" Michael said jovially.

"How are the animals today?" Sapphire asked.

"Bright and cheery as usual. And still lovely too." Emerald said happily, "The ducklings have finally hatched. I watched them waddling to the stream with their parents and they look so cute!"

"Aww, we should try and see them ourselves." Annie said with delight, "I do love seeing baby animals."

"As do I!" Emerald squealed.

She looked around curiously.

"Say, where's Ruby?" the girl in green asked, "Is she still not up yet?"

"She's awake." Sapphire replied, "She's just getting ready. She should be down any minute..."

Then right on cue, Ruby came downstairs. The silver-haired girl was dressed up in her usual red shirt, black leather jacket and black leather trousers. Ruby was the oldest of the three sisters and was hoping to become a supernatural explorer. Last month, she'd discovered that she had a protection spell placed on her, but still had no idea on who was behind it. She'd also had a very close call against the hunters which had ended with her plunging a sword into their boss. She believed that she'd killed Draven and was still troubled by it. She'd managed to suppress her trauma for a while thanks to the focus on getting Luna back home, moving house and readjusting to her new status quo. But it wasn't to last. Recently, she'd begun having nightmares about the incident and it was starting to affect her. She looked tired, evidently the result of another nightmare in the night.

Ruby stretched and yawned, looking like she wanted to go back to bed.

"Good morning Ruby." Emerald said kindly, "How are you?"

"Tired." Ruby said bluntly.

"We can see, bless you." Michael said sympathetically.

"You've had another nightmare, haven't you?" Annie asked worriedly.

"Same old." Ruby muttered, rubbing her eyes.

"This really isn't good for you Ruby." Sapphire said, her voice full of concern, "If you're having nightmares this frequently then clearly you're still troubled up there," she pointed to her head, "I think you should see someone and talk about it."

"I don't need anyone, I just need to give it time and I'll get over it." Ruby said dismissively, "I'm sure the nightmares will stop eventually."

"But what if they don't?" Emerald asked worriedly, "What if they keep on going? You'll just get worse and worse. Maybe you should take Sapph's suggestion and..."

"I'm fine, alright?!" Ruby snapped irritably, "I don't need help and I'm sure as hell not seeing a shrink! How the hell can I waltz up there and say "Hey, I killed the leader of some evil organization" and expect them to take me seriously? They'll think I'm crazy and suggest I be locked up in the loony bin and that'll only make me feel worse!"

Emerald recoiled. This was uncharacteristic of Ruby. Ruby NEVER snapped at her like that! She may say she's fine but it was clear she wasn't. Sapphire frowned at Ruby but Michael stepped in before she could say anything.

"Young lady, we will have none of that thank you." he said, his voice firm but calm so as not to agitate Ruby, "There was no need to snap at your sister like that."

"Your father is right Ruby. We understand how hard things are for you right now, but don't take it out on Emerald." Annie concurred.

Ruby sighed and rubbed her head. She glanced apologetically at Emerald.

"Yeah, that was uncalled for." she acknowledged, "I'm sorry Em. I didn't mean to shout."

"Oh that's alright Ruby. I know you didn't mean it." Emerald said kindly, "I understand that you're having a bad time at the moment. But don't worry, we'll get through it together and we'll help you as best as we can. You know we've always got your back, and your front, and your sides and your up and down too!" she added with a giggle.

Ruby smiled and hugged Emerald in gratitude.

"You know just the right things to say little sis." the silver-haired girl said appreciatively, "What would I do without you?"

Annie, Michael and Sapphire awed. It was one thing they loved about Emerald, how she seemed to be able to brighten up anyone's day no matter how they were feeling.

"I'm sure I'll feel better after today's training session with Rimor." Ruby said, trying to sound optimistic.

"You should do, exercise is a handy way to deal with stress after all." Sapphire noted, "I wonder what we'll be doing in today's session."

"We'll probably have another chance to fight against Rimor's agents and see how good we are now." Ruby thought, "Maybe I'll finally be able to get Karim on the floor for a change."

"Funny, I thought you liked it when he pinned you down." Sapphire joked.

"Very funny." Ruby said sarcastically, "In any case, we have to be at our best and show how far we've progressed. I hope the three of us can impress Idris today."

"You'll be brilliant." Michael said reassuringly, "I've watched how well you three have been doing and you're learning so quickly. I think you'll give Rimor a great demonstration of what you've all learned in the past month!"

It was hard not to feel their father's enthusiasm. Ruby and Sapphire were feeling good about today's training and felt they would ace it with flying colours. Emerald wasn't as confident, but she put on a happy face and tried to feel the same enthusiasm as her father did. She was suddenly interrupted as she felt her phone vibrate in her pocket. Emerald had left it on silent so it wouldn't go off and frighten the horses when she visited them earlier. Emerald took out her phone and glanced at the screen. She beamed with pleasure.

"Ah, it's Tony! I best answer him before we go." she said eagerly.

"We've got an hour before it's time to go." Ruby noted, "You've got time for a good chat, although an hour flies by with you two, so keep your eye on the time Em."

Emerald giggled. Ruby knew only too well how long she and Tony could chat together if they were allowed to go uninterrupted. She went upstairs to her room so she could talk privately with Tony. Emerald sat down on her bed as she answered her phone. Her bed was covered with huge pillows and lots of soft toys to cuddle with at bedtime. As Emerald put it, she liked to go to sleep feeling warm and surrounded by hugs. Tony's face appeared on her screen.

"Hi Tony, glad you could call!" Emerald cooed cheerfully.

"Good morning to you my little gem." Tony said jovially, "I hope you're well."

"I'm great, thank you. I've been out to visit the horses and feed the birds as usual and now I'm waiting until it's time to go to Rimor for more training." Emerald informed him.

Tony understood. He was the one person that Emerald had been allowed to talk to about Rimor, under the condition that it was ONLY him she informed and no one else. Tony was only allowed to know since he was close to the family and had been identified as a potential target for kidnapping by the hunters. It had been Ruby's idea to give Tony some protection and so Idris had employed a couple of agents to watch over the Summers family. Not a single attempt had been made on Tony or his family in the past month but the agents still kept their guard up anyway. When Tony had asked about it, Emerald had been the one to explain everything. It had been a lot for the Summers family to take in, but they understood what was happening and had expressed immense gratitude to Rimor for offering to protect them.

Tony Summers was fourteen years old and Emerald's best friend. The two had first met at infant's school together. Emerald had noticed him looking lonely in the playground and offered to be his friend. Tony was grateful for the kind gesture and the two had been close ever since. He also remarked that Emerald's eyes were like "sparkling little gems", which had coined up his endearing nickname of "little gem" that had stuck with them ever since. Emerald liked Tony for his friendly personality and laid back attitude. She often joked that it was like hanging out with a male version of herself. Ruby and Sapphire were betting to see how long it was going to be before they eventually became a couple, much to their embarrassment.

"Ah yes, how's that been going lately?" Tony asked, "Are they teaching you how to kick everyone's butt?"

"Pretty much!" Emerald giggled, "It's going well enough I'd say. Ruby and Sapph are learning quickly but I feel like I'm still lagging behind them. I'm really, really trying to learn how to fight, but I keep getting scared easily and it's holding me back." she lamented, "I try to keep optimistic, but I'm just wondering if I'm too scared and weak to be a proper fighter."

Emerald thought back to her last training session. She'd been perfectly fine punching and kicking at punching bags but when the time came to actually spar with Agent Judy, one of Rimor's top agents, she kept hesitating and getting scared, which had caused her to fail the session. Judy had sternly told her that yes, it was scary getting into a fight but she couldn't let fear get the best of her or else she was dead, simple as that. Emerald swore she'd do better next time, but now her self-doubts were coming back and she wasn't so sure again.

"You're still learning Emerald. You'll get better and I know you'll get braver too." Tony said reassuringly, "You'll be a great fighter and you'll handle those hunters if they ever try to attack you or your sisters."

"I'm glad you're confident in me. I wish I felt the same." Emerald said half-jokingly, "I want to be strong like my sisters are. I don't want to be weak and let them down."

"You can do it little gem." Tony said supportively, "I know it's hard for now, but you'll get better the more you keep trying. My parents always say that nobody gets anywhere by giving up."

"Oh definitely not." Emerald agreed, "And I'm not giving up either, I'll do my very best and impress the people at Rimor today!" she cried, punching the air excitedly.

"With that kind of attitude, I'm sure you will!" Tony chortled.

"I'm glad you called." Emerald said appreciatively, "I think you came in at just the right time to give me a confidence boost."

"Anytime Emerald. You helped me out back at school; it's only fair I help you out now." Tony said kindly.

Emerald felt her heart flutter with appreciation. What did she do to deserve a friend like Tony? She knew that she'd always feel glad to have him in her life.

"I think that's enough about me for now. Let's talk about you." Emerald went on, "How have you been Tony?"

The teen boy fell quiet for a moment. Emerald was alarmed. Was it her imagination or did her friend look...troubled? He looked uneasy about something.

"Tony? Is everything alright?" Emerald asked.

"Oh? It's nothing little gem, I just..." Tony began.

He paused for a moment. He should tell her. He couldn't keep this a secret forever. But he couldn't find it in him to break the news to her, not if it might put her off of her training. He coughed.

"Forget about it. I'm perfectly fine." Tony insisted, "I didn't mean to worry you."

"If there's something wrong Tony, you must tell me, please. I'd hate to think if there's anything bad happening to you." Emerald said concernedly.

"As I said, I'm fine. There's just...things going on at home that I'd rather not get in to." Tony said uneasily, "It's complicated. But you don't have to worry about me. I'm still good."

"Well that's alright. If there's anything you want to talk to me about, just let me know. I'll happily listen." Emerald offered kindly.

"Of course little gem. You've always been a great listener." Tony said brightly, "Now then, for how I've been, I do miss seeing you at school even though I do understand the reason why you and your sisters can't go anymore. I do still hope that you three can return someday. I'm still doing well in art class..."

The conversation carried on with Emerald and Tony talking about what they'd been up to lately and sharing stories about the days they'd had. The time flew as it always did when the pair chatted, and all too soon Emerald heard her sister shouting up the stairs.

"Em! Finish off that phone call! We're ready to go!"

"OK Ruby! I'll be right down!" Emerald called back, "Looks like it's that time Tony. I have to go now. I'll talk to you later!"

"You get going and ace your training little gem." Tony said encouragingly, "You'll be great, I know you will!"

"Thank you!" Emerald said, beaming happily, "Bye Tony. Have a good day!"

"And you Emerald." Tony replied.

Emerald hung up, her face disappearing from Tony's phone screen.

The brunette boy sighed as he put his phone away and ran his hands through his long hair. He felt so guilty for keeping Emerald in the dark like this. He knew he needed to tell her, but just couldn't make himself do it. How could he possibly break the news to her? It would break the poor girl's heart and he couldn't bear that.

"I'm going to have to tell her eventually." Tony thought grimly, "But...what do I even say to her? How can I possibly tell her that I..."

He put a hand over his mouth and tried not to cry as his emotions began to overwhelm him. He swallowed heavily and slumped back in his chair. Tony knew he had to tell Emerald the news eventually, as much as he may not want to. He couldn't even begin to imagine how hard it was going to be for her when he finally did...

Chapter 3: Sparring Session

Michael drove his daughters to the Rimor headquarters, leaving Annie alone to look after Wilson and the house. Ever since the girls had started training with Rimor, it had always been Michael who took them there and he would stay and watch them train, more to keep an eye on them than anything else as despite trusting Rimor, he didn't want to leave his daughters alone with them. He and Annie both agreed it would put them more at ease knowing at least one of them was watching over the girls and making sure Rimor was taking good care of them. Their first training session had been scheduled a week after they'd settled into their new home and Michael hadn't missed a single one since they'd started.

The Silverlock family arrived at the familiar building that housed Rimor's headquarters. From the outside, it looked like an ordinary office block and was part of Hopper International, a company that specialized in insurance and managing finances abroad. Michael, Ruby, Emerald and Sapphire were among the few to know the truth behind it. Hopper International was merely a front, a means to fund Rimor's true activities. The organization specialized in supernatural exploration and unlike the hunters, they wanted to preserve supernatural life, not destroy it and they were in it as a means to enhance the lives of others. They worked with the Cooper family to send home all the supernatural creatures that had wandered into their world. Ruby thought back to her friend Luna the Luminoid. How was she doing now? She still missed her luminous friend but Ruby knew Luna was very happy to be back home and out of harm's way, safe from Draven's hunters. She also wondered how things had been going at Rimor. As far as she knew, no supernatural creatures had been discovered since Luna had been sent home. Rimor likely had days where sometimes lots of things were discovered and sometimes they went days without finding anything. But that wasn't her concern. She and her sisters were here to train, that was all she had to focus on for now.

Michael parked up and followed his daughters into the building. Winston, one of Rimor's agents, was waiting for them. He knew the Silverlock family were coming today and was pleased to see them here right on schedule.

"Good morning Mr. Silverlock." Winston said politely, "You're right on time. Mr. Hopper and his team are ready for your daughters."

"That's great." Michael said jovially, "We can get started straight away."

"Of course. Right this way." Winston replied.

He led them to the lift that took them down to headquarters. Everyone went inside and Winston pressed his thumb against the fingerprint scanner. The lift accepted and it slid slowly down to the floor below the office block. No matter how many times the girls visited this place, it was the same thrilling feeling for them. The lift doors opened and once again, the Silverlock family stepped into a world beyond anything they could imagine. There were the usual display cases full of ancient texts and magical items, old weapons, pieces of alien technology and the many, many scientists employed by Rimor who studied and made readings of anything they could place under a microscope. It was like a playground for the biggest of science enthusiasts and Ruby never got tired of seeing it. For a supernatural explorer like herself, this was just the place for her.

They walked past everything and went into another room. This was the headquarters' own personal gym, the very place all agents went to practice martial arts, fighting techniques and to exercise in order to remain in shape. Ruby's best friend, Karim Hopper, was already in action with his father Idris watching his progress. Karim was sixteen years old and had black hair with a streak of purple down the middle. He and Ruby had been close friends ever since they first met back at Creak Hill School. Karim had also saved Ruby's life when Draven had tried to kill her. Since then, Ruby had found herself even more attached to him than ever. She watched with awe as Karim battled another Rimor agent, the two currently practicing staff fighting. They were wearing protective body armour. Rimor agents had to be skilled in using a variety of weapons for there was no telling what kind of opponents they'd be up against. The family stayed quiet so as not to disturb the lesson. Ruby found it hard not to watch Karim as his muscles flexed with every movement. The agent swung his staff at Karim but he blocked it and pushed back, then lashed out with his staff and took the agent's legs out from under him. The agent crashed down onto the soft gym mat with a grunt. Karim tried to swing the staff down on him but the agent rolled aside and jumped to his feet. He butted Karim in the gut with his staff, winding him and making him double over. Ruby winced, imagining that must've hurt. The agent barged into Karim with his shoulder and knocked him onto his back. Karim swung his legs up in a backwards roll and manoeuvred himself back onto his feet. He stood up again and parried several strikes from his opponent's weapon, then blocked an overhead strike, pushed back and swung the staff into the agent's stomach. The agent coughed and stumbled backwards. Idris held up a hand.

"That's enough!" he called out, "Karim, you're doing excellently. You're so fast now that I can hardly keep up with you!"

"Even I'm impressed how well I'm doing!" Karim panted, wiping his forehead, "I couldn't keep up with Nick when I started and now I'm actually holding my own against him!"

"So true." Idris chuckled, "He certainly didn't get you down on the floor like last time."

Even Nick chuckled at Idris's joke. Idris was the man in charge of Rimor and the Silverlock family were indebted to him for his kindness in helping them pick up their lives again after their encounter with the hunters. Ruby was thankful to him for being the one that led her to the Cooper family and discovering her protection spell. She still hoped to one day work for Rimor as a supernatural explorer and Idris was considering the idea. He'd insisted that Ruby would need to be able to defend herself first as Rimor couldn't take in recruits who couldn't fight. The Hoppers noticed the Silverlocks for the first time and Idris laughed, half-embarrassed that it had taken him so long to notice.

"Oh do excuse me, I didn't realize you were here." he said quickly, "Were you watching this whole time?"

"We only saw the end of it sir." Ruby confirmed, "Karim was pretty amazing out there."

"Oh, I was?" Karim said shyly, "Thanks! I was working my hardest out there so as not to disappoint dad."

"You were like lightning!" Emerald cried excitedly, "I couldn't even see the staff in your hands as you moved!"

"When we eventually get to your level, you'll have to teach us to move like that." Sapphire declared, "I'd love to be able to move that fast with a weapon in hand!"

"You'll move onto weapons training soon enough girls." Idris insisted, "But we still need to finish off with your basic combat training. We'll wait for you while you get changed into your gym outfits."

"What will the girls be doing today?" Michael asked.

"We'll be evaluating their hand-to-hand combat training and see how far they've come." Idris informed, "Agents Paul and Judy are overseeing the lesson. I'm keen to see how far your daughters have come since they started."

He sounded enthusiastic but the girls couldn't help but feel there was a slight edge to his words, like he was subtly challenging them to do their best today or else they'd disappoint him. Karim just smiled at the girls.

"Don't worry about it. I'm confident you three will do great!" he said jovially.

"Ruby and Sapph will, it's me I'm worried about." Emerald said timidly.

She tried to remember Tony's encouraging words from earlier. She wouldn't get scared, she wouldn't cower in front of her opponent, she would be brave and prove she could fight!

The sisters went into the changing rooms and changed into their usual Rimor provided gym uniforms. They all wore the same, a white sports vest, a pair of blue shorts, sports tape they wound around their hands for protection and sleek, sporty trainers. After getting changed, they returned to the gym and took their places on the gym mats. The trio stood together as Idris addressed them. Michael sat on a bench and watched as the lesson began.

"It has been a month since you began training with us." Idris declared, "And so far, I'm quite pleased with your results. Ruby and Sapphire, you've both been learning quite quickly and are shaping up to be potentially strong fighters."

Ruby and Sapphire smiled modestly.

"I'm afraid I cannot say the same for you, Emerald." the Rimor leader said grimly, "You've progressed well at the start, but when it came for the time to actually fight an opponent, you've been unable to fight back. You're too afraid to actually hurt anyone and you cower when someone has to attack you. I understand that not everyone can be brave, but you must also understand that fear will kill you quicker than anything else on the battlefield. You cannot afford to get scared whilst in battle."

"I know sir and I'm very sorry sir." Emerald said meekly, feeling uneasy being singled out like this, "But today will be different, I promise you, I won't be a wimp this time, I'll be able to hold my own like Ruby and Sapph can!"

"Someone's fired up today." Ruby joked.

"Maybe it's because she had that talk with her sweet Tony and she's eager to impress him." Sapphire snickered.

"You're not funny you two." Emerald muttered.

"Please girls, this is no laughing matter." Idris insisted, "You all need to take this seriously if you're to pass. The Cooper family have actually asked me if I think you three are ready to learn magic and I said after today's evaluation, I'd let them know."

The girls were amazed. So if they passed today's lesson, they'd get to learn magic next. Now they **had** to set a good impression! The Coopers had expressed interest in teaching the girls magic to further defend themselves and also give Galarsfield another family of sorcerers to help close up the barriers between worlds. So far, they'd practiced teaching Ruby to close up dimensional barriers but it was still a work-in-progress and they didn't want to teach her or her sisters more advanced magic powers until they'd learned how to fight. There was no good teaching them magic if they couldn't defend themselves adequately. As Howard had taught them: a disciplined body and mind were key ingredients to being a good sorcerer. Ruby felt excited. She'd been keen to become a sorceress and it seemed her chance was just at her fingertips! But...should she want to learn magic? What if she killed anybody with her new powers? Ruby put the thought aside. No, you've been learning how to fight without killing anyone, she told herself, you don't have to worry about that!

"Are you ready girls?" Idris boomed.

"Ready sir!" the girls replied in unison.

"Then Paul, Judy, let's begin the training." Idris announced, stepping aside so his two agents could take over. Nick didn't stick around as he wasn't needed. He left Paul and Judy to run the whole session.

Paul and Judy were Rimor's top agents, responsible for saving more creatures from death at the hunter's hands than any other.

They were always working together and were such close comrades that some agents liked to joke they were dating outside of their work at Rimor. Paul and Judy would neither confirm nor deny those speculations as what they did in their spare time was strictly private. Both of them were in gym uniforms too with Paul wearing tracksuit bottoms and a vest while Judy wore gym trousers and a sports bra. The clothes further emphasized her strong body, graceful figure and wide hips. Paul was in his sixties and yet with his fit, muscular body and the sporty clothes he wore, he looked much younger. The girls had been amazed at how fast he moved when in action despite being as old as he was. Michael lamented that even he probably wouldn't be that fit when he turned sixty.

The session began as normal with the usual warm-up stretches. The girls copied Paul and Judy's movements as they limbered up. The warm-ups were the easy part for them at this point. Sapphire had struggled the most at first, due to being a bit stiff as she didn't exercise as much as Ruby or Emerald did, something she'd chalked up to being a bibliophile who loved reading too much. But even she was easily bending down far enough to tough her toes with little strain. After the stretching exercises, the girls were made to jog around the hall for a few minutes. They were being tested on their speed and stamina. Ruby had found this easy from the start thanks to her basketball lessons. She was effortlessly able to keep the pace and run ahead of her sisters. Emerald and Sapphire weren't as fast but they were getting quicker. Michael could see that the gap between Ruby and her sisters was smaller than last time. At this rate, the three would be running side-by-side together in a week or two. They'd kept their jogging pace up for ten minutes and were hardly out of breath, so they kept going. Idris smiled happily. They were getting faster and keeping it going for longer periods than before. All their previous training was paying off. The girls stopped after fifteen minutes to have a breather and then resumed for another fifteen minutes. After they were done, they were allowed to stop and have a break. The girls sat down on a bench and greedily gulped down bottles of water to rejuvenate themselves.

"You've managed to hit half an hour's worth of jogging girls. Excellent work indeed." Judy said jovially, "Stamina is important in battle and you three are getting good at keeping it going for longer periods of time. I can see you outrunning the hunters with ease."

"I was outrunning them before I even started training, so they'll never catch me as I am now!" Ruby quipped, wiping her forehead.

"I try to avoid saying the word "never" because inevitably enough, it comes back to bite us in the rear." Paul remarked, "For any agent on the field, the hunters always catch us eventually. Still, we're very pleased with your progress so far. Now let's move onto gymnastics..."

Gymnastics saw the girls practicing flips, rolls, punches, kicks and other kinds of martial arts moves. There were punching bags, climbing ropes and a long mat for jumping practice. Ruby most often used the punching bags and the climbing ropes for she wanted to build up her upper body strength. She'd said on their first day of training that she wanted to be able to grapple with her enemies and maybe pin them down so she needed to strengthen her arm muscles. Her biceps flexed and strained as they worked hard to pull her up the rope she climbed. Karim watched her, entranced by how strong his friend looked as she exercised.

She looks so beautiful working out like that, a perfect combination of beauty and strength! he thought to himself.

Emerald and Sapphire found the climbing ropes hard but they excelled on the long jumps. Emerald especially seemed to almost fly through the air with her leaps and she currently set the record for jumping the furthest of the three, which surprised her as the sisters had expected Ruby to be the best jumper due to basketball practice. Paul suspected Emerald being as light as she was likely helped her jump further. Emerald was still unbeaten now. One-by-one the girls practiced the long jump and Emerald still jumped the furthest distance.

"You're like a rabbit when you jump!" Sapphire remarked, "You proper just fling yourself from one spot to the next!"

"Comparing me to a rabbit is the best praise I could ask for." Emerald said gleefully, "I'd love to be as cute and cuddly as a rabbit!"

"Typical Emerald." Ruby joked.

Half an hour later, the girls were given another break. Ruby, Emerald and Sapphire sat down together and refreshed themselves with another drink. It was tiring work but it was necessary for them and they were feeling very good about themselves. They were performing at their best so far and the training was really paying off. They noticed that Idris looked quietly pleased with their performances today. They looked set to pass with flying colours. But they couldn't celebrate yet. Now they were moving on to the real training.

After their rest was over, Paul and Judy called the girls back and they joined the duo back in the middle of the gym. It was finally time for combat training. In preparation, the girls, Paul and Judy were dressed up in protective gear to avoid any injuries. They wore shoulder, elbow and knee pads and helmets. Emerald held her fist over her heart in worry. This was it, this was her chance to prove she could be brave and be a good fighter.

"You three are doing fantastically." Judy announced, standing up straight with her hands behind her back, "But you have to do more than show us how fit you are. We'll be concluding with another session of combat training. Show me, Paul and our boss how well you've learnt to fight. Don't worry about winning or losing, this is only an evaluation of your combat prowess. I will go first and will pick my first opponent."

She paused for a moment, her face neutral so as to give nothing away. Ruby, Emerald and Sapphire held their breath.

"Sapphire, you will go first." Judy suddenly declared.

"M-me?" Sapphire said shyly, "Oh, o-ok then. I must admit, I'm a little startled at that. Oh well, here goes..."

The blue-haired girl took her place on the mat opposite Judy. They adopted a battle-ready stance and waited for Idris to give the signal to go. Judy's stance was relaxed and confident while Sapphire was shaking a little and her face showed her nervousness. It was as clear as night and day the difference between a skilled agent and a trainee. Emerald clasped her hands together while Ruby folded her arms. Emerald looked nervous, but Ruby was confident her sister would do well. Sapphire had adapted surprisingly quickly when learning how to fight. She would do just fine.

"Battle commence!" Idris boomed.

Judy reacted incredibly quickly, moving so fast that all Sapphire saw was a blur whooshing towards her. She was sure even trained athletes didn't move that fast on the word "go"! She reeled back as Judy backhanded her across the face and she stumbled over onto her bottom. Her head swam and she couldn't make out which way was up. Judy shook her head in disappointment.

"Much too slow Sapphire. You need to be much quicker than that if you're going to survive a battle with the hunters or any dangerous creature out there." she muttered.

"That may be true, but I prefer to fight smarter..." Sapphire said as she rubbed the side of her face.

Judy was taken off-guard as Sapphire suddenly lashed out with her feet and kicked her in the ankles. Ruby wasn't surprised at that. Sapphire had said she would be the kind of fighter who used brains over brawn and she was showing it here. By letting Judy land the first hit, she'd lulled her into a false sense of security and left herself wide open for a counter attack. Paul chuckled.

"I thought we trained you better than to fall for obvious tricks like that Judy." he jeered.

Judy looked annoyed but said nothing. She was quietly impressed that Sapphire had gotten the drop on her like that. But it wouldn't be happening again. Judy picked herself up and threw a flat-palmed strike at Sapphire. The blue-haired girl blocked the hit with her arm. Judy smiled, glad to see that Sapphire wasn't slow after all. She threw several punches and Sapphire blocked every one of them. Then Judy tried to roundhouse kick the teen girl in the side but Sapphire anticipated that move as well and blocked with her own leg. Ruby and Emerald were in awe. For a girl who didn't exercise as regularly as them, Sapphire had become very fit and agile in a short amount of time! Sapphire threw a punch at Judy but the top agent bent over backwards to dodge and then struck Sapphire in the gut with a flat-palmed strike. Sapphire doubled over and spluttered but recovered quickly and stepped aside to avoid another punch from Judy. Judy roundhouse kicked again but Sapphire dived to one side, rolled over and jumped back onto her feet. She scythed the air with her hand as she aimed a powerful chop to Judy's shoulder. Judy intercepted and sent Sapphire reeling to one side as she knocked her hand away. Sapphire staggered and Judy then grabbed her with both arms. She grabbed Sapphire in a tight chokehold and held her in place. The blue-haired girl grunted and squirmed in her opponent's grasp but Judy held firm. Her grip was like an iron vice.

"Oh no, Sapph's caught!" Emerald exclaimed.

"Don't panic Em, the fight's not over yet." Ruby insisted, "Let's see if our sister can get out of this one..."

Sapphire already had a plan. Just last week, she and her sisters had been taught the importance of fighting dirty if it meant getting the advantage over their opponents. In the real world, they couldn't afford to "play fair" as the heroes in storybooks or films did. She butted Judy with her head, making her cry out as their training helmets collided. Her grip loosened and Sapphire was able to wriggle free and then trip Judy up. She landed down heavily on her back and coughed. Sapphire then aimed to pin her down but Judy rolled away and picked herself up. She wiped her face and held up a hand to signal a time out. Panting, she wiped her forehead and smiled at Sapphire.

"Excellent work there young lady. You've improved so much since we started and you fought pragmatically, using any advantage you could find to get one over me. You'd make one fine agent of Rimor if you were to join us."

"Oh I don't know about that..." Sapphire said meekly, "I'd be happy just supernatural exploring with Ruby rather than being a Rimor agent. But thank you anyway."

"You were brilliant out there Sapph! Well done!" Ruby congratulated.

"You had Judy on the ropes there! Great work!" Emerald cheered.

"You really did yourself proud out there my girl." Michael said with pride, "Your mum's going to be so thrilled to hear how you did today."

Sapphire blushed with pleasure. With this fight over, Idris set up the next one. He decided that Karim would go next and he let his son pick the next opponent. Despite being in-training himself, Karim had been at it far longer than the girls had, so in Idris's eyes, he was qualified enough to be a training opponent. It was also as much a training exercise for him as it was for the girls. Karim took his place on the mat and he wasted no time picking his opponent. To no one's surprise, he chose Ruby. The silver-haired teen stood opposite him and balled her fists.

"I'll try not to go easy on you just because we're mates." Ruby replied.

"Good. I wouldn't insult your efforts by asking that of you." Karim said agreeably.

Idris gave the signal and both teens leapt into action. Karim was the first to attack, throwing a punch at Ruby's face. Ruby dropped down to the floor and slid just underneath his punch. Then she jumped up behind Karim and rammed him in the back with her shoulder. Karim cried out, more surprised than hurt, and he fell into a forward roll to soften the blow. He stood back up again and blocked a kick from Ruby that was aimed for his shoulder. He knew what Ruby was thinking: a blow to the shoulder can numb the opponent's arm and weaken their punches. He'd learned that same lesson himself. While the kick did nothing, Ruby was undeterred and she followed-up with another punch. Karim dodged and suddenly spun around towards Ruby, driving his elbow into her ribs. The silver-haired teen yelled and Karim followed up with a punch to the stomach. Ruby staggered but she shrugged off the blow and retaliated. She swung her hand in a chopping attack towards Karim's head. But at the last minute, she suddenly hesitated and stopped herself. No, you can't do that, she told herself, you might kill him! Seizing his chance, Karim charged into Ruby and tackled her. Ruby fell to the floor and Karim suddenly grappled with her. He forced her down and pinned her there. Ruby squirmed furiously but Karim wouldn't let her go. He grinned slyly at her.

"You know, you really need to stop letting me pin you down like this." he teased, "One would think you were enjoying it."

Everyone else giggled at the coy remark.

"It's not my fault that you're more experienced than me." Ruby snapped, angry at herself for not following through again.

"I don't think it's just that." Karim said, his voice suddenly serious, "I think you're holding back. You said you weren't going to go easy on me but it still feels like you're not giving it your all. I want you to give me all you've got!"

"I'm not holding back!" Ruby grunted, "What on Earth gave you the idea that I am?"

"You stopped yourself from striking my head just now." Karim noted.

"I was worried I might do serious damage or worse if I did hit you, so I hesitated." Ruby admitted.

"We're wearing protective gear, remember?" Karim reminded her, "You wouldn't have done any damage if you had hit me. And anyway, you can't afford to hesitate in battle Ruby!" he warned her, "You hesitate, you get killed, simple as that. I know you're still troubled about Draven but you need to accept that if you're going to survive out in the real world, sometimes you may need to kill in order to save yourself!"

"Stuff that! Killing should NEVER be an option!" Ruby shouted disagreeably, "There's always other ways to incapacitate your opponent! I don't care what you or Idris or anyone else is trying to teach me, I'm NEVER going to resort to killing!"

"That still shouldn't stop you from going all out." Karim replied, "Even if you're not fighting to kill, you still can't hesitate or else you'll get killed as well. Just maybe readjust your fighting style so you don't have to worry about landing any killer blows, OK? Don't aim for the head, the neck or the chest, just aim for the arms and legs."

Ruby mulled over what Karim had said. He was right, if she was so determined never to kill again then she should adapt her battle style around that. Aim to weaken and bring down opponents and then she wouldn't feel the need to hesitate anymore. While they'd been talking, Michael decided to voice his own concerns to Idris.

"I'm really starting to doubt if this is a good idea." he whispered, "Ruby's still haunted by Draven's death. Is teaching her how to fight and saying she might need to kill really going to help her?"

"We all agreed it was for her own safety." Idris said firmly, "Even Ruby agreed to this. At least with us, she can learn how to fight without killing. I think we'll be helping her greatly."

Michael was still doubtful. Ever since the training had started, Ruby's nightmares had begun. Doing this was likely affecting her mental state negatively rather than positively. But Idris was right on one thing: with Rimor Ruby could learn to avoid accidentally killing anyone even when acting in self-defence again. And Karim had just the advice to help her put her worries to bed. He and Idris watched as Karim let Ruby go and they started over. The rematch went much better this time with Ruby not holding back. As Karim had suggested, she never once aimed for his head, neck or chest as they battled. She only attacked his arms or legs. The two blocked each other's attacks and then Karim swiped towards Ruby's head. Ruby ducked down and suddenly sprang forwards, tackling Karim to the floor. The two teens landed in a heap and grappled with each other, trying to force one another off. Then Idris suddenly called for the fight to stop. Ruby and Karim picked themselves up, panting heavily.

"We got off to a shaky start there Ruby, but you performed much better after taking Karim's advice." the head of Rimor congratulated, "Here at Rimor, we train our agents to fight in many different ways. I'm confident that if you follow our teachings, you'll avoid another incident like with Draven."

"Thank you sir. That's the kind of combatant I want to be." Ruby declared, "The kind who can neutralize, not kill."

"And you're well on your way there my girl." Idris praised, "You're keeping up well with Karim despite being relatively new to this. In another couple of months, you two might end up being equals."

The two teens beamed. They liked the thought of that. Equals on the battlefield fighting together and defeating the hunters! It was quite an inspiring thought.

"OK Emerald, you're up now!" Idris called over to the brunette girl.

"Oh, m-my t-turn now?" Emerald gasped, "Blimey, that was fast! OK, time for me to prove myself!"

Ruby and Sapphire cheered for their younger sibling as she took her place on the mat. Paul was going to be her opponent. The middle-aged man stood before her and cracked his knuckles. He was completely relaxed, looking as if he knew he had this match won before anyone had thrown a punch. Emerald swallowed heavily. Her heart was in her throat and she could feel her palms sweating. She closed her eyes and breathed in and out heavily. Remember Tony's words, she told herself. She could do this! Idris gave the signal to begin and Paul made the first move. The top agent was gone one second and then back again as he seemed to teleport from one spot to the next. Emerald screamed and tried to protect herself but she was too slow to react. Paul caught her with a flat-palmed strike to the face that threw her backwards. Thankfully her helmet protected her from the worst of the blow. Emerald shook her head and retaliated, throwing a punch to Paul's stomach. Paul side-stepped and jabbed her in the ribs with two fingers. Emerald grimaced, winded by the blow. She cried out as Paul aimed to punch her again and she jumped backwards to avoid it.

"You can't afford to get scared Emerald! Remember, give it your all!" Ruby called to her.

"Don't let yourself get intimidated! You can be brave! You can do it!" Sapphire yelled supportively.

Emerald tried to tell herself the same thing but all her mind could focus on was how badly she was doing. She was going to let everybody down! She had to fight back and do better or else she was going to fail! Emerald used this to motivate her next move. She lashed out with a powerful kick aimed for Paul's legs but Paul intercepted and blocked the move. Emerald tried to punch him but he blocked that move too. He barely seemed to feel Emerald's blows. It was like trying to knock down a steel wall to her. She tried several times to land a hit but Paul blocked every one of them.

"If you keep doing the same thing over and over, maybe you'll eventually hit me." Paul said sarcastically, "Your fighting style is too basic, too straightforward little Emerald. You need to follow your sister's examples. Be more creative and be unpredictable."

"I'm trying but as I'm fighting, all I can think about is trying to hit the opponent!" Emerald wailed, "I can't think of anything else!"

"Then don't think about that. Try and focus on other ways you can get around me." Paul encouraged.

Emerald wasn't sure she knew how to do that. She tried once again to punch Paul but he blocked the attack. Then he jabbed Emerald in the gut with his elbow and knocked her down onto the floor. Emerald winced and then stared in horror as Paul came at her again and aimed another punch at her. Emerald curled up into a foetal position and covered her face. Paul stopped his attack. Emerald lay curled up on her side and whimpered loudly. The top agent shook his head sadly.

"That's no good Emerald. If you do that in a real battle with the hunters, you'd be killed instantly." he said grimly, "We may have to try something else with you. You're simply not brave enough to be a fighter."

"I'm sorry, I'm so sorry! Let's go again! I promise I'll do better!" Emerald begged.

"You promised us at the start of the session and yet look how that went." Paul said, unconvinced, "Oh well, we're still learning. Let's go again."

The match began again but the result was the same. No matter how hard Emerald tried to be brave and put up a good fight, she kept getting scared and hesitating. At one point, she even hesitated despite having the opportunity to land a good hit on Paul.

Eventually, Idris had to put a stop to the session. All Emerald was doing was getting herself pummelled and he didn't want her to get hurt any longer. Michael was relieved as it had been getting hard to continuously watch his youngest daughter getting beat up so many times and struggling to fight back. Ruby and Sapphire stared sadly at their sister. They'd been so supportive but it hadn't helped Emerald at all. Idris looked regretful as he gave his evaluation.

"I'm sorry to say Emerald, but you've proven you're still not yet capable of fighting." the head of Rimor said. His tone of voice made it clear he wished he could be saying otherwise, "Ruby and Sapphire pass today's session, but I'm afraid I cannot say the same for you Emerald. Believe me, I was hoping I could say you all passed today."

Emerald sat slumped on her knees in defeat, her face soaked with both sweat and tears. She'd failed completely. Tony's words of encouragement hadn't helped her at all. She sobbed heavily, holding her head in her hands. It wasn't the beating she'd taken that hurt her so much, it was her own sense of failure that felt like the biggest blow to her.

"I'm a failure! I'm too cowardly to be able to fight!" Emerald howled, "I'm nothing but a weak, pathetic coward!"

"Emerald, don't beat yourself up!" Ruby cried, rushing to her sister's side, "It's OK, you're still learning. There's always next time."

"Of course! You can learn from your failures today and turn them into successes next time." Sapphire said encouragingly, "Don't put yourself down like that Em. You've got plenty of room left to grow."

"But what if I never get any better?" Emerald asked, "What if I keep being a wimp and I don't improve? I'm just going to be a weakling and I'll be holding you two back! Maybe I'm not fit to be a fighter!"

Michael came in and gave Emerald a hug. Emerald threw her arms around her father and sobbed into his chest. Her father's strong, gentle arms around her were just what she needed at this moment.

"I know you're feeling very upset about all this Emerald. It's never easy when you've tried so hard to do something and you can't seem to do it." Michael said sympathetically, "You have always been a gentle and loving person, so maybe fighting isn't for you. We should try to find something that is for you instead."

"Of course Mr. Silverlock!" Karim agreed, "There's more than one way to handle yourself than being able to fight! She can still be a valuable member of the team even if she isn't a fighter!"

"I c-can?" Emerald snivelled, wiping her eyes.

"You can." Idris concurred, "Not everyone who works for me is a fighter, yet everyone at Rimor is valued in one way or another. You're no different Emerald. You can still be a valuable team player even if you can't fight like Ruby and Sapphire can. We just have to find something else that's more suitable for you."

A smile spread across his face as he thought this over, "And I'm sure the Cooper family can help you with that..." he declared.

Chapter 4: So You Want To Learn Magic?

Emerald's head was still spinning. Despite failing the training session, Idris was still suggesting she could learn magic too? It was incredible that he had decided on that. She'd been so sure she'd miss out on everything but no, she would still get to join in after all. As Emerald lay in her bed and tried to sleep for the night, she played back the conversation between her and Idris after training had ended.

"How can I still be a valuable member of the team if I can't fight?" she'd asked.

"Quite simple." Idris explained, "The Cooper family can grant you and your sisters magic powers in the forms of colourful gems. You take those gems, they give you powers. I'll let them explain all the details but basically, there's one colour gem that grants you healing powers. You can be a valuable member of the team as a healer rather than a fighter."

"Ah, I get it. It's like in a game of Dungeons and Dragons where you have the combatants and the team healer, right?" Sapphire chimed in.

"Hey, I love playing that too!" Karim said excitedly.

"Yes, you sure do." Idris chortled, "I remember how you'd spend hours in your room playing that with your cousins a few years ago. But yes, it is like that." he continued, "Ruby and Sapphire are the fighters and you can be the healer. We will still teach you how to defend yourself of course, but with my idea, you won't have to feel useless Emerald. Anyone can be a valuable member of a team, even without being able to fight."

"A team healer..." Emerald murmured, her mind in a whirl over what she'd heard.

Of course, that sounded wonderful to her. She didn't want to feel like she was useless so being able to contribute in some way was just what she needed. And being a team healer was perfect! She was a lover rather than a fighter and liked to make people better so how could she say no to such an offer? It was also perfect for she had one big desire in life, and by sheer coincidence, being a healer tied into that. Emerald still remembered how surprised Idris was when she'd told him about it.

"That's perfect for me Mr. Hopper!" she'd said, "I'd love to have healing powers! Wow, it'd be like I've become a magical nurse!"

"I'm glad you're enthusiastic Emerald." Idris said jovially.

"Why wouldn't I be?" Emerald replied, beaming, "I want to be a nurse when I grow up so magical healing powers is perfect for me!"

Idris looked thrown by her reply. Ruby and Sapphire giggled.

"It's true Idris, Emerald may only be twelve, yet she's already got her mind set on what she wants to do in the future."

"Says the girl who sought to be a supernatural explorer before she'd even turned ten." Sapphire joked.

"True." Ruby acknowledged, "In any case, it's perfect for her. Thanks for suggesting it Idris. I think you've just made Emerald's day."

"I didn't want this session to end on a downer for her." the Rimor boss said kindly, "I'm glad I could put a smile back on her face. You'll have to tell me at the next available opportunity how the magic powers go and what you choose to have. And you three won't be alone either..."

He looked to Karim, who just winked at him. The girls didn't need them to say anything, they knew what was being implied from that exchange. So Karim was going to get magic powers too. He'd said that he didn't want to go on adventures with the girls and be powerless against supernatural creatures or mythical monsters that his basic combat skills would have no chance against so he wanted to be part of the team in that capacity. He and Idris had actually decided on that before the girls had started training but they'd agreed to wait until they'd caught up so all four of them could get their powers together.

"So if the Cooper family can grant magic powers to people, why don't they give everyone at Rimor powers?" Ruby had asked, "Wouldn't that make fighting the hunters a lot easier?"

"They're the only family in this country with magic gems and they don't have many left." Idris said grimly, "They'd never be able to give everyone at Rimor a gem. We all agreed it was best they were saved in case of emergencies. Also, we are in possession of magical artefacts so if we ever need magic, we have our own resources to rely on. We just prefer to use gadgets and weapons when fighting the hunters so we don't risk them destroying our finds from over the years. In this case, you children are going to be big targets for the hunters and you're pursuing the supernatural explorer lifestyle, so you need something extra to defend yourselves, hence you kids will be the first in years to be granted those magical gems."

"We are?" Sapphire said in surprise, "Gosh, that long since they last did it, huh? When was the last time they gave anyone magic powers?"

"When Selina turned five." Idris explained, "Before their daughter, Betty and Howard hadn't given a single gem to anyone. For centuries, the Cooper family have only really given the gems to their descendants as the family line continues. They didn't want to hand out gems to other people in fear of making them targets for the hunters. But as you know, we have to make an exception for you all. You three and my son will be the first people outside of the Cooper family to become sorcerers."

That got everyone excited. Talk about a special occasion! They imagined it must feel special for the Cooper family as well. At long last, they got to share their magical gifts with families outside of their own. The Coopers wouldn't be the only magical family in Galarsfield anymore. Emerald shifted in her bed, her head sinking further into the pillows as she tried to get more comfortable. She wasn't sure if she'd be able to sleep tonight. She was too excited just thinking about tomorrow and what she was being offered. A team healer! Healing powers! She'd been tempted to phone Tony about it and let him know but decided not to in the end. It would be best to wait until she got the powers so she could show him. He'd appreciate a live demonstration.

I get to be a different kind of nurse! How exciting is that? Emerald thought to herself, *Tony will be so impressed! I thought I was going to be useless but it seems I won't be after all. I can see it now: we're in a fight and I can heal up anyone who gets injured. And maybe I can use the powers to fight as well so I'll be extra helpful!*

Emerald tossed and turned for hours but just couldn't get to sleep. It was like waiting for Christmas Day to arrive, how could she possibly sleep given what an exciting day lay ahead for her and her sisters tomorrow?

"And now I need the toilet." she sighed, getting out of bed to go for it.

After she was finished, she headed back to her room to try and finally get to sleep. But as Emerald walked past Ruby's bedroom, she could hear noises. Emerald stood outside the door and listened in curiously, wondering if Ruby was as excited about tomorrow as she was. But as Emerald listened in, she quickly realised that it was nothing pleasant. Ruby sounded troubled. She was muttering out loud to herself and sounded very distressed. Emerald gasped, her sister was having another nightmare! She ran into Ruby's room and dashed over to her bed. Ruby was lying there on the bed fidgeting uncontrollably and muttering continuously. Her head was soaked with perspiration.

"No...please...I didn't mean to...I'm so sorry! I'm so sorry!" Ruby whimpered in her sleep.

"Ruby, wake up." Emerald said gently as she tried to shake her sister awake.

"NO!" Ruby shrieked.

She catapulted out of sleep and sat up in her bed. She panted furiously and clutched her pounding chest. Ruby blinked heavily and looked around wildly. She was back in her room. The nightmare had thankfully ended. Ruby sighed heavily and fell back against her pillows. She ran a hand through her hair and groaned.

"Again...I was hoping last night would be the last." the silver-haired teen moaned.

She turned to look at Emerald. Her younger sister was staring at her with frightened eyes.

"Oh...sorry Emerald. Did I wake you?" Ruby asked.

"No, I was already awake." Emerald whispered, "I heard you and came in to see what was wrong. What was it about this time?"

She clutched her big sister's hand for comfort. Ruby stroked Emerald's hands gently to put her at ease.

"Oh nothing, just another nightmare." Ruby said, trying to sound casual to put Emerald's worries to rest, "You don't have to worry about anything, I'm fine."

"No Ruby, you're not fine." Emerald said sternly, "Please, tell me all about it. You won't feel any better by keeping it all to yourself. You must tell someone about it."

"I don't want to. It's too horrible to relive and I don't want to keep you up all night either." Ruby mumbled, "Please Em, just let it go and get back to bed."

"I'll try to, but I've been unable to sleep because of how excited I am about tomorrow, now I won't be able to sleep because I'll be worried about you." Emerald said sadly.

"You don't have anything to worry about, I'm OK. It's over now." Ruby said, trying to sound reassuring, "Just think about tomorrow when we go to the Coopers to get our magic powers, that'll be something more pleasant to put your mind towards."

"OK, if you say so." Emerald said glumly, "But I still think you need to talk about your nightmares. You really will feel much better if you..."

"Look, I appreciate that you're looking out for me Em, but I don't need counselling." Ruby dismissed, "Talking about it won't do anything except make me feel worse so it's best that I just try and forget about it. Now you go back to bed and don't worry about me, I'm fine."

She pulled the covers over her head and sank down into her pillows to make it clear to Emerald she was in no further mood to chat. Emerald felt hurt. She was only trying to help her big sister and she was being brushed off like she didn't matter to her. Ruby never acted this way towards her or Sapphire before the nightmares started. Despite what Ruby believed, she clearly did need counselling as this behaviour wasn't normal for her. Emerald wanted to put her foot down but she worried that she'd only make Ruby angrier. Instead, she patted her on the arm gently.

"OK...goodnight Ruby." she said tenderly.

Then Emerald picked herself up and walked out of Ruby's room to go back to her own. But she was stopped in the hallway by a door opening up and someone peering out to see her. It was Sapphire. Her long hair was in a mess with some strands wrapped around her face. She brushed it aside and blinked, clearly not fully awake yet.

"Em? What is it? Were you talking to someone?" she asked, yawning loudly.

"It was Ruby. She had another nightmare." Emerald explained, "She still won't talk about it and just wants me to leave her alone."

Sapphire shook her head in disapproval.

"That's not good of her. She can't just brush you off like that." the blue-haired girl said grimly, "She needs to talk about it. It's only going to keep gnawing at her if she doesn't let it out eventually."

Emerald nodded agreeably.

"We can worry about that in the morning. We really should get some sleep for tomorrow." Emerald suggested.

"Of course." Sapphire agreed, "Hopefully in the morning, Ruby will be in the mood to chat."

She hugged Emerald to comfort her and silently reassure her everything would be fine. Emerald returned the hug and the two sisters bid each other goodnight. Emerald went back to her room and lay down on her bed to try and get some sleep. Unfortunately, sleep was the last thing she'd be getting tonight...

It was the same sensational feeling for the girls no matter how many times they visited the Cooper family. They came to Harlow's Wood, they went so far into the woods, came across a fake fence that said the area was off limits, passed through the barrier that kept their house hidden from the world and were greeted with the sight of the Cooper family's cottage on the other side. It truly was an example of true magic on display and they could only wonder how the Cooper family had learned how to do it. It must've been difficult learning a spell like this.

After breakfast, Annie had driven the girls down to Harlow's Wood to visit the Cooper family. Michael had to miss out as he couldn't get today off work but the girls had promised to show him their new powers after they got home later today. Winston had driven Karim to the woods. Idris wished he could be there to watch his son be granted magic powers but his duties as head of Rimor meant he had to stay at headquarters and keep things running. Karim had promised to show him his new powers as well. The teens gathered together with Annie and Winston following close behind as they headed to the Cooper's cottage. Sapphire and Karim were refreshed and ready to take on the day while Ruby and Emerald were tired. They both yawned constantly on their walk through the woods. Even their breakfast seemed to do little to rejuvenate them. Annie was worried for her eldest and youngest daughters. They were likely going to struggle today without a goodnight's sleep. Then again, Ruby had been tired yesterday and yet still managed to perform well at training so maybe it would be fine.

The Silverlock family let themselves into the cottage while Winston stayed outside to stand guard. Betty and Howard Cooper were sat together experimenting with some kind of potion. They had glass jars and test tubes full of goodness knows what and all kinds of colourful bubbling liquids giving off some very unusual smells. It was like walking into some kind of whimsical science lab. Betty poured a drop of boiling blue liquid into a jar of green liquid. However, the concoction in the jar fizzed and popped with a loud bang, cracking the glass. Betty recoiled and Howard picked up the cracked jar, dropping it into a bin beside him.

"And that's another one ruined." he sighed, "This recipe's proving harder to master than we thought."

"I bet I over boiled the blue concoction." Betty muttered, "Let's try boiling it for five minutes less and that should make the difference..."

"Excuse me? We're here for the girls and Karim's magic powers." Annie announced shyly, feeling awkward about cutting in like so.

The wizard and witch duo jumped in surprise and looked up from their work.

"Oh we do apologize! We didn't even hear you come in!" Betty exclaimed in her usual jolly yet loud voice, "Don't mind us. We're trying to figure out this recipe for a potion that's supposed to heal broken bones. Unfortunately, it's just breaking our glass jars instead!" she added jokingly.

"Yeah it's...clearly not going well." Annie said, trying to sound polite.

"Where's Selina?" Ruby asked curiously.

"Not home I'm afraid." Howard said grimly, "She decided to go out for the morning."

"That sucks. I thought she would be here to be part of the lesson." Karim said in disappointment.

As they'd been talking, Emerald looked to one side and saw something walking towards her. It was the Cooper family's pet cat Kiki. Ever since meeting the Coopers, Emerald had practically fallen in love with Kiki and could barely put her down whenever she got hold of her. She ran over to Kiki and scooped her up. Kiki meowed softly to her.

"Aww, good morning Kiki!" Emerald cooed affectionately, "How are you my adorable little friend?"

"I'm just peachy, if you stop doing that stupid voice to me every time you see me, I'll be even better." Kiki replied.

Emerald was so shocked that she nearly dropped the cat in alarm. Ruby, Sapphire, Karim and Annie were equally as astonished.

"No way, Kiki can talk now?!" Sapphire exclaimed.

"She IS a sorceress's cat so nobody should be surprised." Ruby noted.

Then all of a sudden, Betty and Howard burst out in hysterical laughter. The girls and Karim soon saw why as Kiki suddenly began to transform in front of their eyes and morphed from a cat to a human. They were now staring at their friend and soon-to-be-mentor in magic, Selina Cooper. They should've expected it! Selina's speciality was shape-shifting so of course she could pretend to be Kiki and fool them so easily! The real Kiki trotted into the room shortly after, giving a cool wink to the Silverlock family that suggested she'd been in on the prank the whole time.

"I'm so sorry, I couldn't keep a straight face after that!" Betty guffawed.

"It's wonderful to see that despite your change in personality, you still have a thing for pranks." Howard chortled.

"They amuse me, and amusement helps me cope with life's problems, so of course I still enjoy my little jokes." Selina said, her face blank and her tone of voice still blunt and emotionless, betraying any sense that these pranks actually amused her. Selina had first met the Silverlock family at school where she'd been masquerading as some ordinary Goth girl before it turned out she was actually a sorceress. She and Karim went back even further, having first met when they were both five years old at the time. Selina was dressed in her usual attire of a black leather jacket, black skirt, black and red leggings and black and red boots but there was a slight difference to her appearance this time. The usual red streak of hair that hung over the left side of her face had been changed to purple. It was something Selina liked to do every few weeks with her hair. Karim was the first to greet her, approaching her with his hand held out to shake.

"Morning Selina. You're looking well today." the teen boy said jovially, "How are you?"

"Ecstatic." Selina said dryly, taking Karim's hand and shaking it, "Mum and dad are just the same. You should've heard them; they could barely stop gobbing about how so exciting it is that we're going to be mentoring new sorcerers and sorceresses for the first time in years. Even I'm quite thrilled that we're going to have some new magic users outside of our family for a change."

"You don't sound very happy about it." Ruby remarked.

"Oh I'm VERY happy. This is my happy face, see?" Selina said sarcastically, pointing to her stoic expression, "Now if we're done chin-wagging, let's get on with it."

She gestured for the teens to wait here while she left the room to fetch something. A couple of minutes later, she returned. The one thing guests weren't allowed to do in the Cooper house was see their storage supplies so Selina had to go and fetch what was needed. She came back holding a box made of finely polished and varnished wood with sparkling gold jewels decorating it. It looked very pretty but the teens knew that what was in the box was going to be more interesting. Selina held the box out, her right hand resting on the lid.

"You four are about to become the first people in literal **centuries** outside of my family to receive this gift." the Goth girl explained, "So before I open this box, you most swear a solemn vow that you won't abuse these powers and you won't flaunt your new abilities to the world. Remember, these powers are being granted to you for defensive purposes only. They're not a means for you to show off and be a complete idiot. You'll only use these powers to fight the hunters and defend yourself against supernatural threats. Understand?"

"Of course we understand!" Karim declared.

"We won't do anything stupid Selina." Sapphire vowed.

"We'll use our new powers only for good, we'll never do anything bad with them!" Emerald insisted, crossing her heart.

"I only want to keep myself and my family safe from danger and protect the creatures of the world from the hunters." Ruby swore, "I will use my powers to do just that."

Selina nodded, believing how sincere the teens were. She knew deep down they could be trusted but had just wanted that extra reassurance.

"Then behold, the source of your new powers..." she said, her voice low and mysterious to make it sound more exciting.

She opened the box. Inside were six sparkling gems about the size of a two pound coin. The gems were all in different colours: red, blue, green, yellow, purple and black and just by looking at them, the teens could feel the power they contained. The light that shone from them was dazzling. Everyone was utterly spellbound at the sight of them, they were the most beautiful things anyone had ever seen.

"My word...they sparkle so marvellously!" Annie exclaimed, "Imagine how nice they'd look in a ring or something..."

"They're so pretty!" Emerald cried, clasping her hands together with glee, "I can tell just by looking at them that they're magical!"

"I can't begin to imagine how old they are." Sapphire whispered, "They must date back centuries!"

"They do." Selina confirmed, "As far back as ancient times, sorcerers and sorceresses would use these gems to grant powers to people. Magic exists, as you know, and always has done since the day the world was formed. It's just that only those who truly embrace magic and want to master its powers and abilities can actually **learn** it. For those who practice magic, you can learn to cast spells and such as you've seen from mum and dad. But with these gems? You are granted magical powers that you can't get from ordinary magic. So when you take these gems, you'll be able to do things that even mum and dad can't do. That's because these gems were mainly used as weapons for magic users to fight with, a weaponized form of magic so to speak."

"How are they formed? Where did you dig them up?" Sapphire asked.

"Sorcerers of the past created them." Selina explained, "They're not found or dug up from anywhere. It's a very complex process and you have to be **exceptionally** skilled in order to create new gems. The reason there are so few left is because thanks to the hunters, there are so few magic users left to create any more and the few that remain never learned the process. Even we don't know how to create more. We've kept them to ourselves for so long because of this and only passed them down from generation to generation with me as the latest one to receive a gem. It'll take a few more generations yet, but eventually we're going to run out and there'll be no gems left to grant magic powers to anyone."

"That's a shame." Ruby said sympathetically, "I hope you're not feeling upset that we're using them up so quickly given there are four of us at once all asking for magic powers."

"Not at all." Selina said softly, "On the contrary, we couldn't be happier. Sure it means we'll run out a little quicker than before but if it means we get to have more magic users than us for a change, it means the gems are getting put to good use and we can have that little bit of extra magic in the world again."

"Does anyone else have those gems or is it just your family?" Annie inquired.

"In the UK, it's just us." Selina answered, "There are other magic users in the world but not all of them have these gems. Given how rare the gems are, of course those magical families aren't willing to share and hand them out willy-nilly. They've got themselves to look after with them."

"What do each of the gems do?" Karim asked, "I imagine each colour has its own power?"

"Got it one, mate." Selina confirmed, "You might have seen it in fiction where powers are dependent on colours and in a way, it's kind of the reality."

She pointed to the gems one by one and informed the teens of their powers.

"The red gem grants fire powers, the blue gem grants ice powers, the yellow gem grants light powers, the green gem grants earth powers, the purple gem grants psychic powers and the black gem, well you've seen for yourself with me. After taking the black gem, I was given the ability to shadow meld, shapeshift, create duplicates and conjure up energy balls."

The teens were impressed. From those six gems, they had all those kinds of powers at their disposal! It was going to be tough to choose which one to have.

"Excuse me, but which gem gives you healing powers?" Emerald asked, putting her hand up, "Idris said you have a gem that does so."

"Oh that's the yellow one." Selina informed, "It's part of it granting light powers. With the yellow gem, you'll be able to heal small injuries, conjure up balls of light and make light constructs you can use for offence or defence. You no doubt want that one."

"I do, I do!" Emerald said eagerly, "I'd love to be the team healer! I'm too much of a scaredy cat to be a fighter so Idris suggested I be the healer instead."

"And he's right to do so." Selina said, her voice becoming softer and more sympathetic, "You seem to be really struggling to learn how to fight well due to your gentle nature. I understand that. My...my late brother was just the same." she said solemnly, "But with the yellow gem, you'll be able to protect yourself and also heal yourself and anyone else who gets hurt. I'd hate it if someone as sweet as you ever got injured or killed out there, so I'll be happy to let you take the yellow gem."

Emerald beamed with pleasure. Annie was awed by Selina's surprisingly kind comments. It wasn't often she said nice things like that. The Goth girl looked to the others.

"How about you three? Any ideas which gem you want?" she asked, "You don't have to decide right away, but I'd advise you not to take too long either. I'd rather all four of you get started at once."

Ruby, Sapphire and Karim thought for a moment as they mulled over their choices.

"Do we only get one choice?" Ruby inquired.

"I'm afraid so." Selina replied, "You can only ever have one gem. Trying to use more than one can result in an implosion of magic that can wear the body out and cause all kinds of horrible side-effects.

And you can't change your mind either. When you take these gems, they're with you for life. You're making a decision that will change your lives forever, so think carefully on your power and whether you even want to take them."

The teens knew that they wanted to do this already, that wasn't anything that needed a long think over. Ruby, Sapphire and Karim thought about their powers. What should they choose? What powers would suit them best? Sapphire was the first to decide.

"I'd like the blue gem please." she offered, "I like the idea of having ice powers. I suppose it'd be useful for keeping us cool when it's hot too."

"I want the purple gem!" Karim cried eagerly, "I think it'd be pretty neat having psychic powers! Imagine me using them to pick the hunters up and shake them like rag dolls!"

"Oh that's a funny image right there!" Ruby laughed, "Now for me..."

She looked to the gems and pursed her lips with thought. Yellow, blue and purple had already been taken so that left her to pick between the red, green and black gems. She didn't want the same powers as Selina as she wanted to forge her own identity as a sorceress. She also imagined Selina wouldn't be amused if it seemed she was copying her. So that left just the fire and green gems. Ruby knew she wanted magic powers...but should she take any of the gems? She thought back to Draven's death again. If she had powers, she'd only be in a position where she could potentially kill someone again. She had a horrible image in her head of herself accidentally burning someone to death or crushing someone with the earth. But she had the Coopers to mentor her and teach her to use these powers safely. Ruby would be in good hands and could learn how to use these powers without killing anyone. And maybe there was a way to use the powers without being a risk to anyone's safety.

"I probably sound dumb for asking Selina, but if we get these powers, is there a way to use them without...you know, killing anyone?" Ruby asked.

Selina didn't even blink at the question. If anything, she looked as if she was expecting Ruby to ask that.

"You don't want another incident like with Draven." she acknowledged, "Thankfully, you're in luck Ruby. You can indeed use these powers without killing anyone. Anyone who uses these powers is in complete control over how they use them. The ancient sorcerers of the past thought about that when creating the gems in the first place. If you want to kill, you can do so, but if you don't want to kill then you can use them in non-lethal ways. Even the red gem allows you to control whether your flames actually burn anyone alive or not."

"Oh awesome! That's just what I wanted to hear!" Ruby said gleefully, "In that case, I'll go with the red gem. I guess fire powers are the most fitting for me given my fiery passion for what I do and all." she said thoughtfully.

"No, I'd say it's more fitting because of your hot-headed, reckless and stubborn nature." Selina retorted.

Ruby frowned but said nothing. She knew Selina was right on those points.

"Come on Selina, be nice." Sapphire said sternly, "We don't need personal comments like that."

Selina nodded, finding Sapphire's comment to be fair.

"So we're OK with all our choices then?" Selina asked, "You definitely want the gems you've picked?"

"Yes." the teens all said in unison.

They held out their hands, ready to receive them. But before Selina could do so, Annie cut in. She gathered the children together for a quick moment.

"I must confess, I'm a little worried how things may go for you all once you get magic powers." she said anxiously, "The fact it's for life is quite scary in my opinion. Once you gain these powers, there's no going back. I...I just want you to be sure this is definitely what you want."

"It is mum." Ruby insisted, "We need to be able to fight the hunters and protect ourselves on our adventures. It's not just that we want to do this, it's that we **need** to as well."

"Me and dad already talked it over Mrs. Silverlock." Karim informed, "Both me and him are fully onboard with this. I know it'll be strange and might be scary at first, but it's for the best, not just for me but for your daughters too. You can at least feel better knowing they can protect themselves now, can't you?"

Annie nodded. She and Michael had more or less said the same thing when talking about it together.

"Then by all means, go right ahead." Annie urged, "I really couldn't be prouder of you all for making such a big decision like this and willing to go ahead with it."

The children smiled in appreciation. They turned back to Selina and held out their hands.

"We're ready." Ruby declared.

Selina picked out the gems and placed them on their right hands. Ruby was given red, Emerald was given yellow, Sapphire was given blue and Karim was given purple. The green and black gems would have to wait before getting their owners. The gems sat perfectly in the middle of their palms. Ruby, Emerald, Sapphire and Karim stayed still as they waited for something else to happen. Selina stepped back and nodded to Betty and Howard. They stood up from their potions experiment and approached the teens. Then they held out their own hands and began to chant the spell that would bind the gems to their new owners. Both Betty and Howard murmured strange words that nobody had ever heard before. Then all at once, the gems began to glow even brighter than before. A huge breeze swept around the room as if a tornado was starting to build up. Ruby, Emerald, Sapphire and Karim gasped and screwed their eyes shut as the light was too intense to look at. Their hair blew about wildly in the wind. They felt as if they were about to be whisked off their feet. Then the gems started to sink down into their palms. A huge burning sensation spread from their hands all the way up their arms and to their shoulders. They clutched their wrists. They couldn't close their right hands or even move them. It was beginning to feel painful and they cried out loud. Annie put her hands to her mouth in horror but Selina held up a hand before she could say anything.

"Don't panic, that's completely normal, they'll be fine once the process is over!" she shouted over the noise of the wind.

"I sure hope so!" Ruby shouted, "I feel like my hand's about to explode!"

But just as she said that, the process began to simmer down. The burning began to grow fainter and fainter, the pain stopped and the wind stopped blowing. Then finally, the glowing died down and everything returned to normal. The teens panted, overwhelmed by what had just happened. They felt drained, almost like the gems had taken away their energy instead of given them something new. They collapsed onto the floor and clutched their hands. They sat side-by-side catching their breath. Annie knelt down behind them.

"Are you alright children?" she asked.

"A bit shocked, but I think we're alright." Ruby puffed, wiping her forehead.

"Is it like this with anyone who takes those gems?" Sapphire said, her voice hoarse, "That was surprisingly intense!"

"It's completely normal dear." Betty informed, "What you felt was the gem's energy as it sank down into your hands. Once your body and the gem's energy become one, you'll feel much better. It was like that for Selina as well when she chose the black gem."

"I'm sure it was worth it for the powers we now have." Karim said breathlessly, "So how do they work?"

"We'll give you five minutes to recover, then you can join us out in the back for a practice session." Howard replied, "We'll teach you everything about how the powers work and how to activate them."

"I bet we'll have lots of fun!" Emerald said eagerly, "I can't believe it, we're all sorcerers now!"

"Quite so." Ruby concurred, "Oh those hunters are in for a surprise if they ever come for us again!"

"I must admit, even I'm keen to see their faces once they see what you kids can do now." Annie said deviously. She'd been held hostage by them before so this would be sweet catharsis for her if it ever happened.

Once the five minutes was up, the kids followed the Coopers outside. They had the gems, now they had to learn how to use their new powers. Their first day of magic training was about to begin...

Chapter 5: Magic Training

The teens stood in a line out in the back of the Cooper family's cottage. They had no back garden, just the open space of Harlow's Wood to go out in. Everyone had plenty of space to practice in. The barrier that hid their cottage from view would also prevent anyone from seeing them practice as it expanded out behind the cottage. Nobody would ever know that anyone was there and training to use magic. As everyone took their places, something strange began to happen. Ruby wiped at her forehead as out of nowhere, she started sweating heavily. Sapphire hugged herself and shivered as if she was standing out in the snow. Karim felt as if his head had somehow grown two sizes and it was beginning to throb slightly. Emerald was completely fine, even seeming to feel much happier and newly rejuvenated than before.

"Whew, is this a side effect of the gems or something?" Ruby puffed, "I'm feeling a sudden hot flush here."

"And it's g-gotten a b-bit cold for me." Sapphire shivered.

"I feel fine!" Emerald said brightly, "I feel as if everything is fine with the world and like nothing can make me mad or sad or anything negative."

"At least you're OK." Karim muttered, massaging his temples, "My head's suddenly throbbing. Is this normal Selina?"

"Completely." Selina informed, "Your bodies are still adjusting to the new energies you have in you now you've accepted the gems. You feel the side-effects but they'll quickly wear off. It was the same for me. When I first got my black gem, I suddenly felt as if someone had walked over my grave..." she murmured, shuddering, "At least neither of you will feel that."

"I agree." Annie said grimly, "That sounds most unpleasant. Luckily for you all, this is all normal and they won't last long. So is there anywhere I can watch safely? I wouldn't want to get caught up in their practices."

"You can watch from inside the cottage love." Betty suggested, "The cottage is protected from the powers of these gems so if their powers go astray, you won't have to worry about any damage being done. You'll be safer in there."

"Excellent." Annie said happily, "OK my girls, you listen very carefully to the Coopers and do everything they say. They're the experts on how this stuff works." she said sternly, "And good luck to you all."

"Thanks mum. We'll do our very best." Ruby declared.

"We'll be the best students they've ever had!" Emerald cried excitedly.

"Funny, I kinda told dad the same thing." Karim chuckled.

Annie went back in the cottage and stood by the window to watch the children train. The Cooper family stood before the children and began the lesson. As they talked, the teens felt their bodies slowly returning to normal, the side effects beginning to fade away. Ruby and Sapphire sighed with relief as their body temperatures returned to normal and Karim felt as if a weight had been lifted off him after the headache disappeared.

"Now the first rule of magic is how you use it." Betty explained, "The way we Coopers summarize it, magic is essentially turning one's thoughts into power. Might be an overly simplistic way to put it, but its how it is. You want to turn a cat into a dog or make a human grow about twenty feet in height? You learn a magic spell and make it happen! Easy-peasy!"

"But in this case, you're not learning spells, you're learning how to use weapons." Howard went on, "The same principle applies: if you want to conjure up balls of fire to throw at the enemy? You think it up and you make it happen. Same goes for conjuring up icicles or balls of light or simply moving objects with your mind. Your body and mind have to work in tandem with each other to activate your powers."

"That makes sense." Sapphire agreed, "If we can think up what we want to do but can't make ourselves do it, the whole thing becomes a mess. So we turn our thoughts into power..."

"So, if I think of a shield to protect myself, I can make it happen?" Emerald asked.

"Not without proper training of course, but essentially yes, you can." Betty confirmed, "But let's not get ahead of ourselves, we have to start from the beginning. First, you have to know what abilities are available to you for now."

Selina took over for explanations.

"I already explained what the yellow gem does to Emerald, so I just have to cover you three." she said, looking to Ruby, Sapphire and Karim, "Ruby, with the red gem you can shoot flames from your hands, make flaming swords and create fire tornadoes. And as a reminder, you control whether the flames burn or not, so remember that when you're fighting. Sapphire, with the blue gem you can form ice weapons either around your hands or simply to hold, shoot ice shards from your hands and freeze with a flick of your fingers. Karim, with the purple gem you can use telekinesis and form small psychic barriers for defence that can also make your punches more powerful."

"Wow, we can do all that already? That's neat!" Karim cried excitedly.

"Not so fast Karim, we have to learn how to do those things first." Ruby cut in, "We're new to this so we won't be able to do all that straight away."

"Correct." Selina confirmed, "But we'll work our way gradually through the process. First, the warm-up. Anyone who gets the gems has to go through this before being able to do anything. Hold out your hands and concentrate very hard for a minute. Think about forming something in the palms of your hands. If you can do so, then your body and mind are in sync and you're ready to begin."

"I imagine it has to be in relation to our powers." Sapphire deduced, "So like, I have to form an icicle and Ruby has to form a fireball and so on?"

"Yes dear." Betty confirmed, "Don't worry if it takes a few tries. It doesn't take long to master it and even if you need a few tries more than others, you'll get there."

"OK then, let's give it a go!" Emerald said excitedly.

"As they said everyone, close your eyes and concentrate." Ruby reiterated, "Turn our thoughts into power..."

"Exactly Ruby." Howard concurred, "Let's see if you can do it."

The teens closed their eyes and held out their hands. They stayed completely still and made no sound. The only thing they could hear was the gentle forest breeze around them. The Coopers watched them silently, daring not to disturb them. Ruby, Emerald, Sapphire and Karim put all their thoughts towards making something appear in their hands. It was like they were trying to push all other thoughts out of their minds except the one they were trying to visualise. A minute passed but nothing happened. They kept calm and focused. As Betty said, they might not be able to do anything straight away and would have to try again, so they weren't to worry. They kept it going for another minute. Then suddenly, Ruby could feel a rush of warm energy building up inside her, like someone had turned up the thermostat. Nothing was appearing in her hands but she was sure this was the first step towards it. The warmth inside her had to mean something. Shortly after, Emerald began to feel some kind of energy building up inside her as well. It was as if a heavenly aura was being formed in her very heart. It made her feel warm and content. Sapphire felt a sudden chill spread from her toes and all the way up to her head. Karim felt as if he was suddenly lighter than air, almost like he could float away any minute.

"I...I can feel the fires burning within me!" Ruby exclaimed, "Anyone else feeling something too?"

"Yeah, I do!" Emerald cried.

"It's not like our side-effects earlier. This feels stronger...more controlled somehow." Sapphire murmured.

"It's kinda trippy!" Karim said nervously.

"Don't get excited children." Howard warned, "That feeling you have means the magic is flowing through you. You and the gems are becoming one. Don't lose concentration now. Keep focused and you'll pass the test."

The teens followed Howard's advice and kept their focus on their powers. They tried to ignore everything else, even the strange feelings building up inside them and the feel of the forest breeze brushing over. For a couple of minutes, nothing else happened. All they had were the feeling of the gems' power inside of them but nothing manifesting itself physically. The Coopers wondered if they'd even be able to use the gems at all. It had been centuries since they'd been handed to anyone who wasn't part of a magical family like themselves so this might not even work. And then, it happened. The Coopers gasped as all of a sudden, a ball of fire appeared in Ruby's hands. They expected Ruby would get there first as silver-haired humans had stronger connections to magic than others, but it was still both surprising yet rewarding to see her pull it off. Ruby opened her eyes and gasped in amazement at the fireball in her hands. It felt warm and comforting to her and it didn't burn her at all. Her face lit up with excitement.

"Hey everybody, look at this! I did it, I did it! Look!" Ruby screeched ecstatically.

Emerald, Sapphire and Karim opened their eyes and stared at Ruby's hands in astonishment. The proof was right there in her palms, an actual ball of flames blazing away and dancing about as if sharing her excitement.

"Wow, that's so incredible!" Karim exclaimed, "Look at you, you pulled it off!"

"How does it feel?" Emerald asked, "It doesn't hurt, does it?"

"Not at all." Ruby confirmed, "It feels lovely honestly. At least I won't ever get cold in winter again!" she joked.

"Yeah, you'd warm us all up in no time." Sapphire agreed, "Well, you got there first Ruby. Now it's just the rest of us to go. No doubt we have to start again since you broke our concentration." she lamented.

"Ah, sorry." Ruby said sheepishly, closing her hands to snuff out the flame.

"No, it's quite alright." Howard cut in, "You three won't have to "start again", it gets much easier to do it the second time so you'll quickly get back to where you were before. Now let's go again."

"While you three do that, you come with me Ruby." Selina ordered, "You've passed the warm-up, so we may as well get you started on using your new powers."

"Have fun!" Emerald said sweetly.

Ruby smiled with awe. She often wondered how she'd ever live without Emerald's sunny demeanour to brighten up any situation. Selina led Ruby to another part of the forest, leaving Emerald, Sapphire and Karim to continue with the warm-up. Now the two teens were alone, Selina directed Ruby to stand still for a minute.

"OK, you can make a fireball appear in your hands." she acknowledged, "Of course, you can't do diddly squat with just that. You need to do more than just make flames appear. Let's see if you can throw your fireballs."

Using her darkness powers, she conjured up a shadow clone of herself. The clone was identical to Selina in every way except for one thing. The clone had Selina's original red hair streak so Ruby could tell which was which.

"Hit it." Selina ordered.

"OK." Ruby answered, "Good thing it's not a real living being so I won't have to feel bad about killing it..."

"Not that you have to anyway." Selina reminded her, "You control whether the flames burn or not. It's always up to you whether you kill or not."

Ruby nodded. She would try her best to remember that so she wouldn't hold back in a real battle. Breathing in and out slowly to prepare herself, Ruby concentrated again and just like before, the fireball appeared in her hands. It happened instantly unlike before. Now she and the gem were one, it was much easier. Feeling confident, Ruby threw the fireball at the Selina clone. The fireball hit it directly in the head, reducing it to a wisp of magical black smoke that faded to nothing. Ruby punched the air excitedly.

"Alright, I got it first time!" she cried, "I guess all those basketball lessons are paying off!"

"Possibly." Selina pondered, "Playing sports can help magic users be more accurate with their aim. I have a feeling you'll really get the hang of this very quickly."

"You do? Cheers." Ruby said graciously, "You know, is it just me, or are you becoming a little nicer to me lately?" she asked teasingly.

Selina shrugged.

"You three are growing on me. That's all it is." she muttered.

"Sure it is." Ruby teased, "Oh well, let's continue. What do I do next?"

The next couple of hours were spent testing Ruby on her new powers. She was taught to conjure up more than one fireball at a time, to make flaming swords to fight with, to shoot flames from her hands and to create fire tornadoes. In those two hours, she'd only managed to master shooting flames from her hands. The rest would need more practice, which was OK, as even a silver-haired human couldn't master magic immediately. She had a long way to go, but Ruby was off to a decent start. She was able to conjure up flames in her hands on command and shoot rapidly. At one point, Selina created a whole army of shadow clones to swarm Ruby and she was able to shoot every one of them whilst spinning on the spot to hit from all angles. It was so impressive that Selina looked genuinely amazed she'd pulled it off. Ruby swore that for a moment, she'd lost her stoic demeanour and was showing a genuine emotion for once. Of course, Selina had been quick to regain herself and compliment Ruby in her own deadpan way. Ruby was just appreciative that she'd managed to learn something in those two hours and was on her way to becoming a sorceress.

Meanwhile, it had taken an hour for Emerald, Sapphire and Karim to finally pass the warm-up. As they were ordinary humans, it took them longer to tap into their gem's powers and they'd ended up losing concentration a few times, but eventually they'd succeeded. Sapphire was the first, forming a shard of ice in her hands. Emerald and Karim followed five minutes later, forming a ball of light and a ball of psychic energy in their hands simultaneously. They were thrilled that they'd managed it at last. While Ruby and Selina had been training for their second hour together, Howard and Betty had gotten the three started on target practice too. Ruby and Selina came back just in time to watch Emerald, Sapphire and Karim give it a go. Sapphire threw icicles at illusions Howard formed with his magic, Emerald threw light spheres and Karim worked on moving things with a gesture of his hand. He was able to pick up small rocks with his telekinesis but nothing much heavier for the time being. Ruby applauded them excitedly.

"Wow, you all did it! You can use your powers too!" Ruby cheered.

"It took us an hour, but we got there!" Karim confirmed, "How'd it go with you and Selina?"

"Brilliantly." Selina confirmed, "Ruby's learning pretty quickly. She's fast on her feet and a sharp shooter."

"That's our Ruby, always a quick learner!" Emerald said gleefully.

"How about you guys?" Ruby asked.

"Just been doing target practice." Sapphire answered, "We're doing OK for now, but not brilliantly. We don't always hit the target."

"And I'm struggling to pick up lots of things at once with my telekinesis." Karim informed, "I can pick up a few things but if I go too overboard, my head starts hurting and I lose focus." he sighed, rubbing his scalp.

"You're new, you're all learning." Selina said bluntly, "You'll get better the more your practice."

"We know." Emerald concurred, "Say, we can all train together now Ruby's back!"

"Yeah, let's see you all in action at once." Betty said eagerly, "Selina, you take over for target practice."

Selina nodded and formed another army of shadow clones that surrounded the teens. So they knew which one was real, all the clones had different coloured hair streaks to her, leaving the real Selina as the only one with purple. The teens dropped down into battle ready stances and prepared to fight. But Selina held up a hand to stop them from jumping into battle.

"Hold it. You three, your stances are all wrong." the Goth girl said sharply to Emerald, Sapphire and Karim, "Did mum and dad teach you anything?"

"Don't be cheeky young lady." Howard snapped, "We've been teaching them plenty."

Selina ignored him and went over to the teens. She stood behind Sapphire and readjusted her arms and her hips to improve her stance. Sapphire blushed at the feel of Selina's hands on her.

"If you want to be a sharp shooter, you have to be much straighter in your stance." the dark sorceress informed, "And remember to keep both eyes open when you shoot your ice shards, you'll aim twice as well."

"Oh, y-y-yes, o-of course Selina." Sapphire said shyly.

"Same goes for the rest of you." Selina went on as she readjusted their stances, "It may sound silly, but believe me a firm stance can go a long way in battle."

"OK, we'll remember." Karim said agreeably, "Now let's go!"

Selina stepped back and let the teens get to work. The clones advanced towards them, ready to attack. Ruby struck first, shooting flames from her hands to mow down several clones coming towards her. Emerald formed two balls of light in her hands and threw them at her batch of clones. She scored direct hits and the clones were reduced to smoke once the light balls hit. Emerald beamed happily. This was much easier and more fun than learning to fight traditionally in her eyes. Sapphire flicked her fingers and skewered the clones with sharp icicles. Every one she hit collapsed to the ground in anguish, almost like they were real people that had been stabbed to death. Sapphire winced. Did Selina have to make this exercise feel so real? But like with Ruby's fire powers, she was in control over whether she killed or not. She flicked her fingers again and hit some clones with ice shards that were blunt instead of sharp. They formed as she wanted, making her smile. She was in complete control, just as she wanted. Karim held out his hands and used telekinesis to blow several clones off their feet. Then he picked one up with a psychic grasp and threw it into several others, knocking them all down like dominoes. He was having the most fun of the four, laughing with joy as he used his new powers.

"I've wanted to do that my whole life! This is epic!" he cried with joy.

"You're not wrong there! This is fun!" Ruby concurred.

"I knew having magic powers was going to be enjoyable!" Emerald squealed gleefully.

"Hey, I'm glad you're enjoying yourselves, but remember to keep focused!" Sapphire cut in, "We can't afford to get distracted in a real battle!"

"We know, but we can have a little fun at the same time, can't we?" Ruby said casually.

They kept up the fight for several minutes, effortlessly mowing down shadow clones no matter how many kept coming back and being reformed to fight again. The Coopers watched with pleasure. Their first magical students they'd had outside of the family and they were doing so well!

"Oh this could just make me cry Howard!" Betty cried jovially, wiping at her eyes, "I'm so proud of them all!"

"I thought we'd never get to teach anyone else magic after we trained Selina. And yet here we are." Howard murmured with pride.

"I wish Jaime could see this..." Selina said solemnly.

From inside the cottage, Annie had watched the children in action and had a huge smile on her face.

"My girls, I couldn't be prouder of you. You're achieving such incredible things!" she said to herself, "Oh just wait until we tell your father when he comes home tonight. And no doubt Idris will be very proud of his son..."

Fifteen minutes later, the exercise was over and the shadow clones stopped. The Coopers were full of praise for the teens and congratulated all of them. But now it was time for a more advanced exercise. They decided one more test would finish off the day nicely and they could go home to rest. Selina stood before them.

"Now it's time for a REAL test." the sorceress declared, "You have to hit me with your new powers."

"We do?" Sapphire asked incredulously.

"But...won't that hurt?" Emerald asked worriedly.

"I'm magical as well, I can take it." Selina said dismissively, "And remember, you're in control so you can decide how powerful your hits are. You can either give me a big hit or a little hit, though I'd much prefer the latter if you don't mind." she muttered bluntly.

"OK, let's give it a go." Ruby said keenly, "Though I doubt we're going to succeed. She's more advanced than us."

"This'll be easy!" Karim boasted, "I can just do this!"

He held out his hand and used his psychic powers to grab hold of Selina. But to his amazement, Selina broke free of his grip without even struggling, shadow-melded into the ground, reappeared behind him and backhanded him across the head, knocking him down. He groaned in pain and rubbed his head.

"Nice try dipstick." Selina taunted, "Your powers aren't strong enough to hold a magic user like me. You need much more training before you're that strong."

"Now you tell me!" the young boy grumbled.

"Next time, don't assume anything will be easy." Ruby jeered, "Now it's our turn..."

She readied herself for an attack but Selina had already disappeared before the flames even formed in her hands. Selina reappeared behind Ruby and grabbed her in a bear hug. Ruby squirmed furiously and cried out as the dark sorceress flung her aside, not even straining from the effort. Ruby crashed down onto her side and grimaced but wasn't hurt too badly. Emerald flung a light ball at Selina but she weaved to one side and dodged. Sapphire formed an icicle in her hand and threw it as if she was throwing daggers at her enemy. Selina shadow-melded out of the way, causing her to miss and hit Emerald by accident. The icicle had been blunt so it didn't hurt her much, but it still made Emerald cry out. Sapphire ran up to help Emerald but Selina reappeared and tripped her up by grabbing her ankles. Sapphire fell flat on her face and grunted. Selina then pinned Sapphire down by lying on top of her with her hands firmly gripping her arms. Sapphire squirmed but she couldn't get free of Selina's grip. Emerald formed another light ball in her hands and was tempted to throw it at Selina. But she hesitated. No, she might hit Sapphire instead. Instead, she ran towards Selina with the intent of ramming the ball into her face. Selina shape-shifted one of her arms into a tentacle and whipped the ball out of Emerald's hands. Karim caught it with telekinesis and launched it back at Selina, forcing her to let go of Sapphire and dodge it. Selina shadow-melded into the ground again but didn't come back up straight away. The teens were left wondering what she was planning next. They kept their senses alert for her. Betty and Howard watched with amused smiles on their faces. Selina was always a tricky opponent to deal with thanks to her training, and Selina seemed to enjoy this kind of exercise. So how would their students deal with her?

After what seemed like an eternity, Selina suddenly reappeared behind Emerald, tapping her on the shoulder. Emerald freaked out and spun around, aiming to hit Selina with a light ball. Selina ducked down and Emerald ended up hitting Ruby in the back of the head. Ruby span around angrily but stopped herself once she saw Emerald standing there apologizing for the attack. Ruby understood and forgave her. She looked around and saw Selina appear behind Sapphire. She was about to attack but she stopped dead in her tracks, worried she'd hurt Sapphire. Instead, she called out to her sister and Sapphire turned around to see Selina there. She reacted instantly, throwing an icicle at the sorceress. Selina simply reached up and caught the icicle between her finger and thumb, the tip millimetres in front of her nose. She flicked the icicle away.

"Nice shot. You nearly hit me. Now try and ACTUALLY hit me." she taunted.

"You try it when you can't shadow-meld out the way all the time!" Sapphire retorted.

She threw another icicle at the Goth girl but Selina dodged by shadow-melding again. To the teens, it was like some fantastical whack-a-mole game with Selina popping up and down continuously in this match. Karim tried to predict where Selina would show up again by picking up a rock with telekinesis and waiting for her to show up again. He anticipated she'd appear behind him so he spun around. Selina was there and he threw the rock at her. The rock passed through her harmlessly, as if he was attacking a ghost. Karim clicked his fingers in annoyance.

"Damn! She got me with a shadow clone! I thought I had her!" he complained.

"She is tricky." Ruby acknowledged, "Such a slippery opponent. I'd love to see the hunters try and do any better!"

"Knowing them, they'd try and shoot her but she'd shadow-meld out the way and cause them to shoot each other." Sapphire chuckled.

"Not a bad idea actually, I should try that someday." Selina murmured, reappearing directly in front of Sapphire and making her jump back in fright.

Both Sapphire and Emerald launched their attacks together and tried to hit Selina. The sorceress jumped to one side, leaving a shadow clone behind to take the hit. It dissolved into mist upon being stricken by the icicle and light ball. She shadow-melded into the ground again and this time reappeared behind Ruby. Ruby heard her coming and spun around on her heels. She had fireballs in her hands and was ready to strike. She took aim...but didn't take the shot. At the last second, she hesitated, a tiny voice in her head warning her not to fire. No, you might burn her, it was telling her. That hesitation cost Ruby her chance and she was knocked down onto her back as Selina lashed out and punched her in the stomach. Ruby crashed to the ground, feeling as if the wind had been knocked out of her. Emerald and Sapphire gasped in shock. Betty and Howard shook their heads sadly. They'd seen everything and were disappointed Ruby had blown her chance. Karim ran over to Ruby and helped her back to her feet. He patted her back as she spluttered.

"What happened Ruby? You had her and yet she floored you!" Karim exclaimed.

"She hesitated, that's what happened." Selina said grimly, "Why did you do it Ruby?"

"I don't know, I'm sorry, I just froze up for a minute." Ruby said apologetically, rubbing her stomach.

"What did I tell you about hesitating?" Karim said firmly, "What if Selina had a knife on her and she stabbed you in the gut instead of punching you? She could've killed you! Remember, you can't afford to hesitate in battle!"

"I know that!" Ruby snapped angrily, "I don't know what happened, OK? I just froze up and that cost me big time! I'll do better next time, I'm sure."

"If this was real, you wouldn't have a next time." Selina said coldly, "You need to sort out whatever problems you've got or else you're going to get killed, simple as that."

"I don't have any problems!" Ruby shouted.

"Like hell you don't." Selina snapped, "You're troubled. It doesn't take a psychiatrist to see that. I've heard of your reports from Idris. You hesitated during training as well and you're hesitating again here. You clearly have some kind of mental block that's holding you back and you need to deal with it or else you'll end up in real trouble."

"I'm fine, alright?!" Ruby insisted, "Let's move on and get back to the test, OK?"

"No, it's not OK." Selina said grimly, refusing to budge, "You need to talk about your problems. What's holding you back? Is it Draven? Is his death still weighing on your conscience?"

"Selina, please stop, you're not helping here." Sapphire tried to cut in.

"I agree with Sapphire, that's enough Selina." Howard said firmly.

"Is it?!" Selina snapped, ignoring them both.

Ruby found herself in an uncomfortable situation. The last thing she wanted to do was talk about her problems, especially in regards to Draven. But Selina wasn't going to stop, she had to answer her to get her to back off.

"YES! I admit it, OK? His death is still weighing on my conscience!" Ruby shouted furiously, "Maybe it is what's holding me back! But is that such a bad thing, to not want to kill again?"

"Why do you care so much about what you did to him?" the sorceress questioned, "He was a monster who killed innocent creatures, sorcerers and sorceresses with no remorse, he uses mankind as an excuse for his murders and he tried to kill you! You shouldn't give a damn that he's dead!"

"Well I do, alright?!" the silver-haired teen shot back, "Unlike you, I'm NOT OK with murder! Nobody should ever be OK with it! Murder is still murder no matter who it happens to and murder is NEVER acceptable! I could've dealt with Draven in literally any other way than killing him! I could've tried knocking him out or injuring him so he can't fight anymore! Instead, I went with the worst option and now I have his blood on my hands! Every time I go to sleep at night, he's there haunting my dreams and scorning me for taking his life like so! How can I possibly live with myself knowing that I'm a murderer?!"

"A whole lot happier knowing he's gone and will never murder innocent people and creatures again." Selina snapped as if the answer were obvious.

"Are you daring to say I'm sorry he can't kill anymore?!" Ruby yelled in disgust.

"Don't be an idiot. I'm daring to say you shouldn't feel sorry that he's gone!" Selina snapped.

"I'm not sorry about that, I'm only sorry that I had to be the one that did it!" Ruby yelled.

"It shouldn't matter who did it as long as he's gone!" Selina retorted.

"Oh, so are you saying you would've happily murdered him too?" Ruby said coldly, "How would Jaime feel knowing his sister's OK with murder?!"

That did it. Selina lost her temper and shoved Ruby to the ground. Ruby landed on her backside and grunted from the impact. Everybody recoiled in shock. It wasn't like Selina to lose her cool like that.

"DON'T YOU DARE USE MY BROTHER'S NAME AGAINST ME YOU WRETCH!!!" Selina roared, her voice like an enraged demon.

"STOP IT! Just please, stop it!" Emerald wailed, standing in-between Ruby and Selina and holding her hands up, "We shouldn't be fighting each other! Please stop arguing, you're only going to hurt each other!"

"Emerald is right. That's enough from both of you." Betty said, her voice serious, "Selina, you were way out of line and Ruby, that was uncalled for. I'd have thought you'd know better than to make such insensitive remarks."

"Same here." Annie said, coming out of the cottage to break up the fight, "I've taught you better than that Ruby. I'm ashamed of you for saying something so callous."

Ruby and Selina looked away from one another, feeling guilty over their argument and how heated it had gotten. They were in agreement with their mothers. They were both out of line and it shouldn't have gotten that bad. They looked back to each other.

"I'm so sorry Selina. That really was uncalled for. I shouldn't have used Jaime like that." Ruby said, her voice heavy as if she was about to cry.

"You're damn right you shouldn't." Selina muttered, "But I pushed you too far and caused you to make that remark, so I'm mostly at fault here, not you. Jaime wouldn't have wanted us to fight like this...oh and if it makes you feel any better, he wouldn't have been onboard with murder either." she added, "I'm very sorry too Ruby."

Ruby nodded in appreciation. Annie and Betty smiled proudly at their daughters.

"Well done you two." Annie said kindly, "Now then, I think it's best we go home. We've had quite enough for today."

"But mum, we're not finished yet..." Emerald protested.

"We're leaving, now." Annie said firmly.

"I'm with you there, love." Betty agreed, "I think it's best we resume our training when tempers have cooled fully and Ruby has had some time to recover. The poor dear's clearly still damaged from...that moment." she said solemnly.

Ruby looked away sadly. Betty was right on that. She'd never been the same since Draven's death. Annie took her daughters with her and led them back to the car. Karim watched them go and waved sadly to them, sorry that their first magic training session had ended the way it had. Once the girls were in the car, Annie drove away from Harlow's Wood and headed back to the countryside home. Emerald and Sapphire looked to Ruby. Ruby was staring out the window, watching the countryside whizz past her. She'd wanted to be a good fighter and a good sorceress, but Draven's death still haunted her and was impeding her progress. How...just how could she ever learn to forgive herself for his death?

Chapter 6: How About A Holiday?

Ruby sat in silence the whole trip back home. She never once looked away from the window, not even if Emerald or Sapphire tried to talk to her. All she did was sit and stare out the window, looking more lost and unsure of herself than she'd ever been before. Annie glanced in the rear view mirror every so often to see how Ruby was. If she hadn't been driving, she would've been in the back trying to comfort her. But the brunette woman knew even if she could have a heart-to-heart with her daughter, she wouldn't even know where to start. She wasn't a psychologist, and certainly had no experience dealing with traumatic experiences like murder. What could she even say that she and her husband hadn't said already to try and alleviate Ruby's anguish? Despite Ruby's protests, Annie firmly believed she needed help and would try and get it for her. The moment the family arrived back home, Ruby was the first to get out of the car and head into the house. Annie chased after her. As they walked in, Wilson was stirred out of his sleep and he scampered over excitedly to greet his owners. Annie gently shushed him and told him not now. Emerald and Sapphire came into the house and Wilson greeted them instead. Emerald patted him and smiled sweetly. She picked the little dog up and cuddled him. She had a feeling she was going to need Wilson's company with how things were going at the moment. Emerald and Sapphire watched as Ruby tried to go upstairs but Annie stopped her.

"I'm going to my room." Ruby muttered to Annie, "I need some alone time."

"I understand dear, but don't go just yet." Annie insisted, "We need to talk about what happened back there."

"Can it wait until later? I'm really not in the mood right now." Ruby said grimly.

"It absolutely can NOT wait until later young lady." Annie said sternly, "We're all worried about you Ruby. Ever since we've moved here, your moods have shifted horribly and it's clear, despite what you say, you're still very troubled by what happened with the hunters. You're not sleeping well anymore, you've been more argumentative lately and you snap at us, something you never usually do. We can't let you go on like this."

She took Ruby's hand and gave it a soft squeeze.

"Ruby dear, I know you don't think you need it, but you do need help, and a lot of it." Annie insisted, "I'm sure we can find someone you can talk to and..."

"I don't need help!" Ruby shouted, snatching her hand back, "What good would it do me anyway?! There's no therapist in the world that could possibly deal with my anguish! How can I possibly admit to anyone that I killed someone and expect them to give me any meaningful advice? I took a life, there's no turning back from that! There's nothing anybody can do for me except make me feel worse than I already..."

Her voice cracked and she found herself so choked up by her emotions that she couldn't even speak anymore. With tears streaming down her face, she turned on her heels and stormed upstairs. Annie, Emerald and Sapphire winced as Ruby slammed her bedroom door shut. It sounded as if she was trying to smash the door out of its frame. Then they heard the loud sound of sobbing as Ruby threw herself onto her bed and cried her heart out. It made Emerald feel like crying too. Wilson whined, clearly feeling his owner's sadness.

"Poor Ruby!" Emerald said sadly.

"I know." Sapphire agreed, "Our girl's just never been the same since that day. And if she carries on like this, I doubt she'll ever recover."

"She will Sapphire." Annie insisted, "Regardless of what Ruby says, I'm going to take her to see a therapist. I'm not letting her continue like this. She needs to see someone, and she needs it now."

"But who could we possibly take her to see?" Sapphire asked, "Ruby does have a point on how she can't just go up to someone and say "I killed the leader of a criminal organization". Who would believe her? Worse still, she might be arrested if she was to ever confess that to anybody." she noted, "According to Rimor, the hunters work for the government so you KNOW they'll want to lock Ruby up for killing one of their employees!"

"Wait Sapph, maybe Rimor can help!" Emerald suggested, her face brightening, "Maybe they have a therapist or something!"

"I was going to suggest that myself, dear." Annie concurred, "Idris must have someone working for him who specializes in psychiatric evaluation. No doubt his agents need counselling on occasion after what they go through. I'll ring him up and see what he says."

"I know he'll be very happy to help if he can." Sapphire said brightly, "If not, maybe he knows somebody who can, somebody who can evaluate Ruby secretly so the government doesn't hear about what she did."

"Precisely." Annie agreed, "I'll make the call now, you two go get busy elsewhere."

She went into the living room to make her call to Idris. Emerald and Sapphire stayed where they were. The living room was going to be out of bounds for a while as it was likely to be a long call. So what could they do to pass the time? Emerald stroked Wilson's ears and looked down at him softly.

"I bet you wish you could cheer Ruby up." she cooed to the little dog, "I do too. I hate seeing her so sad and angry. It's actually frightening me."

"Frightening you?" Sapphire asked curiously, "Why?"

"Well it's just; Ruby's kind of scary when she shouts at people." Emerald said timidly, "I especially felt scared when she snapped at me yesterday. And then there's her attitude lately and how she's just so angry and sad all the time. What if it gets worse and she..."

Sapphire put a hand to Emerald's mouth to stop her from finishing the sentence.

"Don't say it!" she exclaimed, "We are NOT going there! Mum's going to get help for Ruby, we're not going to let it come to that, OK?"

Emerald looked down at her feet apologetically.

"Sorry about that. I'm just really worried for my big sister." she said anxiously, "I want her to be happy again."

She put Wilson down on the floor and patted him on the back.

"And I'm going to help her in my own special way!" the young girl cried out in determination, "I'll bake some of her favourite cakes for her."

"Em, you're sweet and you're wonderful, but you're not going to cheer Ruby up by baking her a cake." Sapphire said grimly, "I know your heart's in the right place, but not everything can be solved with baked goods and a positive attitude."

"Maybe not, but it's worth a try." Emerald said sweetly, "It'll at least show Ruby she's still loved and we're right beside her. I'm sure she'll appreciate the gesture."

She scampered off into the kitchen to do some baking. If there was one thing Emerald loved to do more than anything, it was baking cakes. If there was anyone who would provide the dessert while Annie made the dinner, it was always Emerald. She'd learned everything she needed to know about baking from Annie since she was a toddler and now she was so good at it that Annie didn't need to help her at all. Sapphire decided to help despite doubting this would do any good. She got out the baking trays and filled them with cake cases while Emerald got out all the ingredients. Her speciality was chocolate buns with white chocolate melted over the top and topped off with a single Malteaser. Ruby had said that those were her favourite cakes, so Emerald had always made them that way. She mixed the flour, eggs, sugar, butter and cocoa powder into a smooth batter and poured it out into each individual cake case, then put the cakes in the oven to bake. Whilst she was waiting, she broke up a bar of white chocolate into a bowl and put it in the microwave to melt. As usual, she and Sapphire couldn't help having a sneaky taste of the melted, gooey chocolate after it had melted. Ruby liked to do the same whenever she was here to join them. She wished Ruby could be here now as she always had fun joining her sisters with the baking. Those days would come back, Emerald was sure of it. If she kept doing what she could to make Ruby happy again and Annie was able to get help for her, her big sister would be back to how she used to be. It made Emerald beam just thinking about it.

Soon the cakes were finished and Emerald put them all on a cooling tray. Then she drizzled the melted chocolate over each bun and topped them off with a Malteaser. Sapphire admired the way Emerald prepared her cakes. It was like for her, she wasn't just making food, she was making art and they had to look as presentable as possible. She and Ruby liked to joke that Emerald should appear on *The Great British Bake-Off* someday, an idea Emerald actually liked the sound of. After the girls were finished, Annie walked into the kitchen.

"Huh, I thought I could smell baking." she said in surprise, "What's going on here?"

"I'm making cupcakes for Ruby to help cheer her up!" Emerald said sweetly.

"Oh bless you, you little sweetheart!" Annie cried with awe, "Sometimes, me and your father agree you're just too pure for this earth. But don't get upset if Ruby doesn't want any." she said, her tone that of a friendly warning, "She might not be in the mood for anything to eat now."

"I know." Emerald acknowledged, "I'm sure she'll appreciate what I'm doing for her anyway."

"She will dear." Annie agreed, "Anyway, I just finished talking to Idris. As it turns out, Rimor may be able to help Ruby after all. Idris even said that he'd been thinking about suggesting if we let one of his agents counsel Ruby. Given how bad she's gotten, I said I'd be happy if he could arrange a session for Ruby. As it turns out, that Paul chap you train with, is one of his agents who is also skilled in psychology."

"That...honestly doesn't surprise me." Sapphire chuckled, "I always got the feeling he was that kind of guy."

"Agent Paul will know how to help!" Emerald said excitedly, "When can Ruby see him?"

"Tomorrow." Annie said brightly, "We will all go down to Rimor first thing in the morning and Paul will have a therapy session with Ruby. I hope that man can help my daughter. He's our best option. If he can't help then we'll really be stuck..."

Emerald and Sapphire nodded. Paul had to be the one to make this work or it was back to square one. Emerald picked up the tray of cupcakes and carried them upstairs. Not only would Ruby appreciate the nice gesture of making her favourite cakes for her, but she'd be happy to know that there was someone who could help her after all. That was certainly going to make her feel better! Emerald approached Ruby's bedroom. She was glad she couldn't hear her crying anymore. Either Ruby had exhausted herself from crying so much or she'd simply finished and might hopefully be feeling better now she'd let all her emotions out. Emerald stood still for a moment, unsure what to do. Suppose Ruby was still upset and she only made things worse? No, Emerald wanted to help Ruby so she had to give it a try. Inhaling deeply and exhaling out again, Emerald knocked on the door.

"Go away." came the blunt reply.

"Um, R-Ruby? It's me." Emerald replied, trying not to sound nervous, "I just wanted to check up on you."

"I'm fine Em, now please leave me alone." Ruby muttered.

"But you're not fine Ruby." Emerald insisted, "And it's why I've come to cheer you up. I made your favourite cupcakes if you want any." she sang merrily.

"Not hungry." Ruby said irritably.

"But they're your favourites Ruby, chocolate with Malteasers on top." Emerald informed, "Freshly baked just for my big loving sister. I thought you'd..."

"Look, unless you've got anything useful to say to me, don't bother!" Ruby shouted angrily, "I've got way too much on my mind to bother about your stupid cupcakes, so do me a favour and sod off already!"

Emerald was horrified. Ruby NEVER spoke to her like that! The realization that Ruby had said those words to her was so shocking that Emerald felt as if she'd been punched in the chest. She was so hurt by Ruby's outburst that she began to cry. Emerald turned away solemnly as tears cascaded down her cheeks.

"OK...I'll g-go. I w-was only t-trying to help..." Emerald sobbed, "B-but if th-this is h-how you th-thank me, then I w-won't bother you a-anymore."

She was about to run off to her own room and cry into her pillow. She even felt tempted to just throw the tray of cakes on the floor. If Ruby didn't appreciate her efforts then why keep them? But to her amazement...Ruby's bedroom door opened and Ruby called out to her. Emerald stopped and turned around. She could see the shame and guilt on her sister's face. If there was one thing that Ruby could forgive herself even less for than killing Draven, it was making her youngest sister cry. "Wait. Please, don't go Em." Ruby said softly,

"I'm so sorry about that. Please stay. I...I could use your company right now."

Emerald wiped her eyes.

"Y-you m-mean it?" she snivelled.

Ruby managed to smile for the first time since she'd got home.

"Of course Em." she said kindly, "Come on in."

Emerald was amazed that things were looking up for her. Maybe the outburst had given Ruby a realization on how she was acting and was now trying to make up for it. She even imagined Ruby had been as shocked as she was that she'd said that to her, and that was what had changed her attitude. Emerald went into Ruby's room and they sat on her bed together. As she'd hoped, Ruby did indeed appreciate the gesture and she ate one of the cupcakes. One habit Ruby hadn't lost since childhood was how she'd eat the cake first and then finish off by eating the Malteaser. Ruby licked her fingers after she'd finished.

"You do make the best cupcakes ever Em." Ruby complimented, "I know it's not going to do much for me, but I can't thank you enough for looking out for me like this. You're such a wonderful sister and I can't stress enough how much I love your kind and caring personality. You really are like that one ray of sunshine that can keep everything bright."

Emerald was so touched that she hugged Ruby in gratitude.

"You've been the best sister I could ever ask for. Why wouldn't I be nice to you in return?" she said kindly, "You're always looking out for me and Sapph, so I want to do the same for you. And I just want you to be happy again." she said solemnly, "It's so sad seeing you as you are now and I want to help."

"I know, and I appreciate it so much." Ruby said graciously, "I really am sorry for being such a jerk to you lately. I'm so disgusted with myself. You're a wonderful person and you don't deserve the things I've been doing to you. Snapping at you, brushing you off and now telling you to sod off...it was horrible of me and I'm so sorry for doing that to you." she finished, choking back tears as they began to well up again.

"Don't be upset Ruby. I forgive you." Emerald said kindly, "I understand what's wrong: you're troubled by Draven's death and it's upsetting you. People lash out when they're upset, but they don't mean to. I know you didn't mean to shout at me like that." she reassured her.

Ruby nodded sadly. She looked away from Emerald and tucked one leg up to her chest, hugging it slightly. She wiped her eyes.

"It's still no excuse for me to treat you like that." she lamented, "I shouldn't be taking my grief out on you, you're too nice to be putting up with my crap. Sapph, mum and dad are right: I do need help, and lots of it. I never want to shout at you like that again. But...just who can I possibly talk to about my problems?" she lamented.

"Mum found the answer!" Emerald piped up excitedly, "I'd meant to tell you this as well before you shouted at me. She rang up Idris and he said Paul can talk with you. He's apparently trained in psychology so he might be able to help you!"

Ruby looked surprised to hear the news. It was just like her mother to never give up on her and try whatever it took to make things better for her children. Ruby was amazed that she hadn't thought of that herself. She supposed she'd been in denial of her problems for so long and had constantly refused help that it never would've occurred to her that there was somebody who could likely help. At least with Rimor, they wouldn't dismiss her or have her arrested for confessing to murder.

"I feel like such a dummy." Ruby muttered, punching the side of her head in annoyance, "Of course, Rimor was right there and I never thought of that! If anyone can help me, it's them! Their agents have no doubt been through what I've been through so they'll know how to help me!"

Her face broke into a hopeful smile as it settled in that maybe there was an answer to all her problems after all. She hugged Emerald in gratitude. Emerald returned the hug, feeling good that her big sister was already starting to cheer up.

"You and mum are the best. Thank you for everything." Ruby said appreciatively.

"You're very welcome!" Emerald said kindly, "I'm just glad to see you smiling again!"

Ruby beamed. Could her little sister be any cuter and sweeter? It was a small start, but it seemed a cupcake and a talk with one of Rimor's agents may go a long way for Ruby's recovery...

The next day went as planned. The Silverlock family all went to Rimor together. Michael had been able to get the day off work so he was able to come too. Ruby wanted both her parents with her for this session for extra support, and it was only right that both her mum and dad got to hear Paul's evaluation at the end. After arriving, Idris quickly led the family into a single room with a chair and a chaise lounge. The chair was for Paul to sit in and the lounge was for Ruby to lie down on. The room had a comfortable atmosphere with its soft carpeted floor and a window providing a nice view outside. The room was meant to make the patient feel at ease and Ruby felt relaxed just by being here. Annie and Michael were in the room with Ruby while Emerald and Sapphire were made to wait outside. Idris sat Ruby down on the lounge. Ruby lay down, allowing her body to sink into the soft fabric of the chair. If it was possible for a piece of furniture to feel like it was actively trying to comfort you, then Ruby may just have found it. She felt as if she could fall asleep on it if she stayed here long enough.

"I'm sorry it took all of us this long to suggest this Ruby." Idris apologised, "Paul even regrets not thinking of this sooner. Still, I hope we can provide the recovery you need. Just relax and Paul will be with us very shortly. Do you need anything to drink before he arrives?"

"Just some water, thank you." Ruby said politely.

Idris gave her a cup of water to drink. Ruby sipped it slowly, wanting to be nice and refreshed for the therapy session. A couple of minutes later, Paul arrived. The top agent was dressed in his usual strange style of clothing: a dark green long coat, black shirt and trousers and a blue scarf wrapped around his neck. Sapphire joked that he looked like he took inspiration from *Doctor Who* for his outfit choice, only for Paul to confess she was actually right as he liked to watch the show in his spare time. Ruby just thought it was amazing that Rimor agents even had spare time. Paul sat down beside Ruby's lounge, a notebook and pen in his hands. He gave the young girl a soft, comforting smile.

"Good morning Ruby. How are you feeling today?" the middle-aged man asked softly.

"Alright." Ruby said casually, "I actually had my best night's sleep in ages after mum thought about asking you to talk to me."

"It was so wonderful to see her looking at peace at long last." Annie said happily.

"That's good to hear." Paul said with delight, "OK, let's begin the session. Start from the beginning Ruby. While we know what's troubling you, I still need to hear it from you."

Ruby finished her water and handed it to Paul. Paul put it on the counter nearby. He lifted his notepad and prepared to write down any notes on what Ruby was going to say to him. The silver-haired girl sighed heavily and began:

"It all started when Draven kidnapped me and Rimor came to rescue me." Ruby recounted, "Me and Karim were fighting Draven for our lives. Draven had me cornered after my protection spell fizzled out and he was about to kill me. Karim distracted him and I picked up Karim's sword. In that moment, I'd intended to wound

Draven, only injure him enough so he couldn't fight anymore. But instead, I plunged it into his chest and...well, you know what happened."

"And I know that you were most distraught about it. When Idris, me, Judy and the rest of our team found you, you were in a flood of tears." Paul said solemnly, "It was heart-breaking for all of us to see an innocent child like you having to go through all that, let me tell you. I especially wish me, Judy or any of us could've spared you from that experience."

Ruby nodded, glad that Paul was feeling the same way about the whole thing.

"So after you killed Draven, you began experiencing nightmares, am I right?" Paul continued, "I hate to ask you, but I need you to recap the nightmares for me. How do they go and is it the same every time for you?"

Ruby swallowed heavily, wincing at the question. She knew Paul was going to ask about the nightmares but it still made her grimace now she was going to have to talk about them. Trying her best to keep her emotions steady, she replied:

"It's the same nightmare for me: I'm there on the battlefield, fighting Draven, then I stab him with the sword and his body collapses to the ground." she recapped, "As he looks at me, the light fading from his eyes, he snarls at me, saying "How Ruby, how could you dare murder me?!" All I can do is apologize feebly to him, but it does no good. He dies anyway, and then I hear the voices of many others calling me a murderer, saying I'm an evil monster who needs to be locked up. It's...it's pure torture and I can't take it anymore!" she whimpered, "I'd do anything to stop those nightmares!"

She clamped her hands over her mouth and forced herself not to cry despite feeling the urge to. Annie held Michael's hand while Michael put an arm around his wife. They couldn't begin to imagine how horrible the nightmare must've been for their daughter. Paul gave Ruby a minute to recover. She sighed heavily and placed her hands over her chest.

"I'm making a concentrated effort not to kill again and I'm following advice from Rimor and the Coopers to avoid ever doing it again." Ruby continued, "But still, Draven burns in my mind and I worry if I may kill again. I want to be able to fight and do magic as it's for my own protection, and I feel as a silver-head, it's in my blood to become a sorceress like the Coopers. But...Draven still lingers in my consciousness, making me hesitate and question myself, and now I worry if I should be taking these lessons or not. I mean, what if I end up killing again as a result of all the training I've done? I can't bear such a thought! How could I ever live with myself if I took a life with the lessons you all taught me?"

She gripped her hair in worry.

"We at Rimor know only too well." Paul sympathised, "It's the sad thing about killing: when you've done it once, there's no going back."

"How do you all cope with it?" Ruby asked, "The whole taking a life thing? You haven't killed anyone as well, have you?"

Paul shook his head grimly.

"Sorry to say Ruby, but I have." he lamented, "Even my hands aren't completely clean here. I still remember how it happened. I was trying to protect a dragon that had been sighted in the Himalayas. The hunters were after it and I fought them off. During the scuffle, I was grappling with one hunter and I threw a punch at him. To my shock and horror, my punch caused him to career to one side and then he plummeted down the mountain to his death. It was horrific. I was responsible for a man's death. I felt the same way you're feeling now Ruby." he murmured, cringing as his past came back to haunt him.

Ruby felt like getting up off the lounge to hug Paul but she stayed where she was.

"So…how did you get over it?" she asked, "How did you eventually make peace with yourself for what you did?"

"I was reassured by my comrades and my boss that the death wasn't my fault and that I wasn't a murderer." Paul went on, "I hadn't intended to kill that man and I took no pleasure in what I did, so that meant I was still a good man regardless of what I'd done. You're only a truly evil person if you relish killing. I didn't, so that meant I wasn't evil and I shouldn't be ashamed of myself. That helped to put me at ease and I've made a mental note to never kill again unless absolutely necessary. Since then, I've been able to avoid repeating the deed."

"That's wonderful Paul." Ruby said kindly, "But it's not working for me. My family, my friends and even Idris himself have given me that same reassurance and I'm still haunted by Draven's death. It's like I feel there's no forgiving myself for what I've done and I just don't know what else to do."

"That's the thing with death Ruby, it affects us all in different ways." Paul murmured, "And we all have to find our own ways of coping with it. So what worked for me won't necessarily work for you, and vice versa. As is, we need to find something that'll work for you."

The conversation continued for a long time before eventually, the session came to a close and Paul was able to give his evaluation. He had written a lot of notes down during the whole talk with Ruby. Annie and Michael congratulated Ruby on her bravery and honesty in opening up during the whole thing. They sat together as Paul went over all his notes.

"So having talked with Miss Silverlock for the past hour and going over everything that we've talked about together, it is my professional opinion that Ruby is traumatized from the experience of killing another and with us training her to fight, we may have unintentionally made it worse for her." Paul evaluated, "I now see it was a mistake for us to go so quickly into combat training so soon after the incident. We should've counselled her beforehand, but we weren't to know how badly Ruby was affected since she did show signs of improvement after we moved the family into the new house."

"Indeed." Michael concurred, "She seemed fine up until after we'd finished moving in and the nightmares only started after she began her lessons with you."

"So what's your suggestion Paul? How can we help our daughter?" Annie asked.

"I'd like to have further therapy sessions to try and help her more with her mental recovery." Paul declared, "But mostly, I suggest the young girl be given a long rest. No more training sessions for the time being. No more supernatural exploring. A good long break away from us and our world should give her time to recover mentally, especially if she won't have to worry about killing anyone."

Annie and Michael nodded.

"I'd agree on that." Michael concurred, "If we can get Ruby to focus on just living a normal life again, she might not have Draven on the mind so much and the thought of killing won't really occur to her if she's not engaged in anything that she might associate with it."

"Absolutely." Paul agreed, "So whether you do this for a month, two months, the rest of the year even, however long it takes to help Ruby's mental state, just keep her away from anything related to the hunters and having to fight them and live as normally as you can. Maybe a good while living normally can help Ruby finally be at peace with herself, forgive herself for what's happened and put it all to bed. It won't be a quick process, but I'm sure we can make it happen."

"I'll try to live as normally as I can sir." Ruby insisted, "And I'll take all your advice to heart too. Thank you so much Paul. I think you've been a big help to me."

"The pleasure's all mine." Paul said kindly, "A young girl like you shouldn't have to be burdened by such a horrific experience like taking a life. I'm sure we can help you recover Ruby. Just remember, we're always here if you need us."

Ruby beamed with appreciation. She was still smiling with gratitude when the family got back into their car and drove back towards home. Emerald and Sapphire were glad to hear the session had gone well and Paul had an idea on how to help Ruby.

"So if Ruby has to take time off to get better, does this mean me and Sapph have to stop training as well?" Emerald asked.

"No dear, of course not." Annie reassured her, "You and Sapphire aren't suffering from any trauma so you two can keep it up."

"You don't have to stop for my sake girls." Ruby insisted, "You two still need to learn how to defend yourselves and all. The hunters could still attack any time. At least if they come for me, you two will be able to defend me."

"True that." Sapphire agreed, "You could maybe still practice your moves at home anyway. You'll be training by yourself with nobody else to fight against so you won't have to worry about hurting or killing anyone."

"That's right." Ruby said with a nod of agreement, "I could still train with my new fire powers too. Once again, if I'm at home practicing with myself, it shouldn't bother me and I'll still be able to recover up here." she finished, pointing to her head.

"We'll all be helping you every step of the recovery process my girl." Michael said kindly, "And I think the first step to that would be for all of us to have a lovely normal day together. No Rimor, no hunters, no supernatural creatures, just us, the dog and our country house."

"It's a lovely idea Michael." Annie said approvingly, "We could all do something fun together."

The sisters agreed it was a nice idea. Just a perfectly normal day would be great for them. But Emerald thought more about the idea. Maybe there was something else that could help Ruby get better?

Something more than just time at home and trying to live normally? Maybe something special for the whole family? Emerald thought about it for a moment. Then suddenly, she had an incredible thought.

"Hey, I know! Why don't we all go on holiday together?" the girl in green suggested.

The entire family gasped with excitement at such a suggestion.

"A holiday! That's it!" Annie exclaimed, "That'll be just what the doctor ordered!"

"We could get out of Galarsfield for a week or two and just have a fun, relaxing time." Michael thought, "Whether it's somewhere else in England or abroad, a holiday will do us all some good. A change of scenery, whole new experiences for us all, that'll take your mind off of Draven for sure!" he said, glancing to Ruby.

"I think it's a great idea!" Ruby agreed, "We haven't had a holiday in ages. Yeah, I think a holiday is just what we need. But what kind of holiday should we have?"

"How about a cruise?" Emerald suggested, "I've always wanted to go on a big cruise ship!"

"It's a good idea." Sapphire agreed, "We can have some fun on the ship and enjoy visiting a new country. Why don't we look into any cruises available and see where we fancy going?"

"It'll be expensive, but we should be able to afford it." Annie said hopefully, "We haven't been anywhere in a while. We'll see what we can afford and then look for the perfect cruise for us."

"Whatever we do, I know we'll have ourselves one fine holiday!" Michael said jovially, "And it'll be fun for all of us!"

Annie, Ruby, Emerald and Sapphire couldn't agree more. A holiday was perfect for all of them. Emerald smiled happily to herself, feeling very pleased that the family liked her idea. She was contributing to Ruby's recovery and it made her feel like the best sister in the world. She looked to Ruby, who grinned in appreciation at her. She didn't need to thank Emerald with words, her face said it all. Emerald beamed back at her. She lay back in her seat and sighed contently.

A holiday cruise will be so much fun! Emerald thought excitedly, *I can hardly wait! And I bet it'll make Ruby so happy too! She's going to get better, I just know it!*

Chapter 7: Cruising To Norway

It was decided that the family would go on a holiday cruise as Emerald had suggested. The moment everyone arrived back home, Annie and Michael fished out their tablet and began looking up potential holiday cruises the family could sail on. They looked up websites from about four different cruise lines before they found one that was more in their price range. The company was called Starlight Cruises, said to be one of the oldest cruise lines in the world. The line was identified by the words "Starlight Cruises" written in silver with a shooting star arched over them. Each ship in their fleet had a space-themed name to it, fitting with how the line had the word starlight in its name. The largest ship in the fleet was called MS *Nova*, named in reference to a supernova. Upon reading all the details about *Nova*, and seeing the prices, Annie and Michael agreed it was the right ship for them. *Nova* cruised around countries like Spain, Portugal and the Canary Islands, but most interestingly it also sailed around the Norwegian Fjords. The Silverlock family had never been to Norway before. They'd had holidays in Spain and Portugal in the past so they decided the cruise around Norway would be the best option as it was a new country for them to explore. Norway was much like Britain in where it was cold during winter and hot during summer. The holiday was booked for the first week of September, giving the family the remaining weeks of August to enjoy. The weather was likely to still be decent in Norway for the beginning of September so Annie and Michael felt they'd picked the right time to go, even if earlier in the summer might've been the most ideal. They could only afford to go for a single week, but they felt it would still be enough.

Once the holiday had been booked, the girls had been quick to inform all their friends about it. Ruby called Karim and let him know what was happening and also suggested maybe he could join them on the cruise. Karim hardly needed any reason to accept the invite.

"I think it'll be great! I don't get to go on holiday much given dad's busy line of work." the teen boy said eagerly, "I'd love to come! Of course, I need to ask dad about it first but I doubt he'll say no. Knowing him, he'll make sure we have a couple of Rimor agents watching over me on the ship." he joked.

"And me, Em and Sapph too for that matter." Ruby joked back, "I'll be thrilled if you can come too Hop. We'll have SO much fun together, all of us!"

"Won't we just?" Karim concurred, "It'll be great for you too as now you won't have to worry about...uh, that stuff." he said quickly, "You can just sit back, relax and enjoy a lovely holiday."

"That's why we're doing this to begin with." Ruby informed, "Paul recommended I take a long break and Em suggested we go on holiday for a bit to really let ourselves go and forget about last month's events, and that's what we're doing. It'll be a great time for us all, but it'll be even greater if...well, if you're here too."

Karim's face lit up with pleasure as Ruby touched her phone screen. They may not be in the same room together, but Karim could feel Ruby's gentle touch through his phone screen as if she was here with him now.

"I'll let you know if dad accepts or not." Karim concluded, "I'll see you later!"

Luckily for both of them, Idris accepted the family's invitation. While he couldn't come as well, he didn't want to stop Karim from having a chance to enjoy a holiday cruise so he let him go. As he'd expected, Idris had insisted that he not go without someone to watch over him and his friends. He assigned two Rimor agents to accompany Karim on the ship, but they were to try and be as invisible as possible so as not to embarrass him or make things awkward.

As for Emerald, she'd let Tony know about the cruise. The brunette boy was thrilled to hear his friend was going on an exciting holiday and Emerald of course had asked if he'd like to come too.

"I'll have to ask my parents about it, but I won't say no to that." Tony said brightly, "I'd love to come little gem."

"I hope they'll say yes!" Emerald said excitedly, "I think you'll have a great time with us! Have you ever been on a ship before?"

"Once or twice at least." Tony answered, "I think it was at least two years ago since our last one. We went around the Canary Islands then, but this one goes around Norway. We've never been there before."

"Neither have we, hence why we've decided to go." Emerald informed, "I'm so happy I suggested a holiday as it's making everybody else happy and excited and now we get to visit a country we've never been to before!"

"I can see you're enthusiastic about it." Tony chuckled, "I do love how adorable you get when you're excited about something."

Emerald blushed in astonishment. Tony paused, looking surprised he'd said that out loud. Both friends giggled shyly.

"D-did you j-just say I'm adorable?" Emerald asked bashfully.

"N-not quite, I s-said I like how adorable you get when you're excited. Not that I'm saying you're not adorable or anything but...oh never mind." Tony said sheepishly, feeling embarrassed about what he was saying.

"No, it's OK. I...I think it's sweet you think that about me." Emerald said appreciatively.

"Oh? That's alright then. I was worried I'd made things weird for a minute." Tony said, sounding relieved, "Anyway, I'll ask my parents and I'll let you know if we're joining you all."

As he finished talking, he suddenly put a hand to his head and blinked heavily. Emerald stared at her phone screen in worry. What was happening to Tony? Her friend looked as if he was about to pass out suddenly. But to her relief, he quickly recovered and shook his head, puffing heavily.

"Oh...sorry about that. Just had a bit of a funny turn there." Tony said, trying to sound casual.

"Has that happened before?" Emerald asked worriedly.

"Only a couple of times, but it's nothing serious." Tony said reassuringly, "Don't worry about me, I'm fine."

Emerald was sure that Tony was lying to her. He must be hiding something. She remembered how Tony had fallen silent when asking him how he was the other day and now he'd had a funny turn. Was he secretly ill and just didn't want her to know? Emerald wanted to ask Tony about it but decided against it. If Tony was unwell, he'd tell her. He wouldn't hide it from her, so he must be alright.

"If you say so Tony, then OK." Emerald said brightly, "Though if this keeps on, you should see a doctor. I'd hate it if you had another funny turn and ended up fainting."

"I will little gem." Tony promised, "Don't worry, I'm taking good care of myself. Now as I was saying earlier, I'll let you know if my parents are OK with joining you and your family on the cruise."

"OK Tony! Hope to hear from you soon!" Emerald said merrily.

And much to her delight, she did hear from him shortly after and it was good news. The Summers family were going to join them too. With Karim and Tony both joining the girls on this cruise, the fun was really going to begin! Of their friends, the Cooper family were the only ones who rejected the invitation. They were grateful for it of course, but they couldn't accept.

"We're not too fond of sailing ourselves and as a family of sorcerers, we have to keep a low profile at all times." Betty had explained, "A holiday cruise is hardly a low profile, wouldn't you agree?"

"You have fun without us." Howard insisted, "And hey, if you see any strange and mysterious creatures there, let us know about them!

We hear that Norway has quite a selection of creatures that have been sighted there."

"Knowing their luck, they'll meet actual trolls or a Nøkk." Selina muttered.

"Yeah, we might." Ruby joked.

"We can confirm that no, you won't." Howard informed, "Trolls and Nøkken are completely fictional. Even with the dimensional barriers open, no actual trolls or Nøkken have ever been confirmed to exist. But we can tell you an interesting story regarding Norway."

"Oh yeah?" Sapphire said with interest, "What's it about?"

"It's about a mystical artefact that is rumoured to be buried somewhere in one of Norway's famous glaciers." Betty explained, "Have you girls heard the story of the Staff of Wishes at all?"

Ruby, Emerald and Sapphire shook their heads.

"Legend has it that the staff was made by Gideon Trammell, one of the most powerful wizards in the history of mankind." Betty explained, "The staff was a weapon of great power. True to its name, it could grant the wish of anyone who wielded it. However, its power had to be limited to prevent it from becoming a threat to mankind. The staff can only grant ONE wish per person, so you have to think VERY carefully about what kind of wish you want. Once you make your wish, that's it and you'll have to let someone else have it. Also, the staff can't grant any wish you want."

"Like any magical artefact should have, it has limitations so it wouldn't cause catastrophe for us all." Howard added, "You can't wish for anyone to die, you can't wish for anyone to fall in love with another, you can't wish for the dead to rise, you can't wish for limitless wealth and you can't wish to be all powerful. Gideon knew that a weapon like the Staff of Wishes had to be crafted carefully and be unable to grant horrible wishes like that. But aside from that, anything else goes."

The sisters were fascinated by the story. A staff that could grant wishes? As incredible as it sounded, it didn't sound implausible to either of them. Thanks to meeting Luna, the girls could believe in the existence of anything at this point.

"Imagine what we could do if we had that staff..." Ruby thought, "I could wish for all the dimensional barriers to close and all the supernatural creatures lost in our world to be back home! I could clean up Matthew Harlow's mess at last!"

"Oh you could." Sapphire agreed, "The hunters would be put out of a job thanks to your wish and all supernatural creatures would be safe from their wrath."

"I wonder what I'd wish for..." Emerald said thoughtfully.

"Don't get too excited." Selina warned them, "Remember, the Staff of Wishes is nothing more than a rumour. While we DON'T doubt it ever existed, it remains unknown if it still exists now. Details of its whereabouts have long since been lost to time. Whether it still exists or has long since been destroyed, we don't know. My family's actually tried looking into it but nothing concrete's turned up yet. The fact we can't go out much due to needing to lay low doesn't help."

"I suppose while we're on holiday, we could ask and see if anyone has any leads we could follow." Ruby suggested, "We'll be sure to let you know if we can confirm the staff's existence."

"That'll be very nice of you." Betty said graciously, "But don't prioritize that over your holiday, dear. For our sakes, just have a good time in Norway. I'm sure you'll enjoy it in a country as beautiful as that."

The girls nodded and made a promise to the Coopers that they would enjoy their holiday. Still, the story of the Staff of Wishes had captivated them and they were curious to find out if it really did still exist. But as part of Ruby's break, she wasn't allowed to do any supernatural exploring so she wouldn't be able to look for it. But if she or her sisters came across any information about the staff by chance, that would be different. She wouldn't get involved still, she'd let the two Rimor agents accompanying Karim handle it. Her business was to just have a normal, relaxing, fun holiday. Any supernatural creatures or magical artefacts were Rimor's business for now. She also reasoned it would be a good idea if they didn't look for the staff. Something as powerful as that was probably best left undiscovered, especially if it meant the hunters didn't get their hands on it. The thought of them using it made Ruby's skin crawl. It was an intriguing mystery, but in the end it was best to leave it unsolved.

For the remainder of August, the Silverlock family carried out their lives as normal with Emerald and Sapphire still attending training lessons at Rimor and with the Cooper family, while Ruby practiced at home to keep in shape. The only time Ruby ever visited Rimor during that time, was for therapy sessions with Paul. Everyone noticed that her moods had started to improve and Ruby even found herself sleeping better since then, no doubt thanks to Paul's counselling and the idea of going on a holiday. Now Ruby had something to look forward to, it meant Draven wasn't on her mind as much anymore and it was doing her a lot of good. It made everyone happy to see Ruby acting more like her old self again.

The big day soon arrived and the Silverlock family headed on down to Southampton to board their vessel. Wilson was staying with Annie's sister Margot while the family was away. If ever they went on holiday, they always left Wilson in her care. Margot was a huge animal lover and loved to look after people's pets. After they'd dropped Wilson off at her house, Margot wished the family a good holiday and waved them off as they drove to the port. It was a long drive, but they arrived in good time. The day couldn't have been more perfect for departure. The sky was a brilliant blue and the sun was still as hot as it was the previous month. It was easy to believe it was still the month of August despite this being the first day of September. The family stared open-mouthed as they got out of the car and cast their gaze over to the vessel they were going to board. Standing in the port proud and mighty was the colossal *Nova*. It was 344 metres in length, 42 metres high and had 19 decks, easily dwarfing every other ship in the port. They looked puny and insignificant compared to it. The Starlight Cruises logo was proudly on display on either side of the ship while its name was on either side of the bow. The vessel was mostly white in colour. It was the single most beautiful and amazing vessel the family had ever seen.

"It's HUGE!!!" Emerald exclaimed.

"I knew cruise ships were big, but this takes the cake!" Sapphire gasped, "It's colossal!"

"Just wait until we see the inside, I bet it'll look incredible!" Ruby cried.

"I know it's exciting girls, but remember to stay close at all times." Annie reminded them, "Once we find our cabins and get settled in, we'll decide on what to do next."

"I fancy checking out the pool first." Michael decided, "Come on everyone, let's get onboard!"

The family joined the queue to get onboard their ship. Ruby was quick to notice that there were a lot of families boarding *Nova* for this cruise; mums and dads with plenty of children. She guessed that because the school holidays were drawing to a close, most of the passengers here were having one last holiday before school started again. At least nobody would look at her strangely or be making fun of her on this trip. As a means to hide from the hunters when out in public, Ruby had dyed her hair so she looked more ordinary. Her beautiful head of silver hair was now black like her father's. It was either that or be a brunette like Emerald and Annie, but Ruby had felt in the end that black suited her more. They made sure to use permanent hair dye so it wouldn't wash off easily if Ruby had a shower or went swimming in the pools. If anyone saw her, they would think she was just an ordinary girl with nothing unusual about her. It also went without saying that the girls would have to hide their magic powers on this trip. They would only start a panic and that might alert the hunters to their presence. They had to be as normal as possible for this holiday to go ahead without any hitches.

After a while of waiting and getting through boarding control, the Silverlocks were finally onboard the ship. Their eyes widened at the sight of *Nova*'s interior. They felt as if they'd stepped into a luxury hotel rather than a ship. There were neatly polished marble floors, fancy lighting and pieces of modern artwork displayed on the walls, almost as if the ship felt the need to show off how much money had been put into building and designing it. As the ship had 19 decks, there were lifts onboard to help passengers get up and down quickly. Emerald wouldn't be using them while onboard the *Nova*. She was very claustrophobic and couldn't take a lift without hyperventilating, so she always used the stairs instead. As the family explored the ship, they saw just how much this one ship had to offer them. *Nova* boasted several eating places ranging from an all-you-can-eat buffet, a pizzeria, a steak-and-burger restaurant, an ice-cream parlour and some fancy restaurants for those wanting to dine in style. There were plenty of bars around the ship that provided all kinds of drinks for the passengers. The ship also had its own shops for people to buy toys, clothes, souvenirs, household items and many other things. For the entertainment side, *Nova* had a few swimming pools, both inside and outside, a cinema, a casino, a games room, a theatre where musical and stage shows were performed and a court on the outside deck for people to play football or basketball. It was incredible how so much stuff had been packed into this one giant vessel and Ruby, Emerald and Sapphire felt they wouldn't know where to start. A week suddenly didn't feel enough for them. How could they possibly do everything on the ship in just seven days?

In the end, they decided to start off with some lunch and dined in the buffet restaurant together. The lunch shift provided a variety of different meats, breaded fish, salads, potato dishes and sweet confections with a drinks dispenser for anyone who wanted water or hot drinks like tea, coffee and hot chocolate. It amazed the family to see how many options there were just for lunch. Breakfast and dinner were likely to have just as much to offer. Karim and Tony were able to join them. Ruby and Emerald had texted them to let them know what restaurant they were in so they could all eat together. Karim and Tony were just as blown away by what they'd seen as the girls were. Tony remarked how the last cruise ship he was on wasn't anywhere near as big as *Nova* was. Ruby also saw who Karim's bodyguards were going to be. Karim pointed to them and Ruby saw, sitting at a table a few spaces away and pretending not to know them, were Paul and Judy. Of course Idris would send his two best agents to watch over them! Paul and Judy were dressed casually in loose shirts, skinny jeans and sunglasses. The idea was to make them look like holidaymakers but to Ruby, it only made them look more conspicuous. At least they were only there to watch them or else she herself might've felt embarrassed by them being here. As they all dined, Annie and Michael talked to Tony's parents, Marcus and Caroline Summers, while the teens chatted together.

"I tell you girls, this ship's got everything including the kitchen sink on it!" Karim exclaimed, "I know cruise ships are huge and have a lot to offer but to see it all for real is just...I'm still barely keeping up with everything!"

"Is this your first time on a cruise ship?" Emerald asked.

"It is." Karim confirmed, "I've only ever flown on planes to other countries or had holidays here in the UK. This is my first time holidaying on the water."

"I can speak from experience by saying you're in for a wonderful experience." Tony said enthusiastically, "Me and my parents enjoyed the last two cruises we've been on."

"It's a first for us too." Sapphire concurred, sticking her fork into her bed of lettuce, "Emerald suggested it because it's something she's always wanted to do, yet we've never been able to because we've either had other holiday plans or we couldn't afford one."

"I'm sure we're all in for a good time, first time cruising or not." Ruby said enthusiastically as she shoved a fish goujon into her mouth, "In any case, Emerald deserves most of the thanks here for suggesting the idea."

Emerald just smiled modestly and tucked into a muffin.

"I always wanted to do a cruise and Paul suggested Ruby take some time off to get better, so I thought now was the perfect time." she said kindly, "I just thought a big new experience like this would make everyone happy. We've been through a lot, so this'll do us all good."

"I agree." Ruby concurred, "And already I'm glad you suggested a cruise because holy crap, I think we're in for an amazing time! There's just so much to do on this ship!"

"It's the same for all cruise ships." Tony informed, "There's always plenty to do no matter which one you're on. Question is, what to do first?"

"We can figure things out after we've found our cabins and put our luggage away." Sapphire suggested, "I know dad's already eying up the pool so we might go swimming with him."

"I definitely want to play in the basketball court." Ruby said eagerly.

"Maybe you could play against me." Karim suggested, "I'll have a game with you if you want."

"Sure thing!" Ruby said enthusiastically, "Just don't use your new psychic powers to get an advantage, OK?"

Karim rolled his eyes as if the very idea was too ridiculous to consider. As if he'd cheat at sports just because he has psychic powers now!

"I'm looking forward to the formal nights." Emerald said excitedly, "We're all going to dress up beautifully and I've got the most adorable dress to wear!"

"I'm sure you'll look beautiful in it, little gem." Tony purred.

Emerald blushed. Ruby and Sapphire giggled. How long was it going to take this boy to just admit he was into Emerald? He may as well come out and say it with how obvious he was being about it.

After lunch, everyone left the restaurant and searched the long corridors for their cabins. Ruby, Emerald and Sapphire had a cabin to themselves while Annie and Michael were in the cabin next door. They'd booked for a balcony cabin so they could sit outside and enjoy watching the sea roll by as the ship sailed. The cabins were very cosy with comfortable beds, soft carpeted floors, a sofa, a TV with a choice of films and TV shows to watch and a shower and toilet. The girls lay on the beds to see how they felt. The beds were soft and almost seemed to absorb their bodies as they lay down on them. They were certainly in for a comfortable cruise. The girls unpacked their luggage. They'd brought a selection of casual and formal clothes for the week along with coats for in case it got cold and something to do in case they needed a break and wanted some time to themselves. They would have no Wi-Fi when out at sea, so they couldn't just play on their phones the entire trip. Ruby had brought her collection of *Pokémon* cards to play with either Karim or her sisters, Emerald had brought a sketchbook and a pack of crayons and Sapphire had a few books to read. At least on this trip they wouldn't be short of things to do whether they were out and about the vessel or just chilling in their cabin.

After settling in for a bit, the family took Michael's suggestion and went swimming next. They went to the indoor pool and spent the next hour just swimming lengths and playing together in the cool water. The indoor pool had a large glass domed ceiling that provided a great view of the sky outside and allowed the bright September sun to shine in on the passengers as they relaxed by the poolside or swam in the water. For the Silverlock family, the holiday was already starting off in the best way possible. No hunters, no supernatural creatures, no trauma from past events. It was just them having a good time together. Ruby was especially having the most fun she'd had in a while. Sneaking up on Emerald and Sapphire underwater and then jumping up and surprising them made her feel like a kid again. Emerald beamed at the sight of her sister's happy face and the sound of her laughter. It was so wonderful to see Ruby finally looking happy again. It was clear she'd made the right choice for this holiday. Annie and Michael were equally as thrilled to see their eldest daughter having fun and enjoying herself. The healing process was clearly progressing nicely.

After the family had finished in the pool, the sisters went to the outside deck so Ruby could play basketball with Karim. The court was empty so the two could play by themselves. Tony joined Emerald and Sapphire to watch the two play their game. He knew that Ruby was a good player from what Emerald had described to him but he'd never seen her play in person before. Paul and Judy hung close by so they could do their jobs, whilst also letting the teens have their own space. Ruby and Karim both took off their jackets so they wouldn't get too hot while playing. Ruby took a moment to admire Karim's strong looking arms and shoulders before the game started. She had the ball first and began by dribbling across the court. Karim intercepted and tried to block her but Ruby weaved to one side, spun on her heels and dodged him, threw the ball up into the air and scored a perfect goal. Emerald and Sapphire clapped while Tony gasped in astonishment. He was sure the ball didn't even touch the sides of the hoop when it went in.

"Blimey, you said your sister was a good player but I didn't expect she was THIS good!" Tony murmured.

"That's how it is Tony, we can tell you how good Ruby but you will never know just how good she is until you see her play!" Emerald cried excitedly.

"You're fast! I couldn't even keep up with you there!" Karim exclaimed.

"I've had plenty of practice." Ruby said matter-of-factly, "And Rimor's training sessions might also be helping out here."

"True that." Karim agreed, "It wouldn't surprise me if their teachings have made you even faster and more manoeuvrable. Still, the game's just beginning so I've got a chance to catch up..."

But he didn't. As the game went on, it was clearly Ruby's to win. She was just too fast and manoeuvrable for Karim to catch up with. Every time he tried to snatch the ball or block her strikes, she would weave circles around him and get past him. Karim was able to score a few goals, but not enough to stand a chance against Ruby. By the time the game finished, Karim was left panting in defeat. He wiped his forehead and puffed.

"You wasted me! Completely and utterly wasted me!" he exclaimed, "I swear you could play competitively with how good you are!"

"Eh, not for me." Ruby dismissed, "I prefer playing for fun rather than competitively. And I certainly had fun playing with you Karim, even if the game was comically one-sided."

"As long as we had fun, it doesn't matter who won." Karim said casually, "Though I'm sure I'll thrash you next time we play." he joked.

"You've got a lot of practicing before you get to my level, mate." Ruby teased.

The two giggled over their bantering. Emerald, Sapphire and Tony couldn't help smiling at them, enjoying their friendly banter and how close the two were. It was clear to anyone that these two were as genuine as anyone could be in their friendship with one another.

Now the game was over, the teens took a moment to just stand together and watch as *Nova* slowly and steadily pulled out of its port. Their parents were watching too. The cruise was finally starting and the long journey to Norway was getting underway. They watched as the giant vessel sailed away and cruised past the coast of England. They stood there staring for a long time as if trying to make the most of seeing their home country before it eventually disappeared into the horizon. They could see the docks slowly fading into the distance, the cars in the carpark beginning to look like toys as *Nova* set sail. Their cruise would start off with a day at sea and then their first stop would be the city of Stavanger. Next they would arrive at Ålesund, then they would go to Olden before their final stop in Haugesund. After that, it would be one last day at sea and then they'd be back home. It made the teens feel tingly just thinking about it. A whole new country to explore! How exciting was that? The girls watched the coastline, their hair blowing about in the wind. The ship cruised slowly and smoothly, so smoothly that the teens wouldn't have been able to tell if they were moving if they weren't outside watching it happen right now.

"It's so beautiful..." Ruby whispered.

"I knew this cruise was going to be fun." Emerald said happily, "And not only is it fun, it's pretty too!"

She snapped several photos with her phone.

"It sure is lovely." Karim agreed, "My mum would've loved this. She was always fond of the ocean and travelling on boats."

The girls were surprised to hear this. Karim very rarely spoke about his mother. They got the feeling that maybe it was too sad a subject for him to talk about. Ruby put a hand on Karim's shoulder.

"You still miss her, don't you?" she asked softly.

"There's not a day that passes where I don't miss her." Karim lamented, "Dad's just the same. He always puts up a brave face, but I can see in his eyes that he misses her too. If only there was something he could've done for her..."

He stopped himself as he felt his emotions welling up. Ruby patted his shoulder tenderly. Karim sighed loudly and collected himself.

"But there's no use dwelling on that, not when we're supposed to be having a lovely holiday." the young boy said, changing his mood to try and lift things up again, "I know mum would want us to have a great time, so let's keep at it."

"Well said mate." Ruby agreed.

"We have a day at sea tomorrow so we have a whole day on the ship to have fun together!" Emerald said excitedly, "What should we do? There's so much on offer!"

"I think checking out one of the shows would be nice." Sapphire said brightly, "I'm sure they've got some performances on tomorrow night."

"I love a good show." Tony concurred, "I'll have to see if my parents are up for watching any too."

"I'd love to go swimming again." Emerald said eagerly, "Hey Tony, why don't you join me in the pool tomorrow?" she offered.

Tony shifted uncomfortably and looked away.

"Oh...um, that's nice of you to offer little gem, but I'll have to pass on that." he said uneasily.

"Oh? Why is that?" Emerald asked.

"You love swimming." Sapphire acknowledged, "Since when do you say no to that?"

Tony winced. Now he'd done it! He really didn't want to tell the girls his secret as that would spoil the holiday. But how could he explain to them the reason why he couldn't go swimming? He supposed a half-truth could work.

"Believe me, I would love to, but I can't this time." Tony answered, "I've unfortunately developed asthma problems lately and it means I can't really do anything too strenuous or else...well, you know." he said grimly.

"Aww, that's sad to hear!" Emerald said sympathetically, "I'm so sorry about that."

"Don't be. It's not your fault." Tony said kindly, patting Emerald on the shoulder, "Besides, I can still have fun even if I have to dial down how active I can be."

"Of course." Ruby said optimistically, "There's no one way to have fun. Asthma or not Tony, I'm sure you'll find a way to enjoy yourself on this holiday."

"Especially while you're here with all of us." Karim said supportively.

Tony managed to smile in spite of everything. At least his little lie had worked and he hadn't spoilt the mood. And his friends were right anyway. He was here with all of them to enjoy a lovely cruise to Norway, he could still have fun even if he couldn't do some of the things he enjoyed.

"You're all wonderful and I'm grateful to have you all in my life." Tony said graciously.

"Same for us!" Emerald piped, hugging her friend.

The teens continued to watch their ship's steady progress across the ocean. In an hour or so, England would be gone and they would be out at sea with nothing but ocean for miles around. The weather was forecast to be good for tomorrow with calm waves and no storms heading their way, just the perfect kind of weather for a cruise.

But little did anybody know was that Ruby's past was coming back to haunt her. There was another kind of vessel making its way to Norway; only this was no cruise ship. It was a huge black submarine. The submarine had no visible name or number on it anywhere and no logo designating who it belonged to. That was the point for the vehicle was to be completely anonymous to anyone. The submarine carried a large crew of several men and women who were not interested in touring, taking photographs and sight-seeing. They were out on the hunt. They'd been tipped off that Ruby had finally come out of hiding and was on a cruise ship. This was their perfect time to get her after what happened last time. The hunters were back, and this time they were bringing someone very special and important with them on this mission. Draven was part of the crew and he was determined to see this mission successfully completed, even if it meant he had to be there in person. The hunters couldn't allow any mistakes this time. Their reputation was on the line and Draven wasn't going to let this mission become a failure...

Chapter 8: Am I A Good Man?

An hour before the cruise began...

The hunters had been very quiet since their failure to secure the Staff of Wishes. The deaths of Barley and his squadron had left them needing new recruits to make up for the lost agents in the organization, and it had taken them a while to find replacements. But it wasn't just that as to why they'd slipped under the radar lately. Ever since the failed mission in Norway, no more supernatural creatures had been sighted so the team had been cooped up in their base just training and keeping in shape for their next mission, whenever one would come up. But the main reason for their inactivity was down to Draven himself.

The cyborg had sealed himself away in his quarters since the deaths of Barley's squad and he hadn't come out in days. Aside from the catering staff leaving him food outside his door for him to take in whenever he was hungry, he hadn't interacted with anyone. He'd been by himself, quiet and contemplative. His mind was in torment. The words of the statue guarding the Staff of Wishes continuously burnt his mind and haunted him relentlessly. His men were considered impure despite all the good they did for the world, so that had to mean he was impure too. And if he wasn't the good man he believed he was, then what was he? Even in his dreams, the words continued to dance around in his head, almost like they were taunting him, refusing to ever leave him be. It made his nights restless and he'd woken up feeling tired and drained every morning since it had happened. His agents had tried to get him to come out and get things going again but Draven had refused to do so, angrily barking at them to leave him in peace. Simon had tried to get him to come out earlier today and the result had been the same. This had caused Simon to lose patience and he gathered together the highest ranking members of the organization to have a meeting about Draven. The meeting room was like any typical meeting room in a typical office, nothing but four plain walls with a long table stationed in the centre and lots of chairs around for people to sit on. Alice Daniels was at the head of the table. As Draven's daughter and second-in-command of the organization, she was the one in charge while Draven was cooped up in his quarters. She sat with her fingers tented in front of her bright red lips while Simon gave the report.

"It's been weeks since our failure in Norway and Draven has made no attempt to run this organization since then." the agent muttered, "He is neglecting his duties as leader and his duties to the government that funds us. They're expecting results and Draven isn't providing any. Our embarrassing defeat at Rimor's hands and Draven's near death have already sunk our reputation quite heavily as it is, and now Draven's making things worse by isolating himself from us and refusing to take charge."

Alice's eyes narrowed into a scowl of fury as Simon said those cruel, unsympathetic remarks. She understood Draven's torment more than anybody and knew he wasn't neglecting his duties as Simon put it. He was just troubled and having a hard time clearing his head. But as if Simon would understand that. Love and compassion for others was a foreign concept to Simon. Alice doubted he would've cared if it were his own parents in Draven's position right now.

"We can't disagree with you there mate." said one agent, "Draven just won't come out of his quarters. Even when Alice tries to talk to him, he brushes her off."

Alice nodded sadly. She'd tried herself many times over the past few weeks and nothing had happened.

"So what do you suggest Simon?" asked another agent.

"That we replace Draven with someone else as our leader." Simon said coldly, "Someone who won't sit around wallowing in self-pity over a failed mission for weeks on end."

Alice slammed her hands on the table and rose out of her chair. Her green eyes had narrowed into pinpricks of blind rage.

"How DARE you suggest such a thing you scandalous little vermin!" she screeched, "My father is the backbone of our organization and is the reason we've been as successful as we have been for the past few years! After all he's done for us, you're quick to suggest replacing him?! Is this how you're going to repay him for all his hard work in keeping mankind safe from monsters?!"

Simon just smirked coolly at Alice, keeping a level head and refusing to be intimidated by her. He'd made his disdain for Alice crystal clear back during the mission to kidnap Ruby Silverlock and he made no attempt to hide it now.

"Why am I not surprised that Draven's pampered little princess is getting upset over what I've suggested?" he sneered, his voice a deliberately mocking tone to get under Alice's skin, "Maybe you should let go of your bias towards your precious daddy and face reality: Draven is unfit to lead us anymore. He's left us essentially twiddling our thumbs doing nothing, so why keep him in charge if he's not going to do his job?"

"Here, here!" cried an agent.

"I'm sick of sitting around watching paint dry!" moaned another agent, "Simon is right! It's time for a new leader!"

"You will all remember your places and show respect to your leader!" Alice snarled, thumping the table angrily, "If father heard all your treasonous words now, he'd have your heads! In fact, is it really that wise that you suggest replacing him when I'm in the room? I remind you, I'm his second-in-command, so if you're so keen to replace father, don't think that gives you free reign to take over. You'll all have ME to answer to instead if father is dethroned. So tell me, would you rather keep father in charge and give him a chance to come back around? Or would you rather answer to me?" she purred, her voice soft and dangerous.

Everyone fell silent. The mere suggestion of Alice being in charge was enough reason to give even Simon pause for thought. If Draven was replaced, Alice would be the new leader and she'd probably have everyone in the room executed just for getting her father kicked out of his position. They supposed having Draven around was still preferable to possibly having their heads blown off the moment Alice took over.

"I think you've made your point quite clear Alice." Simon muttered with loathing.

"Excellent." Alice sneered, folding her arms and smirking, "Father stays as our leader unless he himself either dies or resigns from the position. We'll have no more talk about replacing him, otherwise I'll have some very nasty stories to tell him..."

The agents nodded. The message was clear: play nice and I won't tell him what you said. It was blackmail, plain and simple, but there was nothing anyone could do about it. They had to comply with Alice or else Draven would have them all fired, or possibly even executed for daring to suggest replacing him.

"So what do we do then?" asked a female agent, "Draven won't come out and lead us and you won't let him be replaced, so what now?"

"I'm sure if anything finally comes up, it'll get father to come out." Alice deduced, "I'm sure a new monster sighting will be just the thing to rejuvenate him. I will of course continue trying to coax him out of it. I'm confident that father will return to his old self and we can get back on track at last."

It sounded like blind faith more than anything, but the hunters had no other options. They also supposed Alice had a point. There was nothing for them to hunt, so it wasn't like Draven would've been able to do much anyway. Maybe a new mission would be just the thing to get him back in active duty again.

"OK, we'll compromise." Simon said reasonably, "If we get a new call to action and Draven accepts it, we'll let him keep his position. But if he ignores it, then he really is unfit to lead us and he will have to be replaced."

"Of course." Alice agreed, "If father ignores it, I'll accept in his stead. I do hope working for me won't wound your pride too much Simon." she jeered.

Simon fumed but said nothing. There was nothing else to say. The meeting was over and the agents all returned to their work. Alice strode down the corridor with her back straight and her hands behind her back. The tall woman always liked to keep a rigid posture, even when doing something as simple as walking. She thought it made her look disciplined and well-trained. She had hated Simon's tone of voice and choice of words in that meeting. It was clear the man was still feeling bitter over being demoted for his recent failures and was keen to make some kind of power grab. As long as she was next in line for leadership, Simon was never going to get close to leading the hunters! A part of her actually wanted to take over from Draven so she could sack him and be rid of him once and for all. The day Simon was gone would be a grandest celebration in her eyes.

Alice made her way over to Draven's quarters again. She sighed to herself as she prepared to knock. Please let him finally be willing to open up! She exhaled and then knocked on the door.

"I told you already Simon, I am NOT to be disturbed!" barked the familiar voice of her father.

"No father, it's me, Alice." the dark-haired woman replied, "I just wanted to check up on you."

"Not necessary. I don't need checking up on." Draven muttered, **"Now leave."**

"Please father, stop hiding away in there and let me in." Alice begged, "Your agents are getting restless. They're anxious about you. They just want something to do, but you won't come out and lead us.

We need you father and if you don't come out now, you could lose your position as leader."

A pause followed Alice's words. Then suddenly, the door opened up with a loud hiss. Alice was startled. Draven had only ever opened his door to take in whatever meals the catering staff provided for him since the Norway mission, and yet he'd opened it up now. Was he finally coming to his senses? Maybe the suggestion he could lose his position as leader was what had convinced him to open up at last. Alice felt the pressure ease in her chest. This was a good start. She entered Draven's quarters. The cyborg was sitting by himself in the corner of his room with his back to the door. He wasn't wearing his helmet and cloak. He sat there with his head in his hands, looking tired and full of sorrow. He didn't even turn to face Alice as she came to him. The tall woman approached him and put a hand on his shoulder.

"Please father, just tell me, what's been troubling you all this time?" Alice asked desperately.

Draven's shoulders heaved and he let out a groan of frustration.

"Alice...do you think I'm a good man?" he asked wearily.

Alice was taken aback by the question. She felt as if he'd slapped her across the face.

"Father, however could you ask such a question? Of course you're a good man!" Alice cried, "I can't believe you'd ever ask me that! What could possibly make you think you're not a good man?"

"That wretched statue in the Briksdal glacier." Draven said, scowling at the mere mention of it, **"You remember my report of our last mission, don't you? It said only the pure of heart may enter the cave and retrieve the Staff of Wishes. Barley and his squad were all fine men and definitely heroes in our organization. They were good men, all of them. And yet they were considered "impure". Despite all the good they've done for mankind, the statue judged them otherwise. So if they're impure despite all the**

good they did...that must mean I'm not a good man either. I must be "impure" as well." he growled.

"Father, pay no attention to that statue whatsoever!" Alice insisted, "You seriously doubt your morality because some stupid magical statue thinks our agents weren't pure of heart? It's a statue! What does it know about morality? It's not fit to judge us! It's not some god lording over all of us and it certainly doesn't speak for mankind! You are a good man father and you shouldn't think of yourself as anything less!"

"I try telling myself the same thing Alice." Draven groaned, running his hands down his scarred, tired face, **"But it still plagues my mind, these thoughts that I'm not the good man I think I am. It's making me second guess my entire life at this point. If we're considered impure because of what we do, then are we actually doing a good thing by hunting monsters, aliens and creatures? Is killing them the reason why we're "impure"? Are we the real villains in all of this? I mean most of the time, we are the ones that initiate the conflict rather than them, so that does make me wonder. I find myself asking all of those questions, and it's tearing me apart!"** he yelled furiously, **"It's why I've isolated myself all this time Alice...I just want clarity for myself and all of us, some sign to confirm that we are good people after all."**

Alice felt hurt to hear her father saying all of this and beating himself up like so. It really was unlike him to let the words of some mystical statue get to him like this. She hugged him tenderly.

"We are good people father." the second-in-command insisted, "Everything we do is for mankind's protection. Think of how many lives we've saved from monsters! Think how many have been saved because of us! If we didn't do what we did, the world would've been overrun with all kinds of creatures and mankind would've been slaughtered. We wouldn't have been good people if we'd sat back and done nothing. I bet that statue only thinks we're impure because of the fact we kill otherworldly lifeforms and destroy magical artefacts. It's part of **that** world so it won't think favourably of us. That shouldn't matter to you. The opinions of us humans are all you should care about father, and in the minds of many, you ARE a good man."

Draven mulled over his daughter's words. He supposed there was some truth to what Alice had said. Mankind would be in a worse place if it hadn't been for him. But suppose there could've been a way to deal with these threats that would've proven he was a good man and shown he was pure? He thought back to Rimor and how they handled the supernatural invasion of the past century. If he'd followed their example, he likely would've been considered a true good man. But he had to remember that Rimor's solution didn't solve the problem. There were still creatures showing up and letting them live only caused other problems that could've been avoided if the creatures had been killed instantly. Rimor also allied itself with a family of sorcerers. Magic had caused this whole mess to begin with, and Rimor thought magic would somehow solve everything? All that did was give magic a chance to make things worse. Yes...Alice was right. He and his organization were good and a mystical statue's words shouldn't have him questioning otherwise. He WAS a good man. He looked to Alice and smiled in appreciation at her. Her encouraging words were just the medicine he needed to cure his troubled mind. Alice beamed, glad to see her father smiling again. But before any of them could speak again, Alice's communicator suddenly crackled into life. Alice answered it.

"What is it?" she asked.

"Have you finally got Draven out of his room?" came the voice of an agent, "We've got an urgent message! Repeat, urgent message!"

Draven took the communicator from Alice and spoke into it.

"Gather the troops, I'll be right with you." he ordered.

He handed the communicator back to Alice and picked up his helmet and cloak. He put them on and strode out of his quarters. Alice followed him closely, secretly giddy with excitement. At last, her father was back to his old self again. There he was with that familiar commanding stride and his quick answer to the call. It was as if the last few weeks hadn't happened. The agents all gathered together in the main hub area with the agent who had reported the urgent message standing before the crowd. She was a small nervous looking woman who looked as if she wished she was standing anywhere else other than before the whole organization. Draven made his way towards her, the agents all stepping out of his way to let him pass as if he were Moses making his way through the Red Sea. Several eyes widened at the sight of their boss actually there in person for the first time in ages. Simon balked and tried to look happy to see him. He prayed Alice hadn't told him about the earlier meeting. Draven approached the nervous agent with his hands behind his back and the cold blue light of his optics gazing down at her. The woman stood up straight and saluted.

"Draven sir! You've decided to show up at last!" she declared, "We're all so terribly pleased to see you back again!"

"Report. What is this urgent message you have for us?" Draven said sharply.

"Oh, r-right! Y-yes, of course! Urgent message!" the woman coughed sheepishly and then took out her Cyber Scroll. She opened it up and read aloud from it, clearing her throat nosily.

"We've had a tip-off." the woman reported, "As per your orders, we've been keeping an eye out for Ruby Silverlock. It seems she's come out of hiding at long last. She was spotted boarding a cruise ship at the docks in Southampton. It's called MS *Nova* and is part of Starlight Cruise's fleet. The ship's course is a cruise around Norway."

She linked her Cyber Scroll to a giant holographic projector that Draven usually used to project images of the world itself to make plans and keep an eye on projects abroad. A huge photograph of the docks emerged from the projector. The organization was faced with a picture of several ships docked in at the bay with one of them being the MS *Nova*. The picture showed several people boarding the ship. The woman zoomed the image in on her scroll so the projected image could give them a closer look at the passengers. Draven eyed the picture with meticulous observation. Alice imagined he was committing every person in the image to memory in case he would need that information for later. Then suddenly, his arm shot up and he pointed at the picture.

"There she is!" Draven barked furiously, **"The very child who nearly killed me! It's her for sure."**

Everyone followed his finger and saw that indeed, Ruby was there in the crowd of passengers getting onboard the ship. At first, they thought he was mistaken because the girl in the picture had black hair instead of silver hair, but they quickly realized that she was in disguise. What really gave her away was the presence of Annie, Michael, Emerald and Sapphire with her. If Ruby had been with anybody else, the trick might've worked. Alice smirked.

"Cute. She thinks a dye job can fool us." she sneered.

"It's a clever trick, but we know it's definitely her." Draven said dryly, **"We must mobilize at once. Who knows what chaos Ruby will cause over in Norway with her powers? She's dangerous and we must take her down at once."**

"We'll take our largest submarine and sail there underwater father." Alice declared, "We can sneak our way to the country undetected if we go underwater and Rimor likely won't catch wind of what we're doing. Our submarine will also be fast enough to get us to Norway in a day or so."

"I'd rather we could fly to Norway as that would be faster, but going by water is stealthier." Draven agreed, **"We can't risk Rimor trying to sabotage our efforts again. We need the element**

of surprise on our side. **We will follow the ship to Norway and once they arrive, we'll capture Ruby."** he announced, **"But remember, do NOT try to kill her! You'll only activate her protection spell and she'll become too strong for us to defeat. We must incapacitate her first, bring her back to base, remove her magic and then we can kill her. With her gone, our reputation will be restored and Ruby won't be around to potentially kill anybody else..."** he purred darkly.

He chose his squad and made his way to his submarine. He made sure to bring plenty of agents with him as he wasn't going to underestimate Ruby. She maybe a child, but she was a child with a protection spell on her. He needed plenty of men and women for a job like this. Alice and Simon were part of his team. As much as he'd rather keep Alice behind and out of harm's way, he knew he'd need his best agents for this mission and Alice had also saved his life, so he owed her that much to let her join him on the field this time. He was also coming in person to oversee the mission. He was taking NO chances. It also lessened the risk of things going wrong if he was here to watch over the mission. The hunters filed into the giant submarine and as soon as everyone was onboard, the vessel sank down into the water and torpedoed out of the base. With no time wasted, it was out in the ocean and making its swift journey to Norway. It would go undetected on its journey as it could slip under radar with ease and no sonar equipment on any vessel would pick it up with how silently it cruised through the water. The crew were quite literally invisible to everyone with the darkness of the ocean hiding the submarine from the surface and no chance of it being detected by other vessels. Rimor and indeed any other intelligence agency back on land wouldn't even know Draven and his team had left the country just now. The crew busily worked at their stations on the submarine while Draven stood behind the helmsman and watched the submarine's progress.

Me and my people may not be pure of heart, but if killing dangerous people like Ruby keeps people alive, then let us be judged as so! Draven growled in his thoughts, *I am mankind's protector, and that makes me purer than any person on this planet. And as mankind's protector, I will not let Ruby and her magical abilities go unchecked...*

Once they arrived, the hunters would capture Ruby and try to keep it as discreet as possible. If anyone got in their way, they would deal with them swiftly and ruthlessly. Ruby had nearly killed their boss and she was finally going to pay for it...

Chapter 9: First Step Into Norway

"Ruby, Sapph, wake up! Look outside! We're here, we're here!" Emerald cried excitedly, nearly yanking her sisters out of bed to get them to wake up.

"Emerald, how many times have I warned you I'll mash you to pieces if you wake me up like that?" Ruby groaned sleepily, waving a hand dismissively.

"That's a silly question to ask, do you expect me to give an exact number?" Emerald said cheekily, "Now come on and get your first glimpse of Norway!"

"Come on Ruby, let's just do it. She'll never leave us alone otherwise." Sapphire grunted, stretching and yawning loudly.

The Silverlock family had enjoyed a wonderful day at sea on their ship. For the girls, it was quite a beautiful and serene experience, having spent some of the time looking out of windows or standing outside on the decks and seeing nothing but ocean for miles around and feeling the ocean breeze blowing over them. It also felt a little eerie knowing they were in the middle of the ocean with just an endless carpet of blue as far as the eye could see with was nothing else around, but they weren't afraid. They were plenty safe enough on the ship and no storms had been forecast. Occasionally, they would glance outside and see oil rigs in the distance. The girls had to wonder what it was like to have a job on those. It was hard to imagine getting up in the morning and going to work on a huge platform surrounded by miles of water and drill for oil for hours on end. What were the working hours like? Did the workers spend days or weeks at a time working on those rigs and then go home for a while after their shifts were over? They only knew that they wouldn't want that kind of life.

For their day at sea, Ruby, Emerald, Sapphire, Karim and Tony spent the day exploring the ship and playing together. Karim tried again to beat Ruby at basketball and just like last time, he failed miserably. Tony had to miss out on swimming and basketball but otherwise seemed to be enjoying the cruise in his own way. He was enjoying watching everyone else have fun if anything else. He did find a game he was able to play that wouldn't give him asthma problems for the ship had a shuffle boarding game on one part of the outside deck. Emerald played with him and despite this being her first time playing shuffle boarding, she managed to score quite decently with twenty points. Tony was more experienced for he'd played before, so he beat Emerald quite soundly, not that his friend minded as she was just having fun playing with him. Sapphire visited the games room and played a game of chess with one of the passengers. Her opponent was good, but Sapphire managed to win by the skin of her teeth in the end. Annie, Michael, Marcus and Caroline had some time to themselves, trusting their children to be responsible enough to look after themselves and play nicely together. Paul and Judy still kept watch over them, though that was mostly because they were Karim's hired protection, and even then they still watched from a distance so the teens could still have that bit of independence and their own space.

After a day of games and sports, the Silverlock and Summers families went to one of the fancy restaurants for one of the ship's formal nights. The restaurant was called Hailey's, named after the famous comet that would pass the Earth every 76 years, and served three course meals that consisted of mostly meat or fish dishes for starter and mains and an assortment of fancy cakes, tarts or cheese boards for dessert. Hailey's lived up to its status as a fancy restaurant with its soft carpet floors, neatly laid tables, soft lighting from sparkling chandeliers and smartly dressed waiters. Unless they looked out of the window and saw the ocean again, the two families would've thought they were dining in a posh hotel back on land. The Silverlock and Summers families had dressed up for the evening.

Annie had put on a bit of make-up and brushed her hair neatly and was dressed up in a smart dark red dress that left her arms and shoulders bare. Michael was dressed in a navy blue suit with a striped tie. Emerald and Sapphire wore dresses too with Emerald's being green and Sapphire's being blue, and Emerald had swapped her hat for a cute green bow. Sapphire had brushed her hair so it say neatly around her shoulders. Both wore a pair of flats that matched the colour of their dresses. Ruby took after her father and dressed in a suit as well. Her's was red with a black tie and black shoes. Ruby was the sort of girl that didn't like dresses and preferred wearing a suit. She'd combed her hair so it neatly swept back over her head. Tony, Marcus and Caroline were also dressed smartly, looking as elegant as the Silverlock family did. Once Tony and Emerald saw each other, they'd been quick to comment.

"I was right, you do look beautiful in that dress little gem." Tony said, his eyes wide with admiration.

"Aww, you're so sweet!" Emerald cooed, putting a hand to her mouth and grinning shyly, "And you look quite dashing in that suit Tony."

"You think so? I like to think I do, so I'm flattered you think that." Tony said appreciatively, "And you two also look lovely." he complimented, looking to Ruby and Sapphire.

"You shameless flatterer." Sapphire teased, "Thank you."

"And you all look very nice too." Ruby commented, "I wonder if Karim, Paul and Judy will join us..."

She soon saw that the trio had already arrived before them. Karim, Paul and Judy were also dressed up nicely with Karim wearing a smart shirt and waistcoat with no jacket while Paul dressed in a green suit and Judy wore a blue dress with a ruffled collar. Karim waved to the two families.

"Hey Silverlocks! Hey Summers! You all look smashing!" he complimented.

"Same to you Karim!" Ruby called back, "Never thought I'd see you dress up smartly, yet here we are. You look great!"

"As do you." Karim complimented, "And I see you don't mind standing out a bit." he noted, taking in how Ruby was the only one of the girls wearing a suit.

"Yeah, I've always been more for suits than dresses myself." Ruby confirmed, "Not that it matters as long as we look smart, eh?"

"We're always saying the same thing." Michael concurred.

Everyone sat down to order their three courses. After dinner, they went to see one of the shows before going to bed for the night. The show was a musical performance with a female performer singing a marathon of Queen's greatest hits and everyone enjoyed the show.

And now the girls were waking up to their first sight of Norway. *Nova* had docked at the city of Stavanger very early that morning and the day had dawned bright and sunny, meaning they were getting a glimpse of the city at its best. Ruby and Sapphire eventually pulled themselves out of bed and followed Emerald to the balcony. The three stood outside and took in the view. Stavanger was like no city they'd ever seen before. It was the third largest city in Norway, and yet it didn't look as modern as most cities they'd been to, nor did it look as large and overpopulated. There were a lot of detached houses, some that looked like they dated back centuries and very few tall buildings. The port their ship was docked in was full of boats ranging from sleek yachts to old-fashioned looking vessels. The city in their eyes looked somewhere between modern and vintage at the same time. Stavanger was also more colourful than most cities with more colour to see than just grey and silver. It was the most beautiful looking city the girls had ever seen so far. It certainly beat places like London and Manchester back in England.

"Wow...this looks nice." Ruby said with awe, "Never seen a city quite like this one before."

"I can't wait to see more of it!" Emerald piped excitedly, "I bet it's even prettier up close!"

"No doubt about it." Sapphire agreed, "And there's some fascinating facts about Stavanger too. Did you know it's the oil capital of Norway for example? There's even an oil museum we can visit in this place." she informed.

Ruby and Emerald shook their heads dismissively.

"Boring." they both said together.

"Is there anything else worth looking at around here?" Ruby asked, "See if that guide book of yours has any suggestions."

Sapphire had bought a guide book about Norway to study before their trip had begun. She picked it up and looked through it to see what it had to say about Stavanger. She flicked through the pages before finding what she was looking for.

"Aha, Stavanger has plenty of restaurants so we could probably find somewhere nice for lunch." the blue-haired girl informed, "As for what else there is on offer aside from the oil museum, there's Stavanger Cathedral we can visit, a museum of archaeology, a maritime museum and they have guided hikes that we probably won't have the time for as we're visitors from a cruise and only have so much time before the ship leaves. Oh and there's a Christmas shop open all year round too." Sapphire concluded.

"I want to go there!" Emerald said eagerly, "I bet they've got lots of lovely Christmas decorations on offer!"

"We can talk with mum and dad about it and see what everyone fancies doing." Ruby declared, "Whatever we do, I'm sure we'll have a lovely time exploring this place. And to think this is what a Norwegian city looks like. Just wait til we see the fjords once we arrive in Olden..."

Emerald and Sapphire nodded agreeably. They'd seen pictures of the fjords but seeing them for real would be something else entirely. For now, they had the city of Stavanger to explore and they would make the most of it for their one day in the city before *Nova* had to move on.

After breakfast, the Silverlock family got their bags together and went through security at the ship's terminal before they could leave and step outside into the city. They showed their travel passes to the security personnel. The family was given the all-clear and they were free to carry on. Like their daughters, Annie and Michael were equally as impressed with Stavanger's appearance. They didn't think it was possible for a city to look so pretty. The sky was a perfect blue and the sun shone brightly, casting dazzling light reflections on the water lapping at the shore of the docks. *Nova* stood out immensely from all the other ships in the harbour, easily dwarfing them in size. Some locals stopped for a moment to gape at the enormous vessel and take photographs. The Silverlock family got their own photos to commemorate the occasion, snapping shots of *Nova* in port and photographing some of the city around them. The Summers family and Karim got off the ship and met up with the Silverlocks. Paul and Judy accompanied Karim again.

"Nice place, isn't it?" Karim asked, drinking in the view from all around.

"We all think the same thing." Ruby concurred, "For a city, it's pretty nice."

"I guess Norway's such a beautiful country that even its cities look attractive." Tony joked, "What do you all plan to do while you're here?" he asked with interest.

"We're pretty much winging it." Ruby replied.

"It's a new place to explore so why not just see as much of it as we can?" Michael said casually, "No need to have any real plan. We'll just look at whatever catches our fancy."

"We pretty much have the same idea." Caroline confirmed, "Though Marcus and I at least hope to see the art museum while we're here."

"Hopefully it's not too far from the ship." Annie replied, "You three enjoy yourselves and we'll do the same. Shall we all meet up back here at around the same time to get back on the ship?"

"We don't have to make it the same time, but we'll try and be back at similar times. Maybe around mid-afternoon-ish should do." Marcus suggested, "Do have a good time all of you."

"We will!" Emerald said sweetly, "And you too!"

As much as it would've been nice for the two families to go together, it was better for them to split up so they could do their own thing. They didn't have to do everything together on this holiday. Emerald and Tony waved to each other as the Summers family headed off in one direction to find the art museum while they headed in another direction. Karim decided he would tag along with the Silverlock family so Paul and Judy followed them too. They reminded Karim not to wander off and to stay close to them or the Silverlock family at all times. The last thing they wanted was to have to tell Idris they'd lost his son in the middle of a foreign city. Karim had no intention of wandering off anyway. He walked beside Ruby as the group began to explore the city. But just as they walked away from the docks, something moved in the corner of Emerald's eye. The girl in green stopped for a second and turned around. Was it her imagination or did she see something move in the water? She stared down at the water but saw nothing. She peered more closely but still couldn't see anything. Sapphire noticed Emerald had stopped and ran back to fetch her.

"What is it Em?" she asked.

"Oh, it's nothing. I just thought I saw something, is all." Emerald said dismissively.

"Might've been a fish or something." Sapphire suggested, "Come on, we mustn't lag behind."

The two caught back up with the group and continued their trek. As they began their exploration of Stavanger, they saw a market square with various stalls offering souvenirs, knick-knacks and other things to people passing by, a local park with a huge lake and a sprinkling fountain standing in the middle of it and a street full of colourful cafes and houses that was so pretty to see and walk through. They looked through a souvenir shop and were met with the sight of lots and lots of troll merchandise. Trolls were a huge part of Norwegian mythology and folklore so this wasn't surprising. Ruby looked at the various different troll toys, snow globes, t-shirts and figurines on sale and once again found herself speculating that trolls were probably real after all. After discovering Luna and learning about how supernatural occurrences had happened in the first place, anything was possible now. They visited a local toy shop but didn't buy anything in the end and as Emerald had hoped for, they found the Christmas shop that was open all year round. It had two floors and was full of Christmas merchandise of all kinds. Vintage Christmas tunes played in the background while people shopped, and they were the English versions, which surprised the teens as they would've thought they'd be hearing the songs in Norwegian instead. Ruby, Emerald and Sapphire bought a bauble each, Annie bought a new wreath and Michael bought a Santa Gonk figure just for a laugh. Karim bought some new baubles and a reindeer tree decoration. He was sure Idris would like them and the reindeer was another tribute to his mum.

"They were mum's favourite things to buy at Christmas time." Karim explained, "She loved reindeers."

"That's pretty sweet." Ruby replied brightly, "I'm sure your dad will appreciate the gesture."

"Oh he does. He's always grateful to have anything that reminds him of her." Karim said happily, "To him, it's like she's still here with us even though she's gone."

Ruby nodded understandingly. It was a nice sentiment to live by.

"I feel the same way Karim." Emerald suddenly cut in, "I always carry this with me to remind me of grandma."

She took out a beautiful golden locket from the inside pocket of her hoodie and showed it to Karim. The locket was shaped like a love heart and had the words "Love you grandma" carved onto the front. Inside was a picture of a smiling old woman with grey hair and square-shaped glasses. She looked very friendly and welcoming. Karim had never seen the locket before.

"That's a lovely locket." he complimented, "And your grandma looked like a lovely woman."

"Oh she was the best." Ruby said happily, "You'd have loved her. She was probably the kindest person we've ever known. Mum would always say that grandma's kindness inspired her to pass it on to us when we were born."

"I don't recall a single time she was ever in a bad mood." Sapphire added, "I doubt anything could've upset her."

"That does sound lovely." Karim said with awe, "But given you have that as a memento, I assume she's dead as well?" he asked sadly.

Emerald nodded sadly and clutched the locket close to her chest.

"She died about three years ago." she lamented, "It was awful. She was just slowly wasting away and forgetting about almost everything in her life. All I wanted was for her to get better...but it never happened." she said sadly.

Karim shook his head sadly. He knew what that was like. He'd felt the same about his mother. He patted Emerald on the shoulder in sympathy.

"At least you've got something to remember her by." he said kindly, "In that way, she's still with you even now."

"Exactly!" Emerald said brightly, "Just by bringing this locket with me, it makes me feel like I've brought grandma on this trip with us. I bet she would've loved Norway if she could see it now."

"Oh she would dear." Annie confirmed, "Mum did love to travel and visit other countries. I know she would've loved to visit this one."

"Why didn't she visit Norway?" Emerald asked.

"She had other countries she prioritized over it." Annie answered, "I remember she'd planned for her last journey abroad to be in Norway. As you know, it never happened. But we're here now and I'm sure she's watching us all have a splendid time."

Emerald nodded in agreement. They were having a good day so far and grandma was no doubt feeling thrilled to watch them all from the heavens enjoying their holiday. After they were finished in the Christmas shop, the Silverlock family, Karim, Paul and Judy walked down more streets before finding somewhere to have some lunch. On their travels, Ruby spotted a restaurant called Peppes Pizza and the family decided to check it out. Peppes Pizza was Norway's own pizza chain specializing in American style pizzas. Ruby knew she had to give it a try and it proved to be a worthwhile choice for the pizza was absolutely delicious. The toppings were flavourful and the crust was nice and crispy. If the girls ever decided they want to live in this country, they'd know where to go for pizza. After lunch, they roamed around the streets some more in search of something to do before heading back to the ship. Despite Ruby and Emerald's protestations, Michael, Annie, Sapphire and Judy were interested to check out the oil museum. They managed to compromise in the end for they went in to look around while Ruby and Emerald stayed outside with Karim and Paul. The Rimor agent promised to keep a close eye on the two while Annie and Michael were inside. Sapphire was a little bummed that her sisters didn't want to come in but they assured her it was OK and they didn't want to stop her from having a look.

"If you say so." Sapphire said with a shrug, "Just don't wander off and get into any trouble, OK?"

"They won't sweetheart." Annie reassured Sapphire, "Paul is watching over them. If anything happens, he'll protect them."

"Absolutely he will." Judy declared, "You're all under our protection as much as Karim is, and Paul can be trusted more than any to keep people safe."

"And we appreciate it." Michael replied, "You two be good and wait for us. We'll try not to be too long in the museum."

"No need to hurry dad. Me and Em can wait." Ruby insisted, "We don't want you to rush for us."

Annie and Michael beamed appreciatively at Ruby's consideration. They went into the museum with Sapphire and Judy close behind, leaving Ruby, Emerald, Karim and Paul outside. Paul looked at his watch. It was half past one. The ship wasn't due to leave until the evening so there was time to spare.

"We've still got time. No need to rush." Paul informed.

"That's fine. We can let mum, dad and Sapph have as long as they like in there." Ruby said thoughtfully, "The weather's still perfect right now so why not enjoy a bit of sunshine and enjoying the view?"

"Easy to do considering how nice the views are here." Karim said as he gazed out at the sparkling water around the museum.

Emerald wasn't as enthusiastic.

"It'll be boring just standing around waiting for mum, dad, Sapph and Judy." she muttered, "I'd rather we could see something else."

"I know Em, but we have to be fair to everybody else." Ruby said firmly, "We can't always do what we want. We did the Christmas shop as you asked and we ate at the pizza place as I asked, ergo we wait for Sapph to do the oil museum as she asked. Don't you think that's fair for everybody?"

"Oh yes, of course I do." Emerald said kindly.

"There we go then." Ruby said brightly, "I'll confess that I'm not one to just stand and wait either, but I'll do so for Sapph and the parents."

Emerald nodded. There was something about Ruby's maturity and sense of responsibility that made her admire her big sister. She was only fifteen and yet was already acting all grown-up. She hoped to be as mature and responsible as Ruby when she got older. She was also glad to see Ruby acting so much more like her old self again. Ever since the holiday had started, Ruby had been more settled, less stressed and hadn't snapped at anyone. Even now she was displaying her usual level-headedness. If this had been Ruby from last month, she likely would've been irritable and impatient. The holiday had been just the recovery she needed. But would it last? Once the holiday was over, would Ruby go back to having nightmares again? If so, would it cause her to become angry and depressed like before? Emerald hoped she wouldn't. She glanced to Paul who was watching some ships sailing in the distance as if making sure there wasn't anything suspicious about them. Paul would probably give Ruby another therapy session to see how she was recovering and if she were to relapse, he'd be able to help her. Even when the holiday was over, everything would be fine. Emerald smiled to herself as those words danced around in her head. She had nothing to worry about.

But as Emerald said this to herself, she saw a glint of sunlight reflecting off of something just in the corner of her eye. Emerald blinked as the light dazzled her a bit and she turned around to look. What on Earth was twinkling like that? Emerald looked to her side and gasped as she saw what it was that had caught her eye. There was a man in blue and black armour creeping just up ahead. That was strange. Who was that man? She doubted it was a policeman. Did policemen in Norway even dress like that? Where was he going and why was he heading in that direction? Emerald watched as the man snuck into an alleyway and got himself into position. Emerald's blood ran cold. She didn't like where this was going. She continued to watch as the man suddenly got down on one knee and picked something up. It was hard to see from this distance, but Emerald knew what was going on. The man had taken out a gun and he was aiming it at someone! But who? She looked to her left and gasped. Was the man aiming at Ruby? If so, that was OK since Ruby's protection spell would save her. But if it activated, she'd only draw attention to herself and the locals would see her. If they saw a girl with glowing hair, a mass panic would start. She had to stop that man before any harm could be done!

"LOOK OUT!" Emerald screeched, throwing herself into Ruby and tackling her to the ground.

Ruby cried out as she was brought down heavily into the pavement. She landed heavily, the impact punching the wind out of her. As the girls lay sprawled on the pavement, the man's gunshot whizzed past them, missing them both and crashing down harmlessly into the waters of the bay. Ruby panted heavily as the shock of what just happened settled in on her. Emerald helped her up, her face white with fear.

"We're under attack! There's a man in an alleyway over there and he's shooting at you!" she screeched.

"I can see that!" Ruby retorted, "Good spot Em, not that it would've killed me anyway but it's still lucky you saw him. I can't have my spell activating in the middle of a city!"

"I see him!" Karim yelled angrily, "Let's get him!"

"Stay behind me kids, I'll lead the attack!" Paul ordered.

Paul drew out his sonic blaster and Ruby, Emerald Karim followed from behind as he sprinted towards the alleyway. The man saw them coming and retreated back into the alley. It was clear he thought he couldn't handle all of them at once. The man didn't get very far for the alley had a dead end, with a wall that was too big and too smooth for him to climb up. He was trapped. Paul and the kids quickly caught up to him and Paul pointed his sonic blaster at the man. The man raised his hands in surrender. The kids stayed behind Paul as the Rimor agent advanced on the man. His face was cool and collected despite the anger he was feeling. He recognized the man immediately from his suit of armour and it made him seethe just seeing it here in Norway. Ruby recognized the uniform too.

"A hunter?!" she gasped, "What are you monsters doing here in Norway?!"

"I think you already know the answer, Ruby." Paul said cryptically, "You're here for Ruby, aren't you?" he demanded, keeping the sonic blaster pointed at the man's face, "I knew you hunters were scummy enough to indulge in worthless causes like revenge. So where's the rest of your crew? There's no way they only sent one of you." he said coldly.

The man just smirked at Paul, confirming his suspicions without actually needing to say anything. As Paul prepared to shoot him, pounding feet was suddenly heard from behind. Paul, Ruby, Emerald and Karim spun around as the feet came closer to them. The teens stood beside Paul in anticipation. They had a feeling they might have to use their new powers to fight. The pounding feet and voices they'd heard came into view and just as they'd feared, it was a squadron of hunters. There they were in their familiar blue and black armour suits, large helmets with big visors and huge guns in their hands. Alice was leading this particular squad. Alice held up her gun and pointed it at Paul. He cursed himself mentally. Of course it had been a trap! How could he have been so stupid as to fall for a trap so obvious that even a five year old would've seen through it?

"Alright sir, you have just ten seconds to stand aside and surrender Ruby to us!" Alice growled, "If you don't comply, your friends at Rimor will have to take you home in a body bag!"

Chapter 10: Attack of the Hunters

Seeing the hunters again made Ruby feel as if a hole had been punched through her chest. How dare they come here and show their faces again in a country as nice as Norway and barge in on her family's holiday just so they could come for her! Did these monsters have any standards whatsoever? She wondered how the hunters knew she was even here at all. They must've somehow been tipped off that she and her family were holidaying in Norway. Alice caught sight of her and looked angered to see her. The visor may have obscured her face but her body language said it all. She clearly wasn't happy to see her again, and Ruby couldn't blame her for it. If Alice had killed her father, she'd have felt the same way.

"You!" she growled, her voice like an enraged tigress, "Oh you have no idea how "thrilled" I am to see you again Ruby Silverlock! I've been dreaming for weeks on end of getting my revenge on you, and now that dream's coming true! I hope you enjoyed your little holiday, because now it's coming to an end!" she growled.

"Don't get any ideas." Ruby said coldly, "You know my protection spell will save me if you try to kill me. And even if you do try anything, Rimor will let everyone know that I killed your boss and then your entire organization will be nothing but a joke!" she warned.

Alice chuckled humourlessly.

"Oh Ruby, you poor, misguided fool. That won't work on us anymore, for you see...my father's not actually dead." Alice purred darkly, "You did come close my dear, but not close enough. Draven is alive, and he's NOT happy with you!"

Ruby's eyes widened in disbelief. Karim was equally as incredulous. That couldn't possibly be true, could it? Before they could call out her bluff, Alice took out her communicator and spoke into it. She could tell they didn't believe her and decided a quick call to Draven would be the proof they'd need that she wasn't lying.

"Father, we've located Ruby and we have her cornered." Alice reported, her tone of voice smug and gloating as if she wanted to rub it into Ruby's face that Draven wasn't dead, "Our little trap worked perfectly."

She received a reply and Ruby thought her heart was going to stop as she heard the very voice she thought she would never hear again.

"You've got her? Excellent work Alice." Draven purred with delight, **"You know what to do now. Shoot to stun, not kill, and bring her back to me. Don't bother about the others, only Ruby matters in this mission…"**

Ruby's head spun wildly in disbelief. She couldn't believe what she was hearing! Draven…was ALIVE?! All this time she'd been wallowing in self-pity and feeling guilty over killing him, only for it to be all for nothing in the end as he wasn't actually dead?! She wanted to believe that Alice was lying and trying to mess with her, but it was definitely Draven's voice that had replied to her on her communicator. There was no way that had been faked; it was clearly Draven who had replied to her. Alice also seemed far too gleeful about getting her to hear Draven's voice again and let him know she'd found Ruby. Why would she be so happy to be telling a lie? Ruby didn't want to believe it, but the proof was in the pudding. She found herself in a whirlwind of emotions. On the one hand, she didn't kill him and therefore she had nothing to be ashamed of anymore. She wasn't a murderer! But on the other hand, Draven was still alive and he was here to take revenge. What was supposed to be a nice, enjoyable holiday had suddenly taken a dark turn. Why did this have to happen now of all times?

"I...I didn't kill him after all?" Ruby murmured, her voice quavering as the shock and realization of what she'd been told settled in, "Draven...is alive?!"

"As Idris often tells us, Draven is a hard man to kill." Paul muttered. Unlike Ruby, he had no expression on his face and no emotion in his voice. It was like Draven's survival wasn't even that surprising to him, and all knowing about it meant was he could confirm for definite that he was alive.

"It doesn't matter if he's alive," Paul went on, "We're not letting you take Ruby. If you want her, you're going to have to fight us for her. I'd heavily advise against it though as I'd hate for us to humiliate you all again. Be a pal and stand down so we can all resolve this peacefully for a change, OK?" he demanded.

"Not on your life, Rimor scum." Alice said coldly, "This only ends one way: you dead and we take Ruby, Emerald and Karim prisoner. Not only do we have a score to settle with Ruby, but Idris's son will make a very valuable hostage..." she said coldly, glancing to Karim.

Karim flinched but kept up a brave face. He wasn't going to let Alice or her squad intimidate him. Paul remained cool and collected as if everything was under control and nobody had anything to worry about. He shrugged casually.

"Fair enough. I did try to be reasonable." he sighed, "So you only have yourselves to blame for what happens next. Kids, let's show these people what you've been practicing lately..." the Rimor agent purred slyly.

Ruby, Emerald and Karim nodded. They knew exactly what Paul meant. All at once, the teens struck out with their new powers. While they would've preferred to keep them hidden, they knew that this was the right time to use them. Ruby thrust her arms forward and swept a few hunters off their feet with funnels of flames that whooshed over them but didn't burn. Even if this was to save her own life, Ruby still didn't want to kill anyone. The hunters cried out as the flames whooshed over them. Alice turned away and winced, feeling the heat of the flames as they swept over her. Great, now she was dealing with magic powered teenagers! Could this day get any crazier?! The hunter that had baited them into coming into the alley tried to shoot at Paul while his back was turned but Paul quickly spun around and shot him with his sonic blaster. The hunter was knocked out instantly by the blast and he slumped heavily against the wall. Some hunters tried to blast the group with stun blasts but Karim held out a hand, clenched his fist and drew it back. The hunters yelped as their guns were seized by psychic energy and wrenched out of their hands. Emerald was the last to attack, forming a yellow energy ball in her hands and throwing it directly into Alice's face. Her visor protected her from the blow, but the force of the impact was still enough to send Alice reeling backwards. Her helmet nearly fell off with the power of that blow. Alice stumbling away gave the group an opening and they ran for it. Paul ushered the kids ahead so he could protect them from behind and act as a shield against the hunters. As they ran, he turned around and shot at the hunters to keep them from pursuing.

"We have to get back to the ship!" Paul declared, "The hunters won't dare attack us somewhere as public as a cruise ship, there'll be too many witnesses!"

"I agree! Those guys love to do things secretly, they can't really do that on a cruise ship!" Ruby replied, "But we need to get mum, dad, Sapph and Judy first!"

"The museum's just over there!" Emerald informed, pointing ahead as she saw it come into view, "We'll run in and let them know what's happened!"

"And once we're onboard, we should let dad know about this!" Karim added, "He'll know what to do!"

Paul nodded in agreement. He had the same idea himself. Rimor wasn't based entirely in the UK, they did have other bases abroad and luckily, they had a base in Norway. Idris could contact the Norwegian base and get their agents to help in keeping the hunters off their backs. But as they headed back to the oil museum, more trouble lay ahead. Another squad of hunters led by Simon was running over to join Alice's squad and they saw the foursome coming towards them. Paul reacted incredibly quickly, blasting sonic waves furiously at Simon and his team. They dodged the blasts and Simon shot back. Paul dived behind a parked car for cover while Emerald held up her hands and formed a protective shield to protect both herself and Paul. The shields she formed were yellow in colour and could be formed in either round or rectangular shapes. The shield was more than strong enough to stop the gun shots. Emerald felt every one as it pinged harmlessly away from her. Ruby sprang up from behind Emerald and threw fireballs at Simon's squad. They stopped shooting at Emerald and Paul and dived for cover before the fireballs could hit. Two hunters tried to shoot at Ruby but Karim used psychokinesis to snatch their guns away again. He grinned wildly, enjoying himself immensely. How great it felt to have the hunters looking so helpless while they were on top of this match!

"Not so easy when you're against magic powered kids, am I right?!" Karim taunted.

"So you've got some magical mumbo jumbo to give you an edge. That's hardly going to make me quake in my boots." Simon retorted, "We hunters have lost count of how many magic powered individuals we've slain in our career! You've hardly got an advantage over us!"

"You sure? Because from where we're standing, we've got the upper hand so far." Ruby sneered, "Maybe you and your goons should just go home and forget all about me."

"Fat chance you little brat." Simon growled, "Draven will never let us hear the end of it if we return empty-handed. So use those pesky magic tricks all you like, we're not giving up."

He took aim with his gun and fired a stun shot at Ruby. What should've been a clean shot was intercepted by Emerald as she quickly threw a shield in front of Ruby. Her light constructs were able to be thrown if necessary and it managed to block Simon's shot. Furious, Simon tried to shoot Emerald next but Karim held out a hand to try and snatch Simon's gun away. Unfortunately, Simon was well-trained in fighting against psychokinesis so he kept a good hold on his gun and pulled back. Seeing he couldn't take the gun away, Karim caught Simon off-guard by flicking his wrist and causing the gun to flick upwards. Simon was startled and he fell over backwards from the sudden motion. He grunted from the impact as he landed heavily onto his back. Ruby grinned with satisfaction, glad to see that things were going well for her team. But there was no time to celebrate yet. She quickly had to duck down as more stun shots blasted towards her from behind. Alice's squad had recovered from the earlier battle and had rushed in to help Simon's squad. Emerald whimpered nervously and clutched Ruby's arm while Ruby glared at the hunters closing in on them. Karim stood protectively in front of them both while Paul took up the rear.

"Great, now we've got two lots of hunters to deal with." Karim muttered.

"It doesn't matter how many there are." Ruby said bluntly, "As long as we can get away and back on the ship, we'll be fine."

"As is, we can't keep relying on your fancy new powers." Paul warned, "We'll attract too much attention and cause a scene. A city as big as Stavanger is hardly the kind of place to battle discreetly."

As he said this, Ruby, Emerald and Karim looked around to see that a few civilians had stopped by to see what was going on. They looked curious and scared. As far as they knew, some kind of strange group had come out of nowhere and was attacking what looked like innocent civilians. Had any of them called the police already? It so, then the hunters would be forced to retreat. But Paul was right. If she, Emerald or Karim used their powers now, they'd cause a mass panic. What would the headlines look like on the Norwegian news? "Witches sighted in Stavanger!" most likely. The hunters noticed there were people watching too and Ruby heard Alice and Simon addressing the crowd, presumably in Norwegian so they could understand what they were saying. It didn't surprise her to see the hunters were skilled in multiple languages. She could imagine what they were saying right now: "Stay back everyone! These are evil witches with evil magical powers! We're taking care of them, so stay back before you get hurt!" Neither she, Emerald or Karim could speak a word of Norwegian so they couldn't defend themselves or explain what was actually happening. Paul could, but he knew it was useless to try. It was his word against all of the hunters and considering he was currently defending the so-called evil witches, the crowd was very unlikely to take his word seriously. The hunters held all the cards for now.

"Of course the hunters will stoop so low as to lie to innocent people about what's really happening..." Paul muttered, "The crowd will want to see us all imprisoned or worse now."

"So what do we do?" Emerald asked anxiously.

"We improvise." Ruby declared, "Hopefully all that training with Rimor can help us out here..."

She made the first move by kicking out backwards with her right leg and slamming her foot into the solar plexus of the nearest hunter to her. Her kick winded him and he staggered backwards. Caught by surprise, he accidentally squeezed the trigger of his gun and stunned another hunter. He crumpled instantly as the blast knocked him out. Emerald followed Ruby's example and kicked at the hunter nearest to her. To her amazement, she kicked him hard enough to knock him down onto the pavement. Two hunters lashed out at Karim but he ducked down, leaving them to crash into each other head first. The blow left them both dazed for a moment, giving Karim a chance to trip them both up with a kick to their ankles. Paul used a flurry of punches and kicks to disarm any hunters trying to shoot him and knock them backwards to clear a path for himself and the kids. They didn't have to beat the hunters, just get away so they could get back onto the *Nova* and hide away from them. Emerald was the first to see an opening and she took it. She sprinted away from the battle and towards the oil museum. Her parents, Sapphire and Judy still needed to be warned before she or anyone else went back to the ship. Unfortunately, Simon saw her and chased after her. Ruby tried to follow him but Alice blocked her way and lashed out with a flat-palmed strike to the face that sent the silver-haired girl reeling. Ruby felt as if she'd been whacked in the face with a hammer. She wiped a trickle of blood away from the corner of her mouth and lashed out at Alice, trying to punch her in the chest. Alice intercepted and knocked Ruby aside with a backhanded strike. Then she grabbed Ruby by the neck and began to strangle her. Ruby gagged and gasped for breath. She tried to get free but Alice's grip was too strong. Rimor's training couldn't change the fact she was still a child facing an adult. Alice grinned deviously, relishing the fact she had Ruby at her mercy.

"I know I can't kill you because of that little spell of yours, but I can at least throttle you into unconsciousness!" Alice crowed, "I'll bring you back to father myself, and I'm sure he has a very grisly fate in store for you! I'll even demand that he let me watch as you die at his hands!"

"I'm...not...going...anywhere...near...that monster!" Ruby choked, black spots starting to dance in front of her eyes as consciousness slowly began to slip away, "Whereas you...can...go back...to Draven...in...total agony!"

Alice's eyes nearly popped out of their sockets as Ruby suddenly swung her leg straight up into her groin. The teenager's knee slammed so hard in-between her legs that Alice thought she was about to pass out herself. She let go of Ruby and collapsed onto the floor. This was the worst pain she'd ever felt in her life. She grabbed her tender spot and gritted her teeth. Her eyes watered. As Alice knelt down trying to fight off the pain in her groin, Ruby rubbed her neck vigorously, sucking in air as desperately as she could. It was lucky for her that Alice had let her grudge get in the way of common sense, otherwise she would've been knocked out and back in Draven's hands. Now Alice was down, Ruby continued fighting the other hunters.

Meanwhile, Emerald had nearly reached the museum but Simon had caught up to her. He tried to stun her but Emerald reacted incredibly quickly, blocking the shot with a yellow shield just in time. Growling in frustration, Simon put his gun away. He would just have to deal with the kid with his bare hands. He lashed out at Emerald, punching her in the stomach and sending her hurling backwards. Emerald crashed into a lamppost, the impact knocking the wind out of her. Now she was stunned, Simon grabbed her by the arm and hauled her back to her feet. Emerald squirmed furiously but she couldn't get her arm free. Simon had a grip as tight as a bear trap.

"Got you!" he sneered, "I bet Ruby will give herself up once she sees your life's at stake little Emerald!"

"Let me go, please!" Emerald begged, still struggling to get away.

"No chance!" Simon spat, "Now stop squirming before I have to hurt you real bad!"

"OY!"

Simon was surprised at the voice that had called out to him. He turned around...and was promptly hammered in the face by a powerful punch. He was more surprised than hurt as he let go of Emerald and spun away, the punch nearly taking his head clean off.

He collapsed onto the ground unconscious from the punch. Emerald smiled with relief to see it had been Michael who had saved her. He, Annie, Sapphire and Judy were about to leave the museum and had seen everything. Michael grinned with grim satisfaction. Last time they'd met, Simon had pointed a gun at him to make Ruby hesitate when she and Selina had tried to ransom the hunters. It felt good to have gotten back at him for that.

"Keep your hands off of my daughter!" Michael roared at the unconscious Simon.

"Mum! Dad! Sapph! Thank goodness!" Emerald shrieked with delight, hugging each of them, "You saved me from being a hostage!"

"Where are Ruby, Karim and Paul?" Annie asked, "Are they alright?"

"They're fighting the hunters!" Emerald said frantically, "We need to help them so we can all get away!"

"I can't believe those monsters followed us here!" Sapphire growled, "All we wanted was a nice bloody holiday, but now they've shown up to spoil it! Oh just wait til I..."

"Calm down young lady, you'll only get yourself killed." Judy warned, "It'll be safer for us if we retreat back onto the ship. You two, get going." she said to Annie and Michael, "Me and Sapphire will help the others."

Despite their concerns for their children, Annie and Michael knew they would be foolish to disobey Judy. They'd only make themselves targets if they stuck around. They wished Emerald and Sapphire luck before running off back to the ship. Judy made sure that nobody was following them as they fled the scene. The parents were in the clear so she and Sapphire followed Emerald back to the fight. They were just in time to see Ruby, Karim and Paul fighting off the hunters as best as they could. Ruby kicked one in the gut and made him stumble backwards, Karim roundhouse kicked one in the legs and tripped her up and Paul karate chopped one in the back and winded him. Alice was still in anguish from Ruby's earlier attack. A couple of hunters had to help her back to her feet and take her out of the fight to give her chance to recover. The two squads kept trying to shoot at the trio but their blasts either missed or were blocked. Sapphire seized her chance to get involved. She formed a pair of ice boxing gloves around her hands and punched one of the hunters in the back of the head. The blow cracked his helmet and made him stumble forwards in alarm. Another hunter saw Sapphire and tried to shoot her but Sapphire flicked her fingers and froze the gun and his hand solid so he couldn't pull the trigger. The hunter tried to free his hand but that only left him open for Judy to come in and kick him in the face. Ruby saw Sapphire and Judy and beamed with delight.

"Great timing you two! We needed a little back up!" she called out.

"We can see that!" Sapphire retorted, throwing icicles at two hunters trying to attack her, "Em told us what was happening so we're here to help you all escape!"

"Their forces are starting to dwindle!" Paul observed, "Let's make a break for it before they send more hunters!"

Nobody waited to be asked twice. With many of the hunters either knocked out or injured, now was a good a time to make a break for it. Ruby, Emerald, Sapphire, Karim, Paul and Judy abandoned the fight and began to flee. Any remaining hunters shot at them but they missed. Alice could only watch helplessly as their target was starting to slip away. She had to do something before Ruby escaped! She couldn't let her father down! The tall woman took out her own gun and aimed. But she wasn't aiming for Ruby, and she wasn't aiming to stun anyone either. She hoped that if she shot Paul or Judy, that would stop Ruby and the others long enough for the hunters to catch up and capture them. Also killing two of Rimor's top agents would be a happy bonus. Alice fired the shot...but hit the wrong target. One of the hunters had picked the worst time to get back up after being knocked down earlier and he was now in Alice's way. The gun shot slammed into his back, making him cry out in pain and then he collapsed onto the ground. Ruby and her team had heard the gunshot and spun around to see what had happened. They saw the downed hunter and Alice standing there, her face in total shock over what she'd just done. Her hands trembled. She was so horrified that she dropped her gun. The two hunters with her tried to calm her down but it was no use. Alice was beyond terrified over what her father was going to do to her after such a terrible mistake. She was sure her days as a hunter were over!

"Oh god, oh god, oh god!" she repeated to herself, her face turning white.

"That poor man! He needs help!" Emerald exclaimed.

"Forget about him, we need to get out of here now!" Paul insisted.

But Emerald ignored him. It was against her nature to just abandon someone in need, even if they were the enemy. Ruby and Sapphire didn't fault her. With how traumatic it had been for Ruby thinking she'd killed Draven, neither of them wanted to just leave someone to die. Emerald ran up to the stricken man. He was lying down on the pavement with a horrible scorch mark on his back marking where he'd been hit. Despite the damage, he was still alive, but barely. Emerald knelt down by the man's side and surveyed the damage. She knew that this wound was too serious for her to heal completely, but maybe she could partially heal it so it wouldn't be fatal and then the hunters could take him away and handle the rest themselves. The man panted heavily. Emerald sensed he was fading fast, so she had to act now. Alice snapped out of her shocked state and saw Emerald placing her hands on the man's back. She pointed her gun at Emerald.

"Get away from him!" she snarled.

"No! I can help him!" Emerald shot back, "I have healing powers, so I can save your friend before he dies!"

"I'm not letting you use whatever witchcraft you have on that agent!" Alice growled savagely, "Who knows what you'll do to him! Now get away from him before I shoot you!"

"How about you back the hell off and let Em save your agent's life?!" Ruby shouted angrily, "He's probably got seconds to live right now and you're just going to deny him a chance to live? We could've easily left him to die, but we're not! As crazy as it may seem Alice, Emerald wants to help him, so put that gun down and let her work!"

"Do as she says." Judy commanded, pointing her own gun at Alice, "Emerald's being more than generous. Don't squander it, lest we be forced to shoot you too."

Alice didn't want to let Emerald use any magic on the hunter. She was sure this was some trick to get back at her and her squad for the attack. She was about to argue again until suddenly, her communicator burst into life and Draven's voice called out to her.

"Stand down. Let the girl do her work. Let's see if she can save Agent Rodriguez."

Alice was astounded. Why was Draven of all people letting this continue? He was the last person to let anyone use magic on his agents! But the tall woman did as she was told and lowered her weapon. She imagined Draven had some kind of plan in mind. He wouldn't give her an order without reason. Alice sighed heavily as she put her gun away. She glowered at Emerald.

"Get on with it." she commanded, "But I warn you, no tricks. You're only to heal him, nothing else. OK?"

"I wouldn't be able to do anything else to him." Emerald said truthfully, "It's not like I can place curses on people or something, not that I'd want to. Unlike you people, I'm not horrible and want to hurt and kill others."

Alice scowled at the young girl but said nothing. She ordered the other hunters to stand back and let Emerald heal Rodriguez. Now no one was pointing guns at her, Emerald relaxed and placed her hands on the dying man's back. She felt a little nervous. This was her first time trying to heal a serious injury. During training, she'd tested her healing powers on little cuts and bruises she, Ruby, Sapphire or Karim had received during training, but this was something else entirely. Rodriguez was still breathing heavily. Emerald could feel him shivering. No doubt he was starting to feel cold as his life was slipping away from him. He winced as Emerald's hands touched the wound on his back.

"Keep still. I promise you this won't hurt, sir." Emerald said gently.

The brunette girl then closed her eyes and exhaled softly. For a moment, she was completely still. Then her hands began to glow and a soothing aura emitted from her palms. Rodriguez suddenly came still and his breathing slowed into a sigh of relief. He felt content and at peace from the calming aura that spread across his back. Everyone stared in awe as the golden light from Emerald's hands engulfed Rodriguez. A couple of minutes later, the light died down and the process was complete. Emerald fell over backwards, completely exhausted from the whole thing. Ruby and Sapphire caught her and helped her to remain sitting up. Emerald was completely drained, close to falling asleep. But she'd done her job. Rodriguez wasn't completely healed, but the wound in his back had healed up just enough so he was no longer in danger of dying. He was in a lot of pain, but he was alive and that was the most important thing. For a moment, nobody moved. It was like they were trying to comprehend what had just happened and what they should do now it was over. Two hunters helped Rodriguez up to his feet. They led him away so he could get medical attention back in the submarine. Emerald had done her part, now they could do the rest. Alice was completely speechless. She had no idea what to think of the whole thing. She hated how she'd been forced to let magic be used on one of her men, but she was at least appreciative that she wouldn't have to come back to Draven and explain how she'd killed one of his agents. But most of all, Alice was confused on why Emerald had even saved Rodriguez's life. Just a minute ago, she, Simon and both their squads had been trying to capture her, Ruby and Karim, and yet she still saved Rodriguez? Why didn't she let him die? She looked over to the tired Emerald.

"Why...? Why did you do it?" the second-in-command asked.

Emerald looked back at Alice with groggy, half-open eyes.

"I...couldn't just...leave him to die, could I?" she said wearily.

"Think of us whatever you want Alice, but we're not heartless." Ruby said firmly, "Do you want to know how my life has been since last time we met? I've been waking up in the night from nightmares because I was that traumatized over the belief I'd killed your father. Unlike you monsters, we actually DO care if people die and we get very upset about it! I know me and Draven are enemies, but I never wanted to kill him. As strange as it may sound, I'm actually kinda relieved to know he's alive, because then at least it means I'm not a murderer. And that applies to your agents too: we don't want them to die, even if we are enemies."

"We've done you a favour by saving your agent's life." Sapphire acknowledged, "So I think you should return the favour by letting us go and calling off the hunt for Ruby. Or is gratitude something you hunters have no concept of?" she asked coldly.

Alice was about to retort but Draven's voice boomed from her communicator again.

"Fall back. We'll let them go this once." he commanded, **"The girl is right, we are in their debt for Rodriguez's life. I think it's fair we return the favour."**

"But father..." Alice protested.

"That's an order!" Draven barked angrily.

Alice was in torment. She didn't want to just let Ruby and her family and friends just walk away like that. Ruby still had to pay for nearly killing Draven and she, Emerald, Sapphire and Karim had to be relieved of their magic powers! But she was in no position to disobey her father. She was still sure he had some kind of plan so it wouldn't hurt to play along for now. Maybe Draven was planning to exploit this act of generosity from Emerald in some way. With great reluctance, she gave the order to her men.

"Do as father says. Fall back. We're done here." she muttered.

The hunters obeyed and put away their weapons. They walked away together, heading back to where their submarine was hidden. Alice was the last to leave. She cast one final glare at the Silverlock sisters.

"Don't get comfortable, either of you. Don't think that we're suddenly going to forgive you for my father's near death." Alice warned, "We're only letting you go this one time. Next time you face us, we're not going to be so generous."

"Come after me all you like, we'll only kick your butts again." Ruby scoffed, "As long as I have my friends and family beside me, you're NEVER going to get your hands on me, so if I were you, I'd just give up and not bother coming after me. I'm more trouble than I'm worth."

"Besides, what's the point of it all?" Sapphire added, "Is it really worth risking life and limb and humiliating yourselves just to get petty revenge on someone who wasn't even aiming to kill your boss in the first place?"

Alice didn't even bother dignifying Sapphire's words with a response. She was in no mood to argue. She turned around and stalked off, leaving the sisters behind. Once she was gone, Ruby, Emerald and Sapphire all sighed with relief. Thank goodness that was over! But they knew they couldn't relax completely. The hunters were in Norway and they wouldn't give up the hunt so easily, even if Emerald had saved the life of one of their own. Paul and Judy ushered the girls to come along.

"Let's get back to the ship." Paul said softly.

The girls nodded and walked off with them back towards the *Nova*. Emerald was starting to feel a little reenergized after her healing trick earlier, enough to at least walk without anyone helping her. But she still looked as if she was ready for a long sleep once she got back to the ship. Everyone would have a much-needed rest once they were back onboard. As they walked, Karim looked to Emerald curiously.

"So why did you save that man's life?" he asked, "I know you said you couldn't just let him die, but is there any other reason for it?"

Emerald looked up to the sky thoughtfully as if searching for an answer.

"Well...I suppose it's a bit of wishful thinking from me." the girl in green mused, "It might be silly of me to say, but I guessed if I helped that man, that might convince the hunters to leave us alone. I'm probably an idiot for thinking that, but..."

"No Em, you're not an idiot. Naïve perhaps, but not an idiot." Sapphire said firmly, "There's nothing idiotic about wanting to be kind to others and inspire them to be kind in return. Whether the hunters want to return your kindness or not is on them."

"Besides, it's quite sweet that you did that for that reason." Ruby complimented, "It might be wishful thinking, but it is worth a shot. Maybe the hunters will appreciate the gesture and back off."

"It's not entirely unprecedented." Paul concurred, "Draven does have an honourable side to him. Believe it or not, he can be reasoned with depending on the circumstances. I'm still certain he'll be back for us, but the fact he let us go in thanks for saving his agent's life is something we should be grateful for."

"And hopefully it'll be enough to convince him to call off the hunt." Ruby murmured.

Emerald smiled to herself in appreciation. If her single act of kindness was enough to get Draven to leave Ruby alone, then she would be the biggest hero of the entire family! They'd never have to worry about Draven hunting them down ever again! They wouldn't have to live in hiding anymore and would be able to live normally like before. She couldn't wait to tell Tony all about it first chance she got. Emerald was grateful that he and his family had missed out on the action. The whole thing would've been too much for them if they'd been there. With any luck, it would remain that way if the hunters decided to leave them alone because of her act of kindness.

Meanwhile, Draven was standing in front of his surveillance monitors with his hands behind his back while waiting for his two squadrons to return. He was deep in thought over everything that had occurred. He'd seen and heard everything that had happened. He'd had one of his Cyber Dragons monitoring the situation whilst invisible so nobody would see it. The Cyber Dragon was only for surveillance duties so he could see what was going on during the mission. Had he needed to, he would've gotten involved in the battle. But instead, he'd seen an interesting development that gave him a great idea. He too had been shocked by Emerald's selfless decision to save Rodriguez's life. He was her sister's enemy, and yet she'd saved his agent's life anyway. But Draven had also been fascinated by Emerald's kindness. She was on opposing sides, but she didn't discriminate and still saved lives regardless. Who knew there really were people that kind and generous in the world? He thought the Staff of Wishes mission was a bust...but maybe he'd been wrong. He put a clawed finger to his mouthplate in thought.

"It would seem we've found our pure of heart..." Draven purred deviously to himself, **"Yes...the Staff of Wishes will be ours**

after all. Emerald Silverlock will be just who we need to get our prize..."

Chapter 11: Tony's Secret

Alice and Simon returned back to the submarine with both squadrons filing in behind them. Some of the hunters had to be carried back, unconscious from the battle. Some had to be helped back due to injuries received during the fight. It had been a long retreat, but soon everybody was back in the submarine and it drifted away from shore. There was no need to hang about in Stavanger any longer, not while Ruby was back on her cruise ship. Even Draven would never stoop so low as to attack a cruise ship and threaten the lives of innocent holiday makers. The government wouldn't be too pleased about that. To the public, the hunters had to look like the heroes, not a bunch of terrorists. But Draven was still keeping an eye on Ruby and her family. The Cyber Dragon he'd sent out for surveillance was still on patrol and still invisible to everyone. It would watch MS *Nova* and see where it went next and it was also equipped with long range listening devices so the draconian machine would be able to eavesdrop on the Silverlock family. Draven was carefully plotting his next move. He knew he needed Emerald to get the Staff of Wishes, but he knew he couldn't just go in and kidnap her. The Silverlock family would be expecting that after what had happened with him and Ruby back in the summer. He would also attract too much attention if he tried kidnapping Emerald. He was sure there was a better way to get her to do what he needed without needing to abduct her. The crew could tell he was deep in thought and they kept themselves quiet and busy, daring not to disturb him. Whenever Draven was like that, they knew it was best to let him think. Alice was in no mood for that. Once the submarine had left Stavanger and sunk back into the ocean depths, she stormed up to Draven, her face a mask of fury. Simon followed behind her, trying desperately to get her to stop but she ignored him. Draven kept his back turned and his gaze fixed on the monitors. It was like he hadn't even noticed Alice had entered the room.

"What on Earth were you thinking father?!" Alice roared, her dazzling green eyes narrowed to pinpricks of rage, "This is so unlike you! You never let people use magic on us, yet you let that little brat do goodness knows what to Rodriguez? That was so risky! She could've done all kinds of horrible things to him, why did you do it, and why did you let them go? We could've captured Ruby then and..."

She was cut off as Draven suddenly turned around, held up his arm and deployed his blade. The tip of it was just inches away from her throat. Alice recoiled and gulped nervously. Not even she dared to speak back to her father when he had his blade at her throat. She stood still and whimpered as the blade glistened in front of her eyes.

"Please stop talking Alice. I'm calculating our next move and you're disturbing me." Draven growled.

"I tried to stop her sir, but she just wouldn't listen." Simon said, trying to get in Draven's good graces.

"You stop talking as well Simon." Draven snapped, **"Both of you have been an embarrassment to our organization today. Not only did you fail at the one job I gave you both, but you were defeated by mere children and a civilian. How is anyone supposed to take us seriously as an organization that protects mankind if a bunch of magic powered teenagers and an ordinary citizen can beat you all?"**

"Please father, it wasn't our fault!" Alice protested, "We..."

"And you Alice, your reckless actions nearly caused the death of one of our own!" Draven said sharply, **"You should be grateful to Emerald that she deigned to save his life and save you from having to report his death to me, otherwise I would've had you drummed out of our organization before you can say "protector of mankind"! And on top of that, why wasn't your gun set to**

stun mode? I gave strict orders to shoot to stun, what if you'd accidentally shot a civilian instead of Rodriguez? If our organization was seen attacking and potentially killing innocent civilians, the government would shut us down in a heartbeat!"

"I was trying to shoot the two Rimor agents with the kids, father!" Alice explained.

"And that makes disobeying orders OK, does it?" Draven retorted, "My orders were precisely as follows: don't bother about the others, ONLY Ruby matters! I never once gave you or anyone else orders to kill anyone, yet you ignored me and you nearly got one of our men killed as a result! Why is it every time you get involved in our missions, you just prove my point that you shouldn't be allowed out on the field?" he asked, his voice full of pain and disappointment for his daughter.

Alice felt as if a dagger had been plunged into her heart. How could her own father say that to her? She wasn't that much of a disappointment to him, was she? She wanted to say something else, anything to try and make up to her father. But what could she say other than "I'm sorry"? She just looked down to her feet in shame. She couldn't even look Draven in the eye anymore. The cyborg sheathed his blade and turned his back on both Alice and Simon. But when he spoke again, his tone of voice had completely changed. He sounded more at ease, more optimistic, almost as if everything he'd been ranting about no longer mattered.

"But before you two start feeling sorry for yourselves, I can confirm that the mission wasn't a total failure." Draven crooned, "If anything, it was more of a success than I could've anticipated."

Alice and Simon were gobsmacked. They stared at each other as if Draven had turned into a turnip. They looked back to their boss in confusion.

"A...success, did you say, sir?" Simon asked, completely befuddled.

"You heard correctly." Draven snapped as if Simon was stupid, **"Remember how the Staff of Wishes mission ended in failure because none of our agents were pure of heart? Well thanks to you two bungling this mission, I can confirm the Staff of Wishes mission is ago once more."**

"What do you mean, father?" Alice asked, "Are you saying that..."

She paused as realization struck her like a bolt of lightning. Her eyes widened and her mouth curled into a devious smirk of satisfaction. She knew her father had a plan the whole time! Now it all made sense! He'd only let Emerald heal Rodriguez because it confirmed that she was the one they were looking for to get to the Staff of Wishes. She chuckled slyly.

"Father, you are so brilliant." she crowed.

"To think that Alice's little accident helped us find our pure of heart." Simon sneered, rubbing his hands together excitedly, "Surely the statue will think so too, anyone who would willingly help their enemies and heal people regardless of what side they're on must be considered as such."

"Exactly." Draven purred, **"Ruby's little sister is clearly a very kind and generous soul. And she's taught me a valuable lesson that I'd long since forgotten. There really are pure humans out there after all. I've spent so much time protecting mankind that I often forget what mankind is truly capable of..."**

He cleared his throat, realizing he was suddenly rambling.

"But enough on that. We will recruit Emerald and have her fetch the Staff of Wishes for us." he announced, **"But we have to be smart about it. Ruby and her family and friends will expect a kidnapping. So maybe there's a way to ask her for help instead of forcing the issue."**

"Maybe we could deceive them?" Alice suggested, "We could pretend we're grateful to them for saving Rodriguez and say that in return for their kindness, we'll tell them where they can find the staff and if they get it, we'll promise to leave them alone and we'll let them keep the staff."

"No need to pretend, for I AM grateful for what they've done." Draven insisted, **"I'm not sure if they'd believe us if we were to say we're repaying them for their kindness. They'll likely suspect we're tricking them. Those two agents watching over them will definitely suspect. But suppose they run into a local and the local tells them where the staff is..."**

Alice and Simon nodded agreeably. It would be simple. They knew Ruby and the others were on a cruise, all they had to do was follow their ship to see where their next stop was. Then they could plant an agent under the guise of being a local, and that agent would tell them where to find the Staff of Wishes. Then they would sit back and let Emerald do the work for them. She was going to be their key to victory and also their key to Ruby's undoing...

"...and that's the whole story dad." Karim concluded, "We certainly weren't expecting anything like THIS for our holiday, that's for sure!"

"Certainly not." Idris said grimly, "And it's rather unsettling to learn that the hunters followed you all the way to Norway without anyone noticing. I'll be sure to get as many of our Norwegian allies to be on the lookout for them and keep you and everyone else safe. Emerald may have saved one of Draven's men from dying, but I doubt that'll make Draven change his mind. The fact he even let you go is rather surprising, and also concerning. If he's done so, chances are he's got some kind of plan in mind..."

"You're basically saying that if Draven does anything nice, there's some kind of catch to it?" Ruby muttered bitterly, "That doesn't exactly put me at ease."

"I know Draven better than anyone Ruby, and I speak from experience when I say that you can't afford to let your guard down."

Idris said cryptically, "I'm more than certain that Draven will still be after you, even after what Emerald did, hence why I'll see to it that you all receive extra protection until your cruise is over. I'd even suggest just staying on the ship at all times. Draven won't dare try anything while you're onboard with hundreds of witnesses. It would only make him and the hunters look bad if they were seen to be attacking a ship for seemingly no reason."

"But we can't just stay on the ship." Emerald protested, "I want to see some of Norway while we're here. This holiday won't feel as exciting if we just stay on the ship all day."

"It was only a suggestion Emerald." Idris insisted, "If you don't want to stay on the ship, then make sure you stay in public at all times. Once again, the hunters won't try anything if there are witnesses around. Don't go into any isolated areas or alleyways or anything. Make sure you're always in a crowd so the hunters will have reason to hesitate."

"Sounds sensible." Sapphire agreed, "If Draven sees himself as mankind's protector, then he'll want to try and keep up that image. If he tries attacking us in full view of a crowd of people, that won't exactly make him look very heroic. Mingling with the crowd is our best option if we want to explore Norway without the risk of being targeted by them."

Everybody nodded in agreement. The matter was settled and they knew what they were going to do for the rest of the holiday. The hunters could stalk them all they liked, but as long as there were witnesses around, they were powerless to touch them. Ruby even wondered if Draven realized the same thing and would just call the mission off, but deep down she knew it wouldn't be as easy as that. She got the feeling that Draven was the sort of man where once he had an objective in mind, he saw it through no matter what.

Once everyone had gotten back onto the *Nova*, Karim had quickly called up Idris and the whole group informed him of what had happened. It was lucky that the ship wasn't due to leave for another hour or two as they would've had no Wi-Fi signal out at sea. Naturally, Idris had been disturbed by the news and felt as if it was somehow his fault this had happened. He felt as if Rimor should've kept a closer eye on the hunters and anticipated something like this, but Paul and Judy gently reassured him that nobody could've prepared for the hunters somehow finding out about the holiday. Now they knew what they were up against, they would follow Idris's advice and make sure they stayed in view of the public at all times, be it on or off the ship. Knowing the hunters wouldn't try anything with too many witnesses around at least made Ruby feel safer. She would've felt even safer if the hunters weren't there at all, but knowing she was protected did make it easier to relax. She and her family and friends may still be able to make the most of their holiday despite this setback. Karim hung up and put his phone away. He ran a hand through his hair and puffed out loudly.

"So that's that then, we stick together and stay in view at all times." Karim recapped, "If any hunters try that alleyway trick on us again, we won't fall for it. We'll just leave them waiting for us."

"I only wish there was a way to stop those monsters for good." Annie said grimly, "Why can't anyone just arrest them and be done with it?"

"The hunters aren't technically doing anything wrong." Paul said bluntly, "Thanks to their work with the government and how they've stigmatised the supernatural over the years, there's no law preventing them from actually doing what they do. They're allowed to kill anything and anyone that's abnormal in some way and the police can't do anything about it. Even the press are powerless to expose them as any attempts to villainize the hunters are met with threats and blackmail to keep them quiet about it. All we can do is fight the hunters off and stop them from killing any magical people or alien creatures."

"I guess the only way the hunters could ever get arrested is if they killed any ordinary civilians." Sapphire said gravely, "And I sure as hell don't want it to come to that!"

"Of course not Sapph, it shouldn't have to come to that." Ruby muttered, "Like it or not, we're on our own and the law can't help us. All we can do is hope that Emerald's generous act will convince them to back off."

"I'll be so happy if it has!" Emerald piped eagerly, "We won't ever have to worry about them coming for us again."

"Like dad says, if Draven does anything nice, there's bound to be a catch to it." Karim reminded her, "So I wouldn't get too hopeful."

"While we're on that subject, that brings forth an important question." Michael cut in.

He looked to Ruby and took her hands into his own. Ruby looked back to him, curious what he was going to say.

"How do you feel knowing you didn't actually kill Draven?" Michael asked gently, "Does it feel like a big weight's come off your chest, sweetheart?"

He gently stroked Ruby's cheek. Ruby took his hand into her own and thought for a moment. She was still trying to figure that out herself. Draven's survival meant a lot of things to her, but what was the best way she could communicate that? She looked down at her lap thoughtfully.

"Honestly? Conflicted is how I feel." Ruby murmured, "On the one hand, I'm relieved that he's alive, because it means I didn't actually kill him. I can finally forgive myself and be at peace with what I've done, because I'm not a murderer after all. But at the same time, I kinda wish he was actually dead, because now him being alive means that he can come back to try and kill me again. And it's not just me that's at risk here: all of you are at risk too and it scares me to think of what'll happen if he gets to any of you!" she exclaimed,

"Oh god, I can't bear to imagine you or mum or my sisters being in his clutches!"

Michael pulled Ruby into a hug to comfort her, trying to ease her rising panic.

"Don't worry my girl. You know we'll be alright." Michael assured his eldest daughter, "We'll all do as Idris says and the hunters won't be able to come for you."

"And he's calling Rimor's Norwegian branch for extra security." Annie reminded her, "We'll be perfectly safe, all of us."

Ruby inhaled and exhaled deeply to ease her nerves. She hugged her parents in gratitude.

"I know mum and dad. I'm just looking out for you all as always." Ruby said softly, "But you're right. We'll be fine, all of us."

"We will!" Emerald said optimistically, "Those hunters won't stop us having a nice time while we're here. We'll enjoy the rest of our holiday and have as much fun as we can!"

"I don't care how many times I have to say it Em, but your sense of optimism is too adorable for words." Ruby joked.

Emerald just smiled modestly.

"And might I add that you've proven yourself to be much braver than you believe yourself to be?" Ruby added.

"I thought the same thing." Paul concurred, "As crazy as things got with the battle, I did at least notice enough of what was happening to see that Emerald held her own quite well out there. She didn't panic or get scared once, not like when we were training a while back. She was even the one brave enough to make a dash for it to warn the others while we kept on fighting."

Emerald looked away shyly.

"Oh please you two, I wasn't that brave. I still needed dad to save me when one of the hunters grabbed me." she said meekly.

"I get you, but don't sell yourself short Em." Ruby complimented, patting Emerald on the back, "Paul's right, you were much braver than you were before. You didn't get scared and cower on the floor, you just fought alongside us. You even managed to save me from getting shot multiple times! Heck, it was thanks to you that the hunter in that alleyway didn't stun me right from the start! I think that's something to be proud of."

"Quite so Ruby." Michael agreed, "Your little sister's proven to be more courageous than she thinks!"

"And I couldn't be prouder." Annie said happily, "Well done to you Emerald."

Emerald beamed with pleasure. She supposed her family and friends were right. She really was braver than she believed. It was so strange how training with Rimor caused her to get frightened easily, and yet fighting for real, she just got on with it and never once panicked in the heat of battle. Maybe fighting for real made all the difference as it meant all her thoughts were on the battle itself and keeping herself alive. There was less room to worry about getting hurt when fighting for your life. Emerald was so pleased with herself that she hugged everyone in gratitude. She was determined to have more faith in herself in the future.

The evening came and the passengers aboard the *Nova* were treated to a beautiful sunset as the ship began to sail away from Stavanger and make its way towards its next destination. The ship would sail through the night and early the next morning, it would dock at Ålesund, and the passengers would have a new day in a new part of Norway to enjoy. Emerald thought it was somewhat magical how cruises worked. It was like every time she went to bed at night, she woke up in a new place. It was an experience that no other mode of transport could provide, and it was what made this holiday so worthwhile for her. Flying abroad or driving to holiday destinations were fun in their own ways, but cruises were in a league of their own. Emerald only wished that there was more time to spend exploring the cities and towns they were visiting in Norway.

EMERALD SILVERLOCK: A CRUISE TO ADVENTURE

The strict timetable that cruise ships followed were the only real downside to the whole experience, as it meant only so long could be spent walking around and exploring the country. But having fun onboard the ship was just as enjoyable as seeing the new country. As the ship pulled away and set sail for Ålesund, Emerald watched as Stavanger began to grow smaller and smaller. She waved goodbye to the city and turned her attention to the sunset ahead. The sun was starting to touch down on the horizon. The sky was a brilliant, blazing orange and the sea sparkled like a cave of treasures in the setting sunlight. It was the most amazing sunset Emerald had ever seen. She was the only one watching it at the moment. Ruby, Sapphire and Karim were playing inside with Annie, Michael and Paul keeping watch while Judy kept an eye on Emerald. The girl in green glanced over her shoulder to see the top agent leaning against the rail and watching her rather than the sunset. Judy was standing near two other passengers that were also watching the sunset, one a man in a brown fedora and leather jacket and another a woman with long dark hair. Emerald waved politely to Judy. Judy waved back. Emerald wondered about Judy. What was life like for her before joining Rimor? Did she enjoy being an agent? And why were she and Paul so close? Were they in a relationship or just close friends? Emerald had been tempted to ask, but she worried it would be impolite if she did. Rimor agents likely weren't allowed to discuss their personal lives anyway. For now, she was just happy to call Judy a friend and a guardian and she appreciated how she looked out for her and her sisters, even if she wasn't their mother. Emerald noticed Judy looking over her shoulder. The agent stared for a minute and then glanced to Emerald.

"Your friend's coming." Judy informed.

Emerald turned her head and saw Tony walking towards her, his face lit up with delight. Emerald had wondered how his day had gone and had hoped she and Tony could meet up again after the ship left

Stavanger. Emerald and Tony ran up to each other and embraced. Judy watched, smiling at the tender scene before her.

"Hello there my little gem! I was hoping I'd find you." Tony said jovially, "Enjoying the view out here?"

"I sure am!" Emerald said eagerly, "The sunset is especially gorgeous tonight! How are you doing? Did you have a good day out today?"

"We sure did." Tony replied, "The art museum was interesting to look through. Both mum and dad were quite amazed at what was on display. How about you? Did you and your family have fun?"

Emerald glanced anxiously over to Judy as if needing permission to tell Tony the truth. Judy nodded, making it clear to Emerald that she could tell Tony everything. She turned back to Tony and recapped the whole day from the visit to the Christmas shop to the pizza dinner at Peppes Pizza and the unexpected attack from the hunters. Tony listened to the whole story in shocked silence. His face seemed to drain of all colour as Emerald explained the ordeal to him.

"It was so scary! I was worried that they were going to take Ruby, but thankfully we got away in the end!" Emerald finished breathlessly, "And now we're hoping the hunters will leave us alone because I healed up their agent who got shot. Idris isn't convinced they'll be so nice though, so we're going to make sure we stick with a crowd. The hunters won't attack us if there are people watching."

She gave Tony a minute to let everything sink in. He seemed to take an age to recover, but eventually, he found his voice again and ran a hand through his hair. He breathed out deeply and pulled Emerald into a tight hug as if worried he was going to lose her for good.

"Oh Emerald, that's awful! I can't believe those horrible people followed us here to try and attack Ruby!" Tony gasped, "I wish I'd been there to help. I could've..."

"You only would've gotten hurt Tony." Emerald interrupted, "It was for the best that you weren't there. The hunters probably would've tried taking you hostage, and maybe your parents too. I'm glad you were elsewhere so neither of you became targets."

"I suppose, but I still would've liked it if I could've helped in some way." Tony said solemnly, "I don't know what I'd do if you'd gotten hurt in anyway."

He then reached up and gently brushed his fingers through the sides of Emerald's hair. Emerald smiled briefly, enjoying her best friend's gentle touch.

"You're the light of my life Emerald, and I'd hate to lose you." Tony said softly.

"Aww, you're so sweet. Thank you Tony." Emerald said, taking his hands into her's, "But you don't need to worry. We're all fine and we're taking precautions so the hunters don't come for us. I suggest you and your mum and dad do the same and don't go anywhere unless there are other people around. I don't think the hunters will bother with you all, but we have to play it safe just in case."

"No arguments there." Tony said agreeably, "We'll stay in public view at all times. So, you said you healed that man who got shot." he acknowledged, "Why did you save him? I mean it's good that you did of course and I probably would've done the same thing, but I'm just wondering what your reason is."

Emerald looked out to the sunset again. The sun was halfway down into the horizon, the light gradually growing dimmer as it nearly disappeared. A soft wind blew over her face, toying with her hair and hat.

"Because it was the right thing to do." Emerald explained, "I had to save him. I know he was one of the bad guys, but that doesn't mean he has to die. And I'm also hoping that doing something nice for the hunters will tempt them to leave Ruby alone. I like to think one act of kindness inspires another, and hopefully that'll be the case."

Tony put a hand around Emerald's shoulder and smiled at her.

"I think that's as good a reason as any." he said warmly, "It's a good thing you chose to get healing powers or else that man would've died. Speaking of, I'd meant to ask you about that." he went on, "Why did you pick healing powers?"

"Oh that's easy! It's because Idris suggested I could be the team healer." Emerald answered quickly, "It was all his idea. I've been struggling to fight as well as Ruby and Sapph and I got scared easily, so he thought I could be the team healer instead. When Selina offered out the magical gems that gave us our powers, I picked the yellow gem to get healing powers. I'd meant to give you a demonstration, but with our training and preparing for the holiday, I just never had the chance to do so." she said sheepishly.

Emerald then reached into her hoodie and took out the locket containing her grandmother's photograph. She opened it up to show Tony. Tony had never seen the locket before. He gazed at the photo of Emerald's grandmother.

"But the biggest reason for choosing healing powers is because of my big dream in life." Emerald continued, "I can't believe I've never told you this yet. But when I grow up, I want to be a nurse. And it's all because of my grandma. When she was lying sick in bed and getting worse and worse, I just wanted her to get better. All I could do was wish I had some way to help her..." she lamented, gazing sadly at the photo, "And that's when I decided: I want to be a nurse so I can help those that are sick and dying. I want to help people get better like nurses do, and now I have healing powers, I'm already on my way to becoming one." she finished.

Tony took this in with interest and awe. He thought it was a very sweet gesture. What could be nicer than knowing someone wanted to be a doctor or a nurse out of a genuine desire to help others? His smile quickly faded for Emerald talking about her grandmother dying made him remember his own situation. He looked away sadly.

"I could do with a nurse right now…" the brunette boy mumbled to himself.

Emerald heard what he'd said. She put away her locket and put a hand on Tony's arm. She gazed at him in concern.

"Why? What's wrong Tony?" she asked worriedly, "Please tell me. Is this about your funny turns and your asthma problems you've had lately?"

Tony winced. Now he'd done it! Why did he have to say that out loud? He sighed heavily, his shoulders heaving. There was no hiding it any longer. He had to tell Emerald the truth. He looked his friend in the eye, his blue orbs full of pain and sorrow.

"I didn't want to tell you this until after the holiday as I thought it'd spoil the mood." Tony said sadly, "But I can't keep it from you any longer little gem. The truth is…"

He took a moment to collect himself. Then he went on.

"…I'm dying." he said, his voice heavy with grief.

Emerald put her hands to her mouth in horror and gasped in shock. The deck seemed to lurch under her feet for a minute. She couldn't believe what she was hearing.

"NO! Please tell me that's not true!" Emerald shrieked.

Tony shook his head gravely.

"I could tell you that, but I'd be lying." he said grimly, "I have a rare disease that is slowly but surely killing me. I may seem healthy on the outside, but inside I'm, as the doctors put it, like a battery that's slowly running out of power. I get the funny turns as you've seen and the asthma problems are down to my disease. Anything like swimming, climbing or sports, I can't do anymore or else I risk suffocating myself. My heart could also give out on me if I do anything too strenuous. Doctors estimate I have about three months to live, maybe four. I have to take medication just to keep going as I am now, but eventually that'll stop working. Mum and dad have been trying so hard to help me. The doctors thought my disease was terminal, but they did research on a cure and found that there IS one. The only trouble is, the cure isn't available in the UK. I'd have to go all the way to America for experimental treatment, and that's going to be way too expensive for my parents to afford! So in the end, I've got no choice but to accept my fate..."

He paused as he found himself beginning to well up. His eyes filled with tears. Emerald was crying too. She couldn't believe that her friend was dying. How could someone as nice as Tony be subjected to such a cruel fate? It was like her grandmother all over again, only worse because Tony would be dying so young. He would never make it to adulthood. Tony looked to Emerald, feeling guilty that he'd brought this on her. He wiped his eyes.

"I'm sorry Emerald. I really didn't want to tell you." he said sadly, "But maybe there's a solution. You have healing powers now, so could you maybe...heal me? Cure my illness?" Tony asked hopefully.

That only made Emerald cry even harder. She hid her face behind her hands and sobbed uncontrollably. Tony was confused.

"What? Did I say something wrong?" he asked worriedly.

"N-no, y-you didn't." Emerald whimpered, "It's just...I can't help you! I'm so sorry Tony, but I can't! I only just got the powers! I can only heal small injuries and partially heal big injuries! I'm no use to you at all, I won't be able to cure your illness!"

She threw her arms around Tony and cried into his chest. Judy, who had heard the whole thing, stayed respectfully silent. This was nothing to do with her and she didn't know what to say that wouldn't make things any worse. It saddened her to see the happy and cheerful Emerald looking so heartbroken.

"Oh Tony, I don't want you to die, please don't die!" Emerald wailed.

Tony hugged Emerald in return and patted her softly on the back.

"I wish I wasn't little gem, but unless we win the lottery or find some valuable treasure, there's nothing we can do about it." Tony said solemnly, "All you can do is just enjoy the time you have with me while I'm still here. That's why my parents even agreed to this holiday despite being unsure about it at first. They both agreed that one last holiday would at least bring some light to my situation."

Emerald made a mental note to thank Caroline and Marcus next time she met up with them. Thanks to them, Tony was here to enjoy a wonderful holiday while he still had some life left in them. As sad as it was that he was dying, it warmed her a little to know that this was the reason he was here now. His life would soon be over, so why not make the most of it while he could? But she would rather he lived to enjoy many more holidays in the future. She had to help him! But how? Her powers were no good and Tony's parents couldn't afford the treatment he needed. It seemed hopeless. Emerald had to accept the grim reality that Tony was going to die and nothing could prevent it. Or so she believed.

Unknown to him, Emerald or Judy, the entire conversation had been overheard. Draven's Cyber Dragon was flying invisible over the MS *Nova* and its long range listening devices had picked up every word Emerald and Tony had said. And just a few miles behind the cruise ship, Draven was in his submarine listening to the whole thing. While he didn't care much for Emerald, he did sympathize with Tony's plight. He'd been close to death himself and all he could do at the time was pray he'd live to fight another day. He found it a shame that someone so young had to be dying so soon. But Tony's situation would play nicely into the plan he'd been formulating. Emerald may not think there was a solution to Tony's illness, but he knew there was and that was the critical component he needed to pull off his next gambit. A plan had formed in his head and he grinned to himself as he thought it over. If Emerald knew about the Staff of Wishes, she'd fetch it in a heartbeat. Whether she knew it existed or not was irrelevant as Draven could just give her that information, then let her and the others do the work for him. The staff would be as good as his.

"Do not worry little Emerald. We can help you and your friend find the solution to your problems…" Draven purred deviously.

Chapter 12: The Staff of Wishes

Tony's parents, Caroline and Marcus, found their son out on the deck and came over to him. They'd had a moment in the bar to themselves and now they were done, they wanted to take Tony back to their cabin and settle down for the night. The holiday was as much a distraction from their worries as it was for Tony. Having to live with their only child inching ever closer to death every day of the year was weighing heavily on them and it was the main reason they'd been happy to accept Emerald's invitation. They wouldn't have much time left with Tony, so why not make the most of it with one last holiday with him? But as much as they tried to remain in good spirits, there were occasions like this where they were grimly reminded of what this holiday was about. Their time together at the bar had been spent lamenting how much they wished they could pay for Tony's operation and have his disease treated. Unfortunately, life wasn't so kind to them. There just didn't seem to be any feasible way they could pay for Tony's treatment. It was to the point the doctors told them they may have to just accept that Tony was going to die, but Caroline and Marcus were holding onto whatever nuggets of hope they could that they may eventually find some way to pay for Tony's operation.

Caroline was of average height and had long blonde hair. Marcus was slightly taller than his wife, very thin and had short black hair that was beginning to grey. They were middle aged but they still possessed a lot of youthful energy that showed age was just a number to them. Like their son, they were very friendly people by nature, which made it easy for the Silverlock family to befriend them as well as Tony. They'd taken a huge shine to Emerald ever since the day she and Tony had met, grateful to her for giving Tony his first ever friend when he'd started to school. Emerald even saw the two as a second pair of parents with how nice and kind they were to her. The Summers did their best to keep their faces looking bright and cheerful as they caught up with Tony again. But their hearts sank as they saw he was hugging a crying Emerald. They immediately guessed what the matter was. Tony looked to his parents sadly.

"I know mum, you didn't want me to tell her until afterwards, but I couldn't keep her in the dark any longer." the brunette boy said solemnly, "I had to let her know."

Caroline nodded understandingly. She patted Tony on the back and then looked to Emerald sympathetically. The girl in green wiped her eyes and looked up at Caroline.

"We're so sorry dear." Caroline said softly, "We didn't want to keep this from you but we didn't want to upset you. We also didn't want to dampen the mood for the holiday. But I guess it was only a matter of time before the truth came out."

"I-it's O-OK M-Mrs. Summers." Emerald whimpered, "I'm a-actually glad T-Tony's told me now s-so it won't c-come as a shock when... it happens. But it really is horrible to know that he's going to die..." she added, feeling her eyes well up again. She briefly wondered how she still had any tears left to cry at this point.

"We can't even begin to describe how it felt when the doctors gave us Tony's diagnosis." Marcus sympathized, "We thought we were going to drop dead ourselves! But Tony has three or four months left in him, which does give us a bit of hope. As dire as things seem, there is still a chance we might be able to save him in the end."

"You should see what mum and dad are doing for me." Tony said, his voice full of appreciation for his parents, "Mum's even been buying lottery tickets as often as she can in the vain hopes that we might actually win it and we can pay for my operation that way. The two are very much exhausting all available options at this point."

"That's so sweet of them." Emerald said with awe, "I bet my parents would do the same for me if I was dying."

"Any parent would." Caroline declared, "We're doing all we can to save our son. In fact...if there's any way you could help us dear, that would be much appreciated." she suggested.

"M-me?" Emerald stammered, "Um...I'm not sure how I can help Mrs. Summers. I would love to help, but as I've already told Tony, my new healing powers are too weak to heal anything as serious as a disease."

"Oh, that's not what she meant." Marcus cleared up, "You're friends with that organization that explores the supernatural, right? Apologies if this is a tall order, but maybe your explorer friends could research a way to cure people? I know dabbling into the supernatural could be dangerous, but it'll be worth a shot."

"Maybe Rimor has something at their base they could save my life with?" Tony asked hopefully.

"I suppose I could ask them." Emerald suggested, "But I doubt they'll be willing to share just in case anything goes wrong. Everything Rimor has in its possession has to be kept locked away in their base for safety reasons and so the hunters don't get them. But as Mr. Summers suggested, they could research on ways to cure illnesses maybe. If anyone can find a cure, it'll be..."

Emerald paused for a moment. Her brain whirled as an incredible idea came to her head. What was the story the Cooper family had told her and her sisters about before the holiday began? She thought back to it and her face lit up with delight.

"Hang on...I might have an idea!" she exclaimed.

"Go on, what is it?" Caroline urged.

"Our sorcerer friends, the Coopers, told us about a legendary artefact known as the Staff of Wishes." Emerald explained, "They said it's a powerful staff that can grant wishes. So if we could find it, we could simply wish for Tony's disease to be cured!"

The Summers family looked to each other with interest. A staff that could grant wishes, that was definitely the kind of miracle they could do with to solve all their problems!

"Now that is an idea." Tony said gleefully, "But...do you know where to find it?"

"Sadly no." Emerald lamented, "The Coopers don't know either. The staff is pretty much just a story for now and all we have to go on is, that's if it even exists, it's hidden in Norway somewhere. The staff was forged in this country by a powerful wizard long ago. But we could ask about it. Maybe the locals might know more about the staff and if they can give us anywhere to start looking, we could search in those places and hopefully find it."

"With any luck, we will and we can wish for Tony to be cured." Marcus said hopefully.

"Let's not get too excited Marc." Caroline warned, "We could still reach a dead end here."

"Of course, but that hasn't stopped us yet, has it?" Marcus noted.

"There's every chance the staff exists." Tony said optimistically, "Just as there's every chance it might not. We have to at least look into it and see what we can find."

He embraced Emerald in gratitude.

"Even if we come up with nothing little gem, thank you for even bringing it up in the first place." he said graciously, "At least we have another possible way to save my life with what you've suggested."

"Don't mention it Tony." Emerald said sweetly, "I can only hope that our efforts won't be fruitless."

"I can help." Judy offered, "I can call our Norwegian allies and ask them to look into any possible locations of the Staff of Wishes. They could potentially dig something up."

Emerald jumped and laughed sheepishly. She'd genuinely forgotten Judy was still here watching over her. She'd been so laser focused on Tony and now his parents that it was like Judy had been invisible the whole time.

"That'll be very kind of you ma'am." Caroline said gratefully, "If your allies find anything, do let us know."

"We'll do what we can Mrs. Summers." Judy insisted, "Rimor has found countless amounts of magical artefacts in its long history of supernatural exploration. This'll simply be another one for us to potentially track down."

Caroline and Marcus shook Judy's hand in gratitude. Judy gave them a reassuring smile that told them Rimor would do everything in its power to save their son. Tony beamed with pleasure. For the first time in ages, he found himself feeling that there was a chance he could be saved after all. He had to remind himself that yes, it could be all for nothing and he might still be doomed to die in the end, but there was still that chance the Staff of Wishes could be real and it could save him. Once they arrived at Ålesund the next day, he and his family could ask the locals and see what they knew. Emerald and her family would do the same. Whether it was their families or Rimor, they'd surely find something about the staff...

The next day dawned and the passengers of MS *Nova* woke up to find themselves in another part of Norway. Ålesund was the ninth largest town/city in the country and like Stavanger, it was a town very close to water, with harbours full of vessels both big and small. Like in Stavanger, the *Nova* was easily the biggest ship currently docked in the harbour, completely dwarfing every other boat nearby. The town had a very old-fashioned appearance with many buildings sporting 20th century architecture, with very few modern buildings to be seen anywhere. It gave the town its own unique beauty that couldn't be seen anywhere else in the world. A large cliff towered over Ålesund with what looked like some kind of observatory standing on top of it. This was the Fjellstua Viewpoint, a popular tourist attraction in the town. Many visitors would take a ride up to the top of the cliff and admire the view from the viewpoint. The passengers of MS *Nova* would be among those visitors. But eleven of those passengers had other things on their mind than sightseeing.

Before going to bed for the night, Emerald and Judy had informed the rest of the Silverlock family, Karim and Paul what they'd learned about Tony and that the holiday was now a mission to find the Staff of Wishes and cure his illness. Ruby and Sapphire were as shocked as Emerald had been to hear that Tony was dying, though Sapphire admitted she secretly suspected that there was something up with him the whole time. Paul and Judy had sent the word out to Rimor's Norwegian branch for any help in finding the staff, or at least any kind of information that might suggest it even exists, while the Silverlock family planned to ask around the town and see what they could dig up.

"I was hoping to just enjoy exploring the town like we did yesterday." Annie said sadly, "But of course, the life of a friend must take priority. Tony's such a lovely boy and it'd be a shame for him to die so young."

"Too right mum." Ruby agreed, "Hence we only have one chance at this. We must find that staff and we've only got today, tomorrow and the day after before we sail back to England. Of course, Rimor's allies over here can still look for it when we go home, but it'd just be nice if we got to find it, you know?"

"Of course." Michael concurred, "It'd especially be perfect if Tony could be the one to make the wish and cure himself with the staff."

"Whether we find it or Rimor does, it doesn't matter as long as we find it while Tony's still alive." Emerald insisted, "You remember what the Coopers told us about the staff, right?"

"Yes." Sapphire confirmed, "We can't wish for the dead to come back alive, so if Tony dies, that's it. All for nothing. It's lucky for him that he's got at least three months to live, so that should buy us some time."

"Provided he doesn't keel over dead sooner than estimated..." Ruby said grimly.

"So how will we ask the locals?" Emerald inquired, "Neither of us can speak Norwegian."

"There'll be locals who can understand English as well." Sapphire noted, "But if push comes to shove, we could at least try learning how to ask "Do you know about the Staff of Wishes?" in Norwegian."

"Me and Judy can do that." Paul offered, "Rimor agents are taught to speak several languages as part of our supernatural explorations. A job like this naturally requires a lot of travelling so it helps to be able to speak the local language."

"Dad's even been trying to get me to learn other languages." Karim said with a half-chuckle, "It's...not going too greatly honestly. The best I can do is speak a few phrases of French but that's it." he said sheepishly.

"No worries. Paul and Judy have got us covered." Ruby said brightly, "OK team, let's see what we can find out while we're here..."

After breakfast, the Silverlock and Summers families set out together into Ålesund to begin their search. Although they were on a mission, both families allowed themselves a moment to take in their surroundings and admire the view for a moment. Like Stavanger, they felt Ålesund was a very attractive looking town. It was also more colourful than most towns and cities in the world with most of the houses being painted either blue, red, white or yellow. Its rather vintage looking appearance and the general laidback atmosphere of the town made the place feel somewhat nostalgic to look around. While exploring the town, they passed a bed of beautiful red tulips outside a few shops which Emerald couldn't help but stop and admire. At one point, Tony had another funny turn and looked dangerously close to passing out right there and then. Caroline and Marcus quickly sat him down on a bench and gave him a minute to recover. Luckily, he did so and was able to stand back up again. He massaged his head heavily and blinked several times. Emerald patted him on the back.

"Are you OK?" she asked worriedly.

"I'm getting there." Tony said groggily, "I was worried for a minute I was going to faint. That wouldn't do at all, passing out in the middle of the street."

"He came very close to doing that a few times before." Caroline said grimly, "It didn't half scare us to death when it happened..."

"All the more reason we have to find that staff and wish Tony's illness away!" Emerald declared, "He won't ever have to worry about fainting again."

Unfortunately, their efforts proved fruitless for a good hour or two. On their travels, they asked as many people they came across as they could about the Staff of Wishes. Sometimes they found locals who could speak English and understand them perfectly while others they needed Paul and Judy to ask for them in Norwegian. The result was the same no matter who they asked: nobody knew about the staff or where it was. A handful of people they asked did know about the legends of the staff but had no idea where to find it, nor did they believe it was even real in the first place. As far as they knew, it was just a story. Soon, lunchtime came and the whole group had to stop and refuel at one of the local cafés before they continued. The ship wasn't due to depart until the evening, so they still had time to ask more locals about the staff. But at the moment, they had to admit their situation wasn't looking too promising. If even the locals didn't seem to know anything about the Staff of Wishes or thought it was just a legend, then what chance did they have of actually finding it at all? Maybe the Staff of Wishes really was just a story and wasn't real. Emerald began to feel the weight of despair starting to press down on her. Tony's only hope of survival seemed to be beyond anyone's grasp for now. Tony noticed Emerald's dismayed expression and he put his hand over her's. He tried to smile encouragingly, though Emerald could see in his eyes that he was feeling just as unsure about the whole thing as her.

"Don't worry about it little gem. There's still Rimor helping us." Tony reminded, "They might find something we won't."

"I know." Emerald said, "But what if they don't find anything either? What if this whole thing ends up being a waste of time and there is no Staff of Wishes?"

"Then we look for an alternative, just as mum and dad have been doing." Tony insisted.

"If we found some long lost treasure or something, that'd definitely help." Karim suggested helpfully, "Dad and his agents have often dug up treasures when searching for supernatural stuff, so you never know. It could happen while we're trying to find the Staff of Wishes."

Emerald perked up at this. Finding a long lost treasure of some kind would be a happy bonus and would more than certainly be able to help pay for Tony's operation. Emerald vowed that from now on, she wouldn't give into despair and remain optimistic no matter what. As the old saying goes: every cloud has a silver lining, and there was a chance that they may find it here in Ålesund. After they'd eaten lunch and set back out into town to continue their investigation, that silver lining came in the most unexpected of ways. The Silverlock and Summers families went around asking locals again about the Staff of Wishes. Emerald and Tony went off together to ask the first person they came across, but as they did so, they ended up bumping into someone. Emerald was so thrown by what happened that she nearly stumbled onto her bottom and Tony had to catch her. They'd bumped into a man and he babbled frantically in Norwegian, more surprised than anything by what had happened. Thankfully nobody had been hurt but Emerald and Tony were quick to apologize for what had happened.

"Oh my gosh, we're SO sorry!" Emerald exclaimed frantically.

"We beg your pardon sir, we didn't mean to bump into you." Tony insisted.

"Oh take it easy you kids, it was an accident! No skin off my bones!" the man reassured them, speaking in a Norwegian accent.

Emerald and Tony were relieved he also spoke English so it would be easier to apologize to him and he'd understand what they were saying. The man looked to be in his fifties and sported a large, rough, untidy beard that surely had never been brushed at any point in his life. He dressed casually in a body-warmer, jeans and trainers and a fisherman's cap and he had a friendly, laidback smile on his face. Emerald got the impression that he could suffer through the biggest of inconveniences and yet he'd still find a reason to smile about it. And yet Emerald swore there was something familiar about him. Was it her imagination, or had they met before? She dismissed the thought for the time being.

"We really are sorry sir." Emerald insisted, "Please don't be mad at us."

"I already said, it's nothing to worry about." the man insisted, "Don't worry yourself about it."

"If you say so." Tony said politely, "We're just glad you're not hurt."

"Likewise." the main said brightly, "So what are you kids up to then? You're not from around here, I take it?"

"No sir. We're tourists on a holiday cruise." Emerald informed, "We've come all the way from England to visit Norway and we're having a wonderful time so far. But we're also chasing down an interesting story about the country. Have you heard about the Staff of Wishes, by any chance?"

The man's eyes bulged with excitement.

"Have I heard about the Staff of Wishes?! You bet your high horses I have!" he shrieked ecstatically, "Oh yes, plenty of us folk know about the Staff of Wishes! It was said to have been forged here in Norway after all! It's been part of our folklore for thousands of years!"

He spoke with the clear enthusiasm of someone who knew a particularly good story and had been aching to tell it to someone for a very long time.

"Well can you at least tell us if it exists or not?" Tony asked, almost afraid of what the answer would be.

"You kids really don't know much about Norway, do you?" the man said cheekily, "Of course the staff's real! It's just some of us folk don't believe it is and think it's just a story! Well my family happens to know the truth about it. The staff is real and can be found in a cave in the Briksdalsbreen glacier all the way over in Olden. Not entirely sure why it's been hidden there, but I imagine it's because it would be a lot harder for someone to go in and fetch it if it's hiding in a snow-topped mountain..." he murmured to himself.

Emerald and Tony thought they were going to faint. This man had just given them what they needed! He knew where the staff was and could confirm it was real! They were so delighted that they nearly bounced up and down with joy. Tony had to keep himself calm just in case his body couldn't handle it. Emerald grinned like a child on Christmas Day, her hands trembling with glee. Doing her best not to go crazy, she thanked the man for his answer.

"Thanks so much, sir. We were wondering if the staff was real and now we know. You've been very helpful to us." the brunette girl said graciously.

"Don't mention it little lady." the man said kindly, "Though I am curious why you're interested in the Staff of Wishes. You're not hoping to find it, are you?"

Emerald and Tony paused for a moment. Should they tell him the truth? They imagined he would understand. But there was something bothering the two. If the man knew where the staff was, why hadn't he gone for it himself?

"Well...would it be a bad idea if we did?" Tony asked meekly.

"Depends." the man said cryptically, "According to legend, only the pure of heart can enter the cave and get that staff. If you two are pure of heart, then you have nothing to worry about."

"But what about you sir? You're a nice guy. Why haven't you gone for the staff?" Emerald asked curiously.

"My family believes that the staff is best left where it is so it won't fall into the wrong hands." the man explained, "That and my back wouldn't allow for me to climb such a mountain. It'd be far too painful for me to attempt it..."

He rubbed his back to further emphasize his point. Emerald nodded understandingly. Nobody would be able to climb the glacier with a bad back. Yet that also made her think again to how she thought she knew the man. Something about him and his bad back made her feel certain she'd seen him before. But how could that be? This was her first time visiting Ålesund. Surely they couldn't have met? Emerald shook off the thought again and bowed politely.

"Well thank you again sir. We're glad to know the staff is real after all." she thanked.

"It's been nice to meet you sir." Tony said kindly, "We best be going now. Do have a good day."

"And you too." the man said jovially, "But I warn you, if you decide to look for the Staff of Wishes, beware of thieves and treasure hunters that might seek it too! If I were you, I'd forget everything

I've told you and just leave it be, lest you make yourselves targets for those kinds of scoundrels."

"We won't look for it sir!" Emerald lied, "We promise! Our ship doesn't even go to Olden anyway, so it's not like we can actually look for it. Bye-bye!"

She and Tony quickly left to re-join their group. As soon as they left, the man's smile faded and his gaze became stone cold. Rodriguez was amazed that the fake beard, and a bit of prosthetic make-up to age him had worked as well as it did to fool those children. He was sure Emerald would've recognized him in spite of that, but it looked as if the disguise had worked. He felt a little guilty having to deceive her like that. His aching back reminded him that it was thanks to her that he was even alive, and this was how he was repaying her? By telling her where the Staff of Wishes was just so she could fetch it for his boss? It was wrong, but he knew it was for a good cause. The staff could help the hunters complete their mission for good. That was worth deceiving a child for. He took a phone out of his body-warmer and put it to his ear.

"Draven? It's Rodriguez. The girl fell for my local act completely." Rodriguez informed, "I've told her where the Staff of Wishes is."

"Excellent. Now once the Silverlock family arrives at Olden tomorrow, they'll no doubt look for it." Draven purred, **"Now we wait and let them do the rest..."**

Rodriguez nodded and hung up. He slipped the phone back into his pocket and briskly walked away. His mission was over, so all he could do now was just re-join the hunters and wait for the *Nova* to head to Olden. He only hoped that Emerald would be alright getting the staff as he didn't want her getting hurt or killed in the attempt.

"And it was just like that? The man just told you where the Staff of Wishes is, no strings attached?" Ruby asked, completely flabbergasted by Emerald and Tony's story.

"Yes! Just like that!" Emerald said breathlessly, "Isn't that wonderful? The staff's hidden away in a place we happen to be visiting on our cruise!"

"Indeed so. Olden is next on our travels and that's where the Briksdal glacier is, so we can look for it once we get there." Tony said happily.

Emerald and Tony had caught up with the others and informed them of their encounter with the man. In order to make sure they weren't overheard by anyone, the group went back to the ship and settled down in one of their cabins to talk. Emerald and Tony were practically buzzing when they told everyone they now knew where the Staff of Wishes was located and that they could reach it as it was in a place their cruise ship would be heading the next day. Caroline and Marcus were overjoyed to hear about it.

"Our prayers have been answered!" Caroline cried gleefully, "The Staff of Wishes is real!"

"We'll be able to save our son at last!" Marcus said excitedly.

But Sapphire had her doubts about the whole thing. She hated to spoil the mood, but she couldn't keep quiet about it.

"I don't know, the whole thing seems very...convenient, don't you think?" the blue-haired teen noted, "Like, am I the only one who finds it VERY suspicious that Emerald and Tony just happen to run into a guy who just happens to know where the Staff of Wishes is hidden and he just tells them where to find it without so much as asking for a bribe? I mean doesn't that sound fishy to you?"

"Truth be told Sapph, I'm kinda on the same boat as you." Ruby said grimly, "How do we know this isn't a trick? The man could've been lying for all we know."

"He wasn't lying." Emerald insisted, "He even sounded incredulous when me and Tony asked if the staff existed or not. He answered it as if he knew for a fact it was real."

"But why would he just give you that kind of information?" Sapphire noted, "Usually people would ask you to pay them for big information like that. They wouldn't just tell you where to find some legendary wish-granting artefact and not ask for money. That's what I find so suspicious, that he just gave you this info completely free of charge."

"I understand your excitement Em and Tony, but I don't think we should follow this lead." Ruby said cautiously, "This whole thing just screams "obvious trap" to me."

"But what about our son?" Caroline asked, "We have a chance to cure his illness and you think we shouldn't take it?"

"No Mrs. Summers, I'm saying it's risky because we don't know if that guy is legitimate or not." Ruby insisted, "What if we go and it turns out to be bunk? What if it is a trap and we all fall for it?"

"Don't be ridiculous Ruby, what reason could that man possibly want to lure us all into a trap?" Marcus said as if the whole thing was so stupid that he couldn't believe Ruby had suggested it at all.

"I don't know, but it's just...I don't like it." Ruby said, her voice full of worry, "Sapph's right, the whole thing is just too suspicious for words. We can't go, not unless we can confirm that man's not joshing us."

"We could pass the story onto our Norwegian agents." Paul suggested, "They could confirm or deny it for us."

"And if it turns out to be true, then we can go." Karim said eagerly, "Though I wonder how many of us will actually be allowed in that cave. The man told Emerald and Tony only the pure of heart can go in."

"Well that's easy enough. I can go in! I'm pure of heart, surely!" Emerald said excitedly.

"You're unquestionably pure of heart my dear." Annie said with pride in her voice, "I don't think there's a person on this planet who's as sweet and kind as you are."

"I'd say we all fit the bill." Michael suggested, "We're all very nice people by nature."

Ruby looked doubtful.

"I'm not so sure about me though." she murmured, "I've dealt with bullies rather violently in the past, I did nearly kill a man and a part of me does wish he was dead. I guess that might make me impure."

"I don't think so." Karim disagreed, "I'm sure your positive traits far outweigh the negatives here."

"Maybe, but I think if only pure of heart can enter the cave, then by "pure of heart", it must mean someone who is completely pure with not so much as a trace of evil in their hearts and no feelings of hatred." Sapphire theorized.

"If there's anyone here who definitely fits that description, it's Emerald and Tony." Ruby declared, "These two haven't got an evil or hateful bone in their bodies."

"But I can't go." Tony lamented, "My disease has weakened me to the point anything too strenuous could kill me, and a climb up a mountain will definitely be too much."

"So I'll go it alone then." Emerald volunteered, "I'll get the staff and once I have it, I'll give it to you so you can make the wish Tony! It's only right if you cure your own disease."

"But you're claustrophobic." Annie noted, "Are you sure you'll be OK going into a cave without anyone with you? I don't want you to get too scared and you end up panicking in there."

"But who can go with her?" Karim asked, "Unless we're considered pure of heart too, we won't be able to go in as well."

"I guess our best bet is to accompany Emerald to the cave entrance and if we're not allowed in as well, then we can just call down to her and remind her to keep calm." Michael suggested, "If anyone else can enter like me or Annie for instance, then we can go in with her."

"I'll go alone if I have to." Emerald insisted, "I may not like small spaces, but if I have to brave them to save my best friend's life, then I'll do so! I can't let my phobia get in the way of that."

Ruby and Sapphire smiled in amazement at their sister.

"You really are becoming braver and braver." Ruby applauded, "I think training with Rimor might've done more for you than even we expected."

Emerald beamed with pleasure.

"So what's the plan for tomorrow?" Caroline inquired, "I doubt the tour guides will let us just climb up the glacier."

"Suppose we could get in before it opens to the public?" Marcus suggested, "We'd probably have to be up really early for that."

"We could arrange a pickup." Judy offered, "Get a couple of Rimor agents to bring us to the glacier by bus while it's still dark and then we get to the glacier just as dawn arrives. If we're quick, we can be up there and down again before the tour guides open up."

"It'll be risky." Annie said nervously, "And suppose we get caught? We could potentially be arrested."

"Not if nobody sees us." Paul reassured her, "We'll be able to sneak off the vessel and get to the glacier no problem. If anyone does chance to see us, I'm sure we can spin some kind of story to explain what's happening and why we're doing what we're doing."

"So how many of us are going?" Ruby asked.

"We're all going." Annie declared, "I know it could be dangerous, but I'd rather not let our kids go out there alone, not with those dreadful hunters around..."

"And we'd rather be there with Tony to keep an eye on him, and also to watch the moment the staff grants his wish." Caroline offered.

"At least with me and the girls' powers and Rimor agents watching our backs, we'll be safe if the hunters do try to attack us!" Karim said confidently, "I think we're all set for this mission!"

"Provided the man's intel isn't malarkey, that is." Ruby reminded him.

"Me and Judy will pass it on to our allies now." Paul offered, "We'll see if they can confirm its legitimacy for us. For the rest of the day, all we can do is wait."

"That's settled then." Annie said, sounding relieved that they'd finished talking over the whole plan, "So what do you kids want to do until the ship leaves?"

"How's about we explore more of the town?" Emerald asked, "Now we don't need to look for the staff, we can have a proper walk around and really take in the sights some more."

"I think that's a great idea." Michael concurred, "We could all do with something more relaxed before we go to Olden tomorrow."

"Yeah, let's see as much of Norway as we can while we can." Ruby said casually, "That's what we're here for."

The two families left their cabin and headed out of the ship to walk around Ålesund again. The Staff of Wishes was supposedly in a glacier in Olden, that much they knew. And if it turned out to be true, they would be going into the glacier to get the staff. It all sounded very straight-forward, but even the best laid plans could go wrong. All the Silverlocks and the Summers could do was hope for the best and that they could get the staff...

Chapter 13: Into the Glacier

It didn't take long for Rimor's Norwegian branch to confirm the legitimacy of the man's intel. Paul and Judy passed the story onto their allies and a few hours later, they got a response. They were able to confirm that yes, the man's story was legitimate. Some of their agents had heard the same story that the Staff of Wishes was hidden in the Briksdal glacier and in order to make doubly sure about it, they'd sent a drone out to fly over the glacier and perform a scan for any energy signatures that would suggest there was something magical in there. The drone had to fly around the glacier for a long time and scan the whole place over and over before they were able to fully confirm that there was at least some kind of magical item hidden in the glacier. The drone was able to pick up a faint energy signature that was clearly no natural energy source on Earth. They found it matched other energy signatures that emitted from magical items they'd found before, confirming for definite that what they'd picked up was magical in nature. The man was clearly telling the truth about the staff's location. There was no way the whole thing could be a trap now they knew the staff was real and it was indeed hidden in the glacier. It was late at night when Paul and Judy got the updates. The Silverlock and Summers families were both asleep at the time so they weren't informed until around 5:00am the next morning. Paul went into Annie and Michael's cabin to wake them up first while Judy went into wake up their daughters. She moved slowly up to Ruby, Emerald and Sapphire and gently shook them awake. Emerald was the quickest to wake up, sitting up in her bed and rubbing her eyes.

"What is it?" she asked sleepily.

"The mission's ago." Judy whispered, "Our allies were able to confirm the story. Their drones detected an energy signature like magic inside the glacier, chances are that it's the Staff of Wishes."

No sooner had Judy spoken those words, all three girls were out of bed and rushing to get dressed right away. That was just the news they'd been waiting to hear. Once everyone was dressed, the group gathered together in the hallway, making sure not to make any noise, and they crept their way to the ship's terminal. While most of the passengers were asleep, some of the staff were still awake. The security personnel at the terminal were puzzled to see eleven passengers up and about with clear intentions to leave the ship. Before they could challenge anyone about it, Paul and Judy simply pointed some kind of device at them and shone a light in their eyes. The staff's faces became blank and their eyes stared ahead vacantly. They didn't move again, allowing the group to carry on unimpeded. The device was a handy gadget that Rimor agents usually carried in case they needed to slip in and out of places without one getting in their way. The light flash hypnotized anyone who stared at it and left anyone who saw it frozen for a couple of minutes. After the spell was over, they would carry on as normal and not remember anything that had happened before the light flash. Unfortunately, it only worked on weak-willed individuals so anyone using the device had to hope for the best when they did. Ruby lamented that it would've been funny to see them use it on Draven.

After everyone was outside, the Silverlock and Summers families found themselves looking at one of the most tranquil and beautiful places in the entire world. The Norwegian fjords were the kind of place where photographs couldn't do them justice. Seeing them in person, it felt to the group as though they were standing in the physical personification of serene beauty. Despite the early hours of the morning, it was light enough to see everything clearly, as Norway had longer hours of daylight in the summer like the UK did. The water was crystal clear and they could see forests of green for miles around. Once the sun was up, the group would be treated to an even prettier sight. This was the kind of sight that couldn't be truly appreciated in the dark. Once the mission was over, they'd return to the ship and then mingle with the crowd as the tour to the glacier opened up. The only downside was that going to the glacier wouldn't feel so special afterwards since they would've already been. But the two families would be sailing back to England knowing something that few others did about the famous tourist spot, and that alone would give them a unique experience that no other holidaymaker could lay claim to.

Paul and Judy signalled ahead and all at once, a dark shadow suddenly lit up with two beams of light jumping ahead and it trundled with a low rumbling noise towards the group. A team of Norwegian Rimor agents had come to the port by bus to pick them up and take them to the glacier. Ruby wondered how long the agents had been waiting for them. The bus hissed as it stopped and the doors opened up to let everyone in. Paul and Judy sat at the front row alongside some other agents while the Silverlocks and Summers sat at the back. It was like they'd just come off the ship to catch a tour bus to the glacier as normal, only the early hours of the morning, the mostly dark sky and the blunt faced agents accompanying them reminded them that this was no tour. They were more like spies going out on a top secret mission. Everyone fastened their seatbelts and Paul signalled to the driver. The bus pulled away and drove off down the road. Nobody spoke as the bus made its way to the famous glacier. Even Emerald was quiet, gazing out of the window at the view outside as it rushed by her. She wasn't actually admiring the view. She was lost in her own thoughts, feeling the anticipation build for the coming mission. Emerald wanted to get the staff and save her friend, but she was still incredibly anxious about actually going through with it. Suppose the staff was deep down into the cave and it was too dark to see? What if it was very short on space? What if a cave-in happened and she was crushed to death? Emerald began to wonder if she could even do this. But one look over at Tony was enough to chase those doubts away. She had to do it. She *needed* to do it! Tony's life depended on her or anyone else getting that staff so he could make his wish. Emerald vowed to herself that she wasn't going to let her best friend down.

A while later, the bus arrived at the stop where the tour guides normally began. The troll cars weren't going to be operational this early in the morning, so the group would have to make their way to the glacier on foot. They headed on up the same road that the troll cars would've taken them on a regular tour. The Norwegian agents led the way while the two families followed them. But as they made their way up, Caroline and Marcus grew concerned for Tony. A walk like this might be too tough for him to manage as his current condition meant he would run out of breath quickly. One of the Norwegian agents had a handy solution for him. He'd brought a special gadget with him to make it easier to get up the glacier without having to waste time on gathering mountain climbing gear to get up it. It looked like a giant silver disc but as he placed it on the road and switch it on, the disc whirred softly and rose slightly off the ground. It was a hover pad, a gadget Rimor's Norwegian branch had invented themselves. Paul and Judy lamented how the UK branch was having trouble replicating it, even with their Norwegian friends trying to help them. The hover pad was mostly used to make climbing places easier on their expeditions and it would help Tony as now he could follow everyone else without needing to walk. He sat on the hover pad and kept himself steady so as not to overbalance and fall off. The gadget hummed as it carried him effortlessly up the road. Tony couldn't help but grin in amazement. He thought it was pretty fun riding on the pad like so. Emerald beamed, happy to see Tony enjoying himself. She'd get her turn once they arrived for she guessed they would get her to use the pad to fly up to cave and get the staff.

The whole time everyone walked up the trail to the glacier, the Silverlock and Summers families drank in the view. Mountain walks like this always had a spectacular view to admire and this was no different. There were trees everywhere and a few waterfalls roared down the mountain side. It was sights like this that served as a fond reminder on how incredible nature could be. The supernatural explorer in Ruby couldn't help but wonder if other worlds had anything like this. All the supernatural creatures that had wandered into their world, did they have a view like what they were seeing now? Did they like how Earth appeared and find it an attractive world to live in? It would be worth asking if she ever met any creatures that could talk. Ruby also found herself seeing things through Draven's eyes a little. While she didn't agree with his beliefs, she supposed she could understand why he was so protective of mankind. He likely wanted to preserve all of this and prevent any potentially dangerous creatures from destroying it. Ruby wouldn't want to see a view as beautiful as this wiped out either. Once they got the staff, the perfect solution would be there in her hands. Ruby would wish all the supernatural creatures of the world back to their home worlds and for all the barriers between worlds to be closed up. The hunters wouldn't be needed anymore and everything would've been resolved peacefully and humanely, just was Ruby wanted. But then what of Rimor? Would they end up being obsolete with nothing supernatural to explore? She didn't like to think that she'd be putting so many people out of a job, but Ruby guessed they'd be able to adapt and find something else to do with their resources. Maybe they could be explorers of a different kind instead.

It was around 6:30 am when the group reached their destination. By now, it was dawning and it was much lighter than before. The sun slowly began to rise up from the horizons and the group were treated to a breath-taking view of what lay before them. Standing tall and proud was the Briksdal glacier. Just like everything else they'd seen, it looked grand. This was a view like no other. There was something strange yet beautiful about the large towering mountain topped with snow that had a long white trail snaking its way down to the bottom. The glacial lake nearby was equally as beautiful, so crystal clear that the two families wondered if it would be drinkable. They were glad to have dressed up in warm coats and gloves for the occasion as it was very chilly this high up. Even then, the group felt the need to zip their coats up as far as they could and blow into their gloved hands. Ruby, Emerald, Sapphire, Karim and Tony all stared in wonder at the famous glacier.

"So this is it, the Briksdal glacier." Ruby murmured.

"It's even more beautiful in person…" Sapphire whispered in awe.

"It looks like someone spilled ice-cream all over it!" Emerald joked, pointing at the snow at the top of the mountain.

"A really big ice-cream at that!" Karim chimed in, "This thing's huge!"

"Given how it's 1,910 metres at its highest elevation, it sure is big." Sapphire agreed, "I can see why someone hid the Staff of Wishes inside it. A place like that's as good as any to hide anything."

"Quite so." Tony concurred, "I am curious as to who hid it in there in the first place."

"Probably the guy who made it." Ruby suggested, "So now we're here, we can go get the staff."

"We shall." Paul agreed, "Emerald, you take the hover pad and an agent will fly you up there." he ordered, "The hover pad can only carry up to three people, so who else wants to go up with Emerald?"

"I'll go up with her." Michael volunteered, "I don't want my baby girl going in there without someone to support her."

"Thank you dad, you're the best!" Emerald said appreciatively.

"Anything for my little girl." Michael said kindly.

"You two take care up there." Annie said anxiously, hugging her husband and child as if she wouldn't see them again after this, "And please Emerald dear, if it's too scary for you, come straight out of the cave."

"I understand what you're saying mum, but I have to get that staff." Emerald said bravely, "Claustrophobia or not, I won't let anything stop me from saving my friend!"

As anxious as she was for her daughter's safety, Annie couldn't help but smile proudly at Emerald.

"Oh my baby girl...when did you become so brave?" she asked with admiration.

Emerald just smiled modestly. She turned to Tony. The teen boy just smiled encouragingly at her.

"Good luck up there little gem." he said supportively, "I do hope you make it back out with the staff."

"I will Tony!" Emerald declared, "You wait there for me. I'll be back before you know it!"

She climbed onto the hoverpad with Michael and one Rimor agent. The agent was in charge of steering and driving the pad. He pressed a button that made the device rise up even further off the floor as it entered flight mode. The agent, Emerald and Michael were given magnetic clamps to wear around their feet so they wouldn't fall off. The magnets were powerful, effortlessly holding them into place on the hover pad. The pad whirred nosily as it ascended up the glacier. Ruby chuckled. It was almost like watching a UFO take off due to the device's disc shape. Everyone watched as Emerald and Michael grew smaller and smaller the further up they went. Annie held a fist close to her heart.

"Be safe you two..." she said to herself.

"They'll be fine mum." Ruby reassured her, "I'm sure of it."

"To think we'll soon be holding a magical artefact from centuries past..." Sapphire murmured with fascination, "I'm kinda giddy just thinking about it!"

"We should definitely tell the Cooper family about it when we get home." Karim declared, "They'll be so excited!"

All the others could do for now was wait for Emerald and Michael to return. The two soon arrived at the cave entrance. The hoverpad flew over the ledge and lowered back down into hover mode now it was back over solid ground. The agent turned the pad off and he, Emerald and Michael headed to the entrance. They were met with a huge rusty door with a bird sculpture in the centre. There didn't seem to be any actual handles on the door. Michael observed the door quizzically. So how was it supposed to open if there were no handles or buttons anywhere? The agent guessed the bird somehow opened the door. He pushed down on its wings but nothing happened. He then tried pushing down on the head. It worked and the door slid open, groaning nosily as if the effort of opening was too much effort for it. Emerald shuddered as the ground rumbled beneath her feet. Michael held tight to her. The door fully opened and everything became silent and still. The trio entered the cave. They came up to another door, this one more rusted than the one outside, and found themselves staring at a huge angel statue. Emerald imagined that when it had first been made, it must've looked dazzling and shiny with its gold paint. Now there was barely any left and the statue looked eroded and weather worn. Michael observed it for minute. There didn't seem to be any obvious way into the cave. The angel statue didn't appear to open or anything and there was nothing to grab onto and open the door with.

"Well this is puzzling. How do we get in if this thing's in the way?" Michael murmured.

"We'll never be able to shift it." Emerald said glumly, "None of us will be strong enough to..."

They were cut off as the angel's eyes suddenly lit up. An ominous red glow lit up the room as the eyes stared at the trio. Emerald yelped in surprise and Michael stood protectively in front of her. The agent held up a hand, signalling them to stay calm. The statue glowered at the trio, staring so intently that Emerald felt it was trying to see into her soul.

"REVEAL THYSELF." the statue demanded.

Emerald swallowed heavily. Her heart was in her throat. This was it! Would the statue allow her inside? Emerald came out from behind Michael and stood to attention, gazing back up at the statue.

"G-g-good m-morning Mr. St-Statue." she stammered, "We d-do beg your pardon for intruding like this..." she coughed nervously and forced herself back on track, "Wh-what I meant t-to say was: my name is Emerald Silverlock sir! And this is my dad," she gestured to Michael, "We've come to claim the Statue of Wishes, so we demand that you let us in!"

Silence.

"...please?" Emerald added meekly.

The statue didn't respond for a minute. Emerald wondered if it was making up its mind on what to do. Did this statue even have a mind for that matter? Michael felt uneasy. He had a nasty feeling that something terrible was about to happen. Then...

"PROCEED." the statue boomed, "YOU ARE BOTH ELIGIBLE TO ENTER THE CAVE. BE QUICK: I WILL NOT STAY OPEN FOR LONG..."

That only made Emerald feel more anxious. Now they had a time limit to be in and out of the cave to worry about? As if this mission wasn't nerve-racking enough already! Why was there even a time limit anyway? Perhaps it was to convince people to hurry up so they wouldn't linger about. The statue then suddenly shuddered and the cave rumbled nosily. Emerald and Michael were tempted to run for it, fearing a cave-in was about to happen. But they soon saw that it wasn't. The statue was actually rising up off the floor, revealing the doorway to the cave behind it. It was like it was ascending to heaven as it slowly rose up towards the ceiling. It stopped when the space had opened up about ten feet. The way into the cave was narrow and slightly triangular in shape. It looked as if there was a tunnel that went a long way down. The Staff of Wishes was down at the bottom. Emerald approached the entrance, but then she hesitated. Her claustrophobia was playing up and she began to feel scared. The tunnel was too narrow and she was worried about the angel statue coming back down and trapping her inside. She threw herself into Michael's arms.

"I can't do it! I can't go in there! It's too small and scary!" Emerald whimpered.

"That's fine kiddo. I'll go in for you." Michael offered.

"NO! Please don't go without me!" Emerald begged, "I don't want to be alone, and I don't want you to get trapped in there!"

"I won't get trapped Emerald. I'll be quick like the statue said." Michael insisted.

"I'd get a move on." the agent urged, "Time is of the essence. I doubt the statue will wait for you to finish deciding what to do."

Emerald was in torment. She didn't want to go inside, but she also didn't want Michael to go in himself. She hated the idea of waiting for him and worrying he wasn't going to make it. Her powers would at least guarantee his survival. She also hadn't come this far just to chicken out at the last minute. She was going in and that was final.

"I'll go!" Emerald declared, "I have to be brave, I have to get that staff for Tony!"

Michael smiled encouragingly at his daughter. With their minds made up, Emerald and Michael entered the tunnel. The agent stayed where he was, his pistol in hand and a watchful eye out for intruders. He would make sure nobody untoward would interfere with the mission. Emerald and Michael made their way down the tunnel. It went down into the cave but neither one could see the bottom. Emerald and Michael had brought torches with them so they could see their way in the dark, but even then they still couldn't see where it ended. Emerald began to breathe in and out very fast. She was feeling closed in thanks to the narrow tunnel and she was sure that it was getting narrower the further down they went. Her heart was racing to the point she couldn't register the individual beats. She was creeping dangerously close towards a panic attack. Michael could sense his youngest child was getting scared and he put a hand on her shoulder.

"It's OK sweetheart. We won't get trapped." he said softly, "We'll be in and out in no time."

Emerald nodded but said nothing. She was so anxious that she'd lost the ability to speak for now. She closed her eyes for a few seconds. Don't think about the space, think about Tony, that was what she told herself repeatedly as she tried not to let it worry her. But as she opened her eyes again, she gasped in astonishment. They could see the bottom of the tunnel. That was lucky, it didn't seem as far down as they thought. A minute later, they reached the end of the tunnel and found themselves in a large, wide-open area. It looked as if some giant creature had hollowed out this room in order to make space for itself. Emerald began to relax now she was in a more spacious area. To her surprise, she could actually see without needing her torch. Some kind of light was emitting from the room. She and Michael entered the room and their eyes lit up with glee as they saw their prize. There, standing proud and majestic on an ancient plinth in the middle of the cave was the Staff of Wishes. It was unmistakable, it truly was real. The stories had all been true. The staff was long and made of solid gold. It had a spherical head and two large angel wing like structures on either side. A dazzling red jewel sat in the centre. The staff emitted a soft, heavenly glow that lit up the cave that made Emerald and Michael feel warm and content just looking at it. Emerald ran up to the staff, her stomach tingling with excitement. She grabbed the staff and picked it up. It was surprisingly light despite its solid gold make. She expected it to be much heavier.

The staff was an incredible sight. It had been down here all this time and yet there wasn't so much as a speck of dust or dirt on it anywhere. It looked brand new, like it had only been put there yesterday.

"This is it! We've got it!" Emerald whispered excitedly.

"That we have." Michael said hastily, "Now let's quick get out of here before the statue closes."

Emerald nodded and jumped away from the plinth so the two could leave. But as she was about to go, something appeared in the corner of her eye. She stopped and turned to her left. The staff's light allowed her to see that the cave had drawings on the walls. The drawings were old and faded, but she could still make out their image. Emerald aimed the staff at the wall so she could get a good look at the drawing. The picture seemed to be depicting some kind of battle. From what Emerald could make out, there appeared to be an old looking person in a large cloak holding the Staff of Wishes. Was it the man who invented the staff? His opponent appeared to be some skeleton-faced monster in black robes and holding a cane. What on Earth was that thing? Emerald took her phone out and snapped a picture. She was sure Ruby and Karim would be interested to see it and maybe the Coopers would know who they were.

"I wonder what that's all about..." Emerald murmured to herself, "And just who is that man and the monster he's fighting? I hope the man won."

She was shaken out of her thoughts by a sudden rumbling noise. Emerald nearly jumped out of her skin. Was the cave about to collapse on top of them? Michael quickly realized what was happening.

"The statue must be closing down!" he shouted, "Quick, back to the entrance!"

Emerald was charging up the tunnel before Michael had even finished talking. She ran like she'd never run before. The narrow tunnel no longer mattered to her, all she cared about was getting out and fast! Michael bolted after her. The two could see that the angel statue was indeed moving back down again. They could already see the way out starting to close. Please let them get out in time! Emerald could already see herself being trapped inside as it finally closed. She pushed herself harder, forcing herself to run even faster. The statue was halfway down by the time Emerald and Michael reached the top of the tunnel. Emerald screamed desperately as she threw herself forwards in a mad leap to escape. She cleared the entrance and made it back out just in time. Michael looked as if he might not make it, but he timed his leap just right and was able to get out of the way with seconds to spare. Both Emerald and Michael lay sprawled on the floor, gasping and panting with a wave of relief rushing over them. Emerald was amazed her heart hadn't stopped beating. She looked to the staff, glad that it was still in her hands. In hindsight, they really hadn't needed to rush like that. They could've just used the staff to wish themselves out of the cave if they'd ended up trapped inside. In their mad rush to get back out again, the thought had never occurred to them. Michael was the first to recover, climbing to his feet and running over to Emerald to help her back up. Emerald's nerves were tingling, but she was unharmed, much to Michael's relief.

"That was a close call, wasn't it kiddo?" Michael said half-jokingly.

"That was scary! I thought we weren't going to make it!" Emerald shrieked, "Thank goodness we did!"

She looked down at the staff.

"We got it, now I can get this to Tony and he can wish his illness away!" Emerald said gleefully.

"You could always do that now you have it." Michael noted.

"Well, yes I could, but it would be just right if Tony makes the wish." Emerald insisted, "He's the one who's dying, so he should get to wish himself better."

Michael nodded understandingly. He supposed he couldn't really disagree with Emerald. The two turned to leave the cave, only to see that they were no longer alone. Emerald screamed as she saw Draven and Alice standing at the mouth of the cave. The cyborg leader of the hunters was there in person, his blue optics bearing into Emerald and Michael. Alice was beside him, gun in hand and prepared to shoot if anybody so much as stepped out of line. Michael noticed that she'd already shot one person. Lying dead on the ground just a few feet away was the agent who had brought him and his daughter to the cave. Emerald clutched the staff tight to her chest, her eyes wide with horror. She hadn't met Draven before, but she knew it was him regardless. Ruby had described him to her before and she doubted there were many other cyborgs in capes roaming the world. Draven stepped forward, his menacing gaze fixated on the staff in Emerald's hands.

"Thank you so much for fetching the Staff of Wishes for me." Draven purred, his voice full of mock gratitude, **"Now if you'd be so kind as to hand it over to me, we can avoid any unnecessary violence. You did save the life of one of my own, so I'm willing to be reasonable. Hand over the staff, and I will let you and your entire family live, even Ruby. Please don't try anything foolish, I'd hate for Alice to have to shoot you both…"**

Chapter 14: I Make This Wish…

Emerald couldn't believe what was happening. What should've been a successful retrieval mission was about to go horribly wrong. How could this have happened? How was Draven here without anyone knowing and how did he know they'd even be here to get the staff? Emerald could feel herself beginning to hyperventilate. It was like being in a nightmare, only this one wasn't going to end with her waking up. Michael spoke up for her.

"How did you get here without being seen?" he demanded, "And how did you know we'd be here? There's no way you could've known we'd be here!"

"Me and Alice travelled here inside my Cyber Dragon, which has cloaking technology." Draven explained, **"Your group had no chance of spotting us as we flew through the sky towards the cave. As for your other question, I had one of my agents feed you information that would divert you here. After Emerald very generously saved my agent's life, I knew she was the pure of heart I needed to get into the cave and get that staff. It was as simple as that: I had my agent steer you in the right direction and you get the staff for me."**

Emerald felt sick. Ruby and Sapphire had been right to be suspicious all along! It had been a trap and they'd fallen right into it! Now she understood why the guy in Ålesund who had told her where to find the staff looked familiar. He must've been one of Draven's hunters the whole time and the reason he'd told them where to find the staff was just so Draven could take it from them once she'd gotten it. How could they have been so stupid? They'd suspected there was a catch to it all and they still fell for it! Draven advanced on Emerald, his hand stretched out. The light of the staff glinted off of his sharp, metal claws.

"Now my sweet little Emerald, the Staff of Wishes please." he purred.

Emerald stepped back, still clutching the staff close to her.

"N-no! I w-won't let you have it!" she stammered, trying to sound brave.

Draven rolled his eyes. He looked more bored than irritated by the whole thing.

"Don't try my patience, child." he sighed irritably, **"You really do have no other options here. Alice could shoot you or your father dead before the thought of making a wish even crossed your mind. Give it to me or your father will die."**

Alice pointed her gun at Michael, her finger tight around the trigger. Her bright red lips were curled into a cruel, sadistic smile. Unlike Draven, she was relishing this moment and enjoying the look of terror on Emerald's face. Michael tried not to be intimidated, but Alice could see it in his eyes, he was terrified too. To think a few months ago, Simon had held him at gunpoint to make Ruby hesitate when she'd been her hostage, and now she was getting to do the same to make Emerald comply. Emerald looked helplessly to Michael. She wanted him to do something, pull some miracle out of thin air to save them both. Michael just looked back at her, looking completely defeated. She could tell just from his face what he wanted to say to her: don't worry about me, just get out of here with the staff! But Emerald wasn't going to abandon her father. She would never forgive herself if he died because she'd been a coward and fled. With tears in her eyes, Emerald looked back to Draven.

"O-OK, i-it's y-yours." she whimpered, "Just p-please d-don't kill my d-dad."

She threw the staff at Draven as hard as she could. It was a futile attempt to maybe stun Draven and distract him long enough for the two to make a run for it. But Draven simply caught the staff with one hand. The movement had been so fast that neither Emerald nor

Michael saw it happen. Alice kept her gun raised just to make sure neither one tried to get the staff back. Emerald looked to Michael, her eyes streaming with tears. Michael looked back at her, gently reassuring her with his eyes that he understood why she had to do it. Draven stared down at the staff as if he'd found a nugget of gold that would make him financially independent for life. He couldn't believe that he was actually holding the genuine article right there in his hands. He'd thought he'd never get his hands on the staff, and yet now he had it. His wish would finally come true.

"At long last...I have the staff!" Draven crowed, sounding like a scientist who had made an incredible discovery and couldn't believe the results he'd found, **"Now all supernatural creatures and magic will be gone forever!"**

"Our mission will be complete father! Once and for all, mankind will be safe forever from otherworldly threats!" Alice said excitedly, "Oh mother would be so proud of us both!"

"Yes. I only wish she could be here now to see us accomplish what she'd set out to do all those years ago..." Draven said wistfully, **"In her name, I will finally eradicate the biggest threat that mankind is up against for good!"**

He clutched the staff tightly with both hands and held it up high. The cyborg was about to make his wish until Emerald spoke up. She was surprised she could even find her voice again with how scared she was.

"NO! Please Draven, don't make your wish!" Emerald begged.

"Why shouldn't I?" Draven snapped, **"My duty is to protect mankind from supernatural threats! With this staff, I can finally fulfil my duty!"**

"But it's wrong of you to do this!" Emerald insisted, "You can't just wish for so many innocent creatures to die like that! That's a horrible thing to do! And I can't let you make your wish for you might use the staff to kill Ruby!"

"I'm not going to wish for your sister to die." Draven retorted, **"I'm only wishing for supernatural creatures to die and magic to be gone. All that will do is take Ruby's protection spell away."**

"So THEN we'll be able to kill her." Alice sneered, "I've even insisted that father lets me do the honours."

But to Emerald and Michael's surprise, Draven shook his head at that.

"No Alice, once Ruby's magic is gone, she'll no longer be a threat." he said matter-of-factly, **"There'll be no need to kill her."**

Alice looked as if she'd been slapped across the face. Emerald and Michael were equally as astonished.

"What?! But father, she almost killed you!" Alice screeched in anger, "You can't just let that brat get away with it! She needs to pay for her actions!"

"We've been over this already Alice." Draven said coldly, **"This is a mission to save mankind, not get revenge. Revenge is such a worthless cause and I will not have you risking our mission by making it personal."**

"But she..." Alice tried to say.

"SILENCE!" Draven thundered.

His voice echoed all around the cave entrance. Emerald and Michael recoiled. Alice was stunned silent, unable to say a word. She couldn't even move. It was like Draven had blasted the life out of her with that single shout. He cleared his throat and turned back to the Silverlocks.

"Do excuse my daughter. She's always been very...temperamental." Draven muttered, almost sounding embarrassed about Alice's behaviour.

"Am I delirious, or did you just say to Alice that you're NOT going to kill Ruby?" Michael asked, still trying to make sense of everything.

"You really mean it Draven? You won't kill my sister?" Emerald asked, still stunned by what Draven had said earlier.

"You have my word." Draven confirmed, **"Consider it me returning the favour for you saving my agent's life. Unlike Alice, I was never motivated by revenge against Ruby. I just didn't want her to be a threat. Now I have the staff to make my wish with, Ruby will be an ordinary girl with no magic to potentially make her dangerous. There's no need to kill her now."**

"And here I thought you hunters had no standards..." Michael scoffed.

"I'm glad you won't kill Ruby, but that doesn't change the fact your wish is still wrong!" Emerald countered, "You're still going to kill lots of innocent creatures just because you're scared they might be a threat! And you want to take magic away, even though magic can do good things for people! It's thanks to magic that I saved your agent! And you want to just take that all away? I like my powers and I want to continue doing good with them! My sisters and Karim want to do the same with their magic too! Please Draven, please don't make your wish!" she pleaded, clasping her hands together.

Draven shook his head in refusal.

"Mankind must come first my child." he said, his voice gentle as if he was a father trying to reassure his child that he was doing the right thing, **"I understand the way that you feel, but I must put the lives of the entire world above your idealistic beliefs about the supernatural and the magical..."**

With everything settled, Draven turned back to the staff.

"Now then...the wish." the cyborg leader purred, **"Oh mighty staff, I ask for you to grant me my one wish."** he chanted, **"I wish for all supernatural creatures to be destroyed and all traces of magic to disappear forever."**

Emerald clutched her father worriedly. Michael hugged her tight. All they could do was watch the wish unfold now Draven had made it. But strangely...nothing happened. The staff didn't do anything. It just continued to shine brightly there in Draven's arms, but no magic came out of it or anything. Draven stared curiously at the staff as if thinking "Is this thing working or what?" Just as he was about to speak again, the red gem in the centre of the staff flashed and a heavenly voice suddenly spoke to him.

"I cannot grant your wish." the staff said to him softly, *"It is forbidden for me to grant wishes that bring death to others and take away the powers of others. Make another wish."*

The gem stopped flashing. Draven stared at the staff, feeling as if he'd been punched in the stomach. It was as if the staff had somehow been mocking him when it told him his wish was denied. Emerald sighed with relief. She should've guessed that Draven's wish couldn't come true. The Coopers had told her and her sisters that the staff couldn't grant wishes that killed or took powers away. At least nobody would be losing their magic now. But most importantly, no innocent creatures were going to be heartlessly slaughtered. Draven was still for a few seconds. Then suddenly, he burst back into life with a thunderous roar of rage.

"WHAT?!?!" he bellowed, **"I WENT THROUGH ALL THIS JUST TO BE DENIED MY CHANCE TO SAVE MANKIND ONCE AND FOR ALL?!"**

Emerald saw an opportunity to get the drop on Draven. He was ranting furiously, distracted by rage, so she was able to form a golden energy ball in her hands and throw it at him before he even realized what was happening. Draven just had time to see something heading towards him before it slammed into his face and exploded in a ball of bright light. The impact was so powerful that his visor cracked. He reeled back and roared with anguish, momentarily blinded by the energy ball attack. Draven dropped the staff and clutched his face. Alice jumped back in alarm. Now her attention was away from the Silverlocks and onto Draven, Michael saw his chance to tackle the tall woman down to the ground. Both Alice and Michael hit the stony floor with a thump, the impact knocking the wind out of them. Alice tried to aim her gun at Michael but the big man was much too strong for her. He kept the gun away by restraining her wrist and forcing her gun hand down. He eventually managed to force Alice to drop the gun. Now she was disarmed, Michael jumped to his feet and rushed to the cave entrance. Emerald followed him, grabbing the Staff of Wishes along the way. However, Draven's Cyber Dragon was waiting for the two and just as they were about to escape on the hover pad, the black and gold machine fired a beam at them and stopped them completely. Both father and daughter were completely immobilized. But luckily for them, they could still talk, albeit through gritted teeth. Just as Draven and Alice were about to catch them, Michael managed to make a wish.

"I...wish...we...were...back...down...the mountain!" he grunted, trying as best as he could to speak while frozen to the spot.

The staff's red gem glowed brightly and in a flash of light, the wish was granted and Emerald and Michael were free from the Cyber Dragon's beam. They reappeared down at the bottom of the glacier just a few feet from the glacial lake. The others saw the flash of light and ran over to the two. Emerald and Michael took a moment to catch their breath as the rest of the family approached.

"Michael, Emerald, what happened? Are you both alright?" Annie asked worriedly as she helped her husband to his feet.

"Look, they got the staff!" Ruby cried excitedly, "They did it!"

"Oh how wonderful!" Caroline cheered, "Now we can save our son's life at last!"

"Don't get too excited." Sapphire warned, "Something's not right here."

She could tell from how frightened her sister and father looked that something bad had happened. Emerald was the first to recover, snapping out of her daze and throwing herself into Ruby and Sapphire's arms.

"We need to get out of here, now! NOW!" Emerald shrieked, her voice full of terror.

"Em, calm down! What's wrong?" Ruby asked with concern.

"Draven's here!" Michael cut in, "He tricked us! He had an agent lead us all here so he could take the staff from us!"

Ruby, Sapphire, Karim, Paul and Judy stared in horror as they let the news settle in for a second. Of all the worst things that could've happened! Draven had to be here now just as they were carrying out an important mission! Ruby kicked at the ground and swore angrily.

"Oh I knew it! I knew this was a trap and we still fell for it!" she ranted furiously, "How could we have been so stupid?! It all makes sense now! That guy in Ålesund must've been in on the whole thing and that's why he told you and Tony where the staff was free of charge!"

"I said the whole thing was too convenient." Sapphire muttered, "But there's no use beating ourselves up about it, we need to get out of here now as Em said."

"What's going on everyone? Who's Draven?" Caroline asked worriedly.

She soon got her answer as suddenly, a huge shape crashed down behind everyone, the impact so large that a huge shockwave blew everyone off their feet. The Silverlock and Summers families crashed down onto the rocky ground, more startled than hurt. They lay sprawled on the ground, grunting in pain and shell-shocked for a few seconds. Emerald had dropped the staff after being flung aside. It had splashed down into the glacial lake nearby. The two families looked up and found themselves staring at a very angry Draven with both blades deployed and his large cape billowing out behind him. He had literally jumped off the glacier and thanks to his cyborg armour, he'd taken the impact without any damage done to himself. He'd made a small crater upon impact with how heavily he'd crashed down. Alice followed after him, riding on the back of their Cyber Dragon. Tony stared, his bright blue eyes wide with terror.

"E-E-Emerald? I-i-is that him?" he stammered.

"That's Draven." Emerald confirmed, "He's the leader of the hunters and the one who tried to kill Ruby."

"And now it looks as if he's here to kill all of us!" Marcus exclaimed, pulling both Tony and Caroline close as if to protect them.

Ruby thought her heart was going to stop. She never thought she would be in this situation again: staring face-to-face with her arch-enemy and preparing to fight for her life. She'd been so sure that she'd seen the last of Draven that night she'd plunged a sword into his chest. But here they were, facing each other down like last time. Draven's optics fixed on the silver-haired girl. If hatred had a face, Ruby imagined it would look like Draven. Alice jumped off the Cyber Dragon and stood beside her father, her gun in hand and ready to shoot. Paul and Judy drew out their weapons and prepared to shoot. Ruby took a deep breath and clenched her fists. This was what she'd been training for, now she had to show what she could do.

"You..." Ruby hissed venomously.

"Ruby Silverlock...there you are." Draven crooned dryly, **"How I've longed to see that face again. You nearly killed me last time we met, and that makes you dangerous. I was hoping to use the staff to kill all supernatural creatures and rid the world of magic permanently. At least then, I wouldn't have to kill you since you'd no longer be a threat to mankind without your magic. But the staff refused, so I have no choice but to do this the hard way."**

"We don't have to do this Draven!" Ruby protested, "Why do this when there's a solution to all our problems that can avoid any unnecessary killing?"

"Yeah!" Karim added, "If you just back off and let us use the Staff of Wishes, we'll make a wish that can solve everything and make everyone happy! We were planning to wish all the creatures back home and the dimensional barriers to be closed! If we do that, everyone wins. Mankind's safe from supernatural threats and no creatures have to be killed. Doesn't that sound like a good idea?"

"It sounds like a temporary solution to the problem, not a permanent one." Draven scoffed, **"What good will sending the creatures back do? It'll just give them an opportunity to come back to our world again! And closing the dimensional barriers won't solve anything either. They got opened up by Lord Hallows, so who's to say anyone else can't do the same thing, especially if magic is still allowed to thrive? Your wish will only solve one problem and not another! Supernatural creatures AND magic both have to be eradicated if mankind is to truly be saved!"**

"No they don't!" Ruby shouted, "Magic may have caused all this, but magic is also the solution to the problem! It's thanks to magic that we have a means to close the dimensional barriers at all! If you hunters put aside your stupid bigotry for one second and actually cooperated with magic users instead of killing them, then Hallows's mess would've been cleared up by now! It's because of you morons being unable to let go of your hatred as to why what should've been a simple solution is taking longer than it should've done!"

"We will NEVER cooperate with witches and the like!" Alice screeched, "Anything mystical and abnormal is wrong and must be destroyed, for all our sakes! Now give us the staff or else we'll kill you all!"

"Go to hell!" Ruby snarled, "We're never giving you the staff!"

"You want it, you'll have to take us on!" Sapphire dared.

"ALL of us!" Karim shouted bravely.

Emerald just stood beside her sisters and balled her fists, trying to look brave. Paul and Judy stood beside them. Annie, Michael,

Tony, Caroline and Marcus all stepped back. They knew that they were out of their depth here and shouldn't make themselves targets. They would leave all this to the children and Rimor now. Draven allowed the parents and Tony to leave. He didn't want them to become collateral damage in this fight. Once they were gone, he turned back to the kids and Rimor agents. He crossed his blades in front of his face. The blades were so shiny that Ruby could see her face reflected in them. It was like they were showing her through her reflection that she was their next target.

"Fine, I'll take you ALL on!" Draven roared.

He threw his cape off and charged towards the group like a snarling beast. Ruby, Emerald, Sapphire and Karim braved themselves, ready to attack with their new magic powers. Now they would see if their training with both Rimor and the Coopers would pay off in this battle...

Chapter 15: Returning The Favour

Draven's blade came slashing down towards his opponents. Ruby, Emerald, Sapphire and Karim all jumped back to avoid the attack, the blade just missing Ruby's face by inches. Draven struck the ground, leaving a neat groove into the rocky ground where his blade hit. He pulled himself free without even struggling and swiped at Ruby a second time. The silver-haired teen held up her hands and blasted Draven with a jet of flames that forced him to back off. His armour was heat-proof so he was in no danger of getting burned, but the attack was still enough to push against him. Draven slashed away at the flames. At this moment, he looked like a demon that had risen from Hell and was walking through the flames towards the foolish mortal that dared to stand in his way. Ruby could see that this wasn't going to work, so she tried throwing fireballs at Draven's face instead. She launched a few, but Draven was too fast and managed to cut through each one. Sapphire saw an opportunity to ambush him and formed ice around her fists. She punched Draven in the back. The punch didn't even leave a scratch on his armour. Draven spun around and kicked Sapphire in the gut, throwing the blue-haired girl off her feet. Karim used his psychic powers to save her from a painful fall and managed to catch just her inches above the ground. Sapphire stood back up and attacked again by throwing icicles at Draven. The cyborg walked through the attack, completely unflinching. Sapphire may as well have been throwing pebbles at him for all the good it was doing. Desperately, Sapphire flicked her fingers and tried to freeze Draven to the spot. Ice formed around his feet but he broke free with one casual tug on his legs. Draven grabbed Sapphire by her coat and threw her straight into Ruby, the teenager seeming to weigh nothing in his hands. The two sisters lay sprawled on the ground, winded by the blow. Draven advanced on the kids, aiming to try and knock Ruby out before she could get up again. He knew trying to kill her was pointless since her protection spell would activate. He aimed a powerful punch towards her head, only for Emerald to form a yellow barrier in front of Ruby and block the attack. Draven turned and lunged for Emerald. Screaming in fright, Emerald jumped back, leaving her attacker to claw the ground in front of her feet. She formed an energy ball in her hands and threw it at Draven's face. It made him stagger a little, but he quickly recovered and carried on as if nothing had happened.

"Did you kids really think getting magic powers would do you any good?" Draven crowed, **"I've had years of experience dealing with witches, magicians, sorcerers and the like. My armour has been upgraded enough times that magic barely even fazes me anymore. You may as well be fighting me with toy swords for how effective your powers are..."**

"You forget Draven, me and Ruby beat you without magic powers, so I think our chances look even better than before now we have them!" Karim crowed, "Also, it means we can get more creative with our fighting, like THIS!"

He thrust his arms forward and Draven suddenly found himself reeling backwards in shock and pain as a huge rock slammed into him as if fired from a gun. Karim reckoned that using the environment to his advantage could give him and his friends a hand in this battle. The rock broke to pieces and Draven's visor cracked even more. If this carried on, it would break entirely and his eyes would be exposed. Karim picked up several smaller rocks with his psychokinesis and he threw them at Draven. The rocks bounced off of his armour as he walked through them. He lashed out, aiming to punch Karim in the face, but the teen boy jumped away to dodge him. He then drew out his sword, the very same sword he'd used to fight Draven last time, and the two clashed weapons together. Ruby watched for a second, finding herself transported back to that night when she and Karim had been fighting for their lives against the cyborg. Unlike last time, she wasn't going to let it end with her nearly murdering him. Karim and Draven crossed blades and pushed against each other. Ruby saw her chance and blew fire at Draven. He was caught off guard and that distracted him enough for Karim to slash at his arms with his sword, creating a shower of sparks as his blade scraped over Draven's armour. However, the damage was only superficial and Draven kicked Karim, knocking him aside. Then he lashed out and punched Ruby in the stomach. Ruby fell down onto her back and grunted as the impact nearly punched the air out of her lungs. Alice grinned wickedly and aimed her gun at Ruby. At this close distance, she couldn't possibly miss. One single stun blast and she'd be out cold, ready for her father to take her prisoner. They'd take the other kids prisoner too and find some way to get rid of their magic. But Alice didn't get a chance to shoot as Sapphire sprinted up to her, catapulted herself into the air with one mighty leap and kicked her in the face. It had been an impressive feat and even Sapphire was impressed with herself.

"Good shot!" Ruby complimented, "That was quite a flying kick!"

"Like something out of a movie!" Karim added.

"Looks like all that training's paying off. I was never this athletic before!" Sapphire exclaimed.

Paul and Judy nodded with admiration. They were glad to see Rimor's training hadn't been for nothing. They'd been kept busy by Draven's Cyber Dragon as it had tried to intervene with the battle, but their Norwegian allies were now shooting at it so the two finally got their chance to join in. The two noticed that Draven was sneaking up on the kids, aiming to ambush them from behind, so they intervened. Paul and Judy shot at Draven with their guns. His armour protected him from the shots, but he felt them and he spun around furiously.

"Now, now, let's play fair, shall we?" Paul said disapprovingly as if scolding a child, "Someone like you shouldn't have to resort to underhanded tactics like that."

"In a battle, all that matters is winning." Draven retorted, **"You can't afford to play fair when fighting for the fate of others..."**

He ran towards Paul and Judy and tried to attack with his blades. Both of them pulled out a staff each and parried his attacks. Loud clanging sounds rang through their ears as metal came into contact with metal, but their staffs held firm against Draven's blades. His weapons were sharp, but even they would take a long time to cut through the staffs. Draven sliced and slashed at both Paul and Judy, but they managed to block every attack. Unlike the kids, they were skilled adults with years of training under their belt, making this a more even contest. Draven remained undeterred as he continued clashing weapons with them. He swiped at Paul, missing his chest by millimetres as he bent over backwards and Judy somersaulted through the air and landed behind him. She butted him in the back with her staff, catching Draven off-guard long enough for Paul to swing his own staff up into Draven's chin. His head snapped backwards, his helmet nearly flying off from the hit. Paul and Judy pole-vaulted into their opponent and kicked him in the stomach. The two of them attacking simultaneously was enough to knock Draven backwards. He stumbled but remained standing. He shook off their blows and retaliated by springing towards them, springing into the air and hurling himself towards them as if he'd been thrown by an invisible, giant hand. Paul and Judy were forced to dive out of the way to avoid Draven crashing down on them. He landed and the force of the impact caused the two agents to trip and stumble over. Judy quickly scrabbled to her feet but Draven kicked her staff away before she could grab it. The Rimor agent attempted to roundhouse kick her opponent, only for Draven to block and then punch her in the side. Judy cried out in anguish as she felt a rib crack from the punch. Paul picked himself up and whipped out his sonic blaster. He shot Draven three times, but the sonic waves did no good. He shrugged them off effortlessly. He lashed out with a punch that would've shattered Paul's skull to pieces if it had hit. The Rimor agent ducked down and retrieved his staff. He swung it up, pummelling Draven in the face with it. He aimed another attack, but he was forced to dive for cover as a powerful laser blast suddenly fired at him. Draven's Cyber Dragon had managed to shake off the other Rimor agents for now and was flying in to help its master. Ruby, Emerald, Sapphire and Karim could see that the Rimor agents needed help dealing with a powerful machine like this, so they ran in to help. With their powers, they at least had a fighting chance. The Cyber Dragon blasted furiously, each laser shot punching a crater into the ground. It wasn't able to hit Paul as he dodged every shot. Ruby stepped in and threw fireballs at the machine. Unfortunately, they were useless as like Draven's armour, the robotic dragon was heatproof too. But Ruby had got its attention, giving Paul a moment to help Judy. Paul helped Judy to her feet, his partner wincing from the pain in her side. She was in no condition to fight anymore, so Paul had to help her off the battlefield. The kids and the Norwegian agents would have to handle this without them. The Cyber Dragon shot at the kids, but Emerald threw energy balls to intercept them. Sapphire threw icicles and Karim used psychokinesis to catch the lasers and throw them back. The Rimor agents shot at the Cyber Dragon. Draven watched as his machine fought off the whole group. Just one Cyber Dragon was tough enough to deal with, so he was confident that it would turn the tide in the battle. He turned to Alice.

"Look for the staff." he ordered, **"Me and the Cyber Dragon have got this."**

"Yes father." Alice purred.

With nobody to stop her, Alice ran off to look for the Staff of Wishes. She already knew what she was going to with it: she'd use the staff to wish for everyone to surrender and give up the fight so she and her father could put a quick end to the whole thing. Then she'd give the staff to Draven in the hopes he'd be able to find some kind of loophole to allow his wish to be granted. But where had the staff gone? Nobody had seen where it had been dropped. Alice smirked to herself as she whipped out an energy detector. Being a hunter came with its perks. But as she was about to track down the Staff of Wishes, someone watched and saw what she was doing. Annie, Michael, Caroline, Marcus and Tony had taken cover in some nearby bushes and had been watching the fight unfold. It was all very intense for them and they could only pray that Rimor would win the fight. Tony had been the only one to see Alice heading into the glacial lake, clearly in search of something. He had a nasty feeling he knew what she was looking for.

"Oh no...that woman's looking for the staff, and everyone else is too busy fighting to notice!" Tony murmured to himself, "I have to stop her!"

He imagined Ruby, Emerald and Sapphire would've done the same thing. Without any hesitation, he leapt out of his hiding place and sprinted towards the lake. Caroline saw him run off and her face went white with horror.

"TONY, COME BACK HERE!" she screeched at the top of her lungs.

But her son ignored her and carried on running. Marcus stood up and sprinted after him.

"Stay there Carol, I'll get him back!" he called to her.

Caroline wanted to stop him, but she let him go in the end. Someone had to stop their son from doing something foolish. She stayed put and Marcus ran off after Tony. All the while, Alice was wading through the lake in search of the Staff of Wishes. She counted her blessings that she'd dressed warmly for even with her thick coat, trousers and boots on, the lake was still incredibly cold. Just walking into it was enough to nearly take all the breath out of her. She hoped the staff hadn't landed anywhere too deep as she didn't fancy having to swim through the lake to get it. Luckily, she managed to find it at a shallow area where the water only reached her knees. Alice could see the red gem in the staff's head glowing faintly under the water. Chuckling to herself, she reached down and grabbed the staff. It was her's and everybody was too occupied with Draven and the Cyber Dragon to stop her. Alice ran her hand delicately over the red gem.

"I may not be one for magic, but a chance to have my wish granted is worth making an exception for." the tall woman crooned darkly to herself, "Now, staff, I wish that..."

She got no further as all of a sudden, she heard splashing sounds from behind and she spun around to see Tony advancing oh her, his eyes full of determination. Scoffing, Alice backhanded him in the face, sending him falling down into the water with a splash. She had no idea who he was, nor did she care. Tony tried to get back up again only for Alice to press down on his back with her foot. Tony scrabbled helplessly but Alice was too strong for him. She intended to keep him pinned down until he drowned. But then she heard someone else splashing towards her and this time, she wasn't quick enough to react. Marcus clasped both fists together and socked her in the side of her face. Alice dropped the staff and reeled to one side. Now she was away, Tony was able to stand up again, gasping for breath. Marcus quickly helped Tony up to his feet and pulled him to safety. Alice was left on her knees, trying to regain herself after that hit had knocked all her senses out of order. Once Marcus and Tony were out of the lake, Marcus was quick to scold his son.

"What were you thinking out there?!" he cried, "You could've gotten yourself killed!"

"That woman was looking for the staff. I had to stop her from getting it." Tony protested.

"You didn't need to endanger yourself like that!" Marcus snapped furiously, "You're in no condition to help as you are! We could've let one of those agents know and they would've dealt with it!"

"They're busy with Draven and that robot." Tony protested, "I had to act or else..."

He then suddenly trailed off as he began to feel faint and he swayed alarmingly, looking ready to pass out. His disease was acting up again and just the act from running, going into freezing water and nearly drowning had been too much for him. He promptly collapsed in his father's arms. Marcus gasped in horror and lay Tony down on the ground. He wondered if his son was about to die right then and there. The doctors had warned him that too much strain on his body could cause his heart to give out on him and he was sure that was what was happening. He had to revive him and quick! As he quickly tried to revive his son, Emerald saw what was happening and her eyes widened with shock. Tony was passed out and she guessed from Marcus's frantic attempts to revive him that it was deathly serious. Tony couldn't die now, not when she'd been so close!

"No, don't die Tony! I'm coming for you!" Emerald pleaded.

She hated having to abandon the fight, but Ruby ushered her to go and help Tony before it was too late. Emerald charged over to her friend and knelt down by his side. Marcus did several compressions on Tony's chest and then went mouth-to-mouth on him to try and revive him. He saw Emerald kneeling beside him and looked to her.

"Quick, find the staff and make the wish!" he said frantically, "Tony might have seconds left!"

"Where is it?" Emerald asked.

Marcus gestured to the lake. Emerald took off again, rushing towards the lake. Luckily, she saw Alice picking the staff up again.

She'd finally recovered from Marcus's earlier punch and she had the staff in her hands, but not for long. Emerald threw an energy ball at Alice with such force that Alice was knocked off her feet. She splashed down into the water again and dropped the staff. Emerald quickly grabbed it. She ran back to Tony and Marcus before Alice could stop her. Now she had to hope she wasn't too late and Tony hadn't died, or else the wish wouldn't work. Panting heavily, Emerald looked to the staff.

"Staff, I wish Tony's disease was gone and he's completely healed!" she yelled frantically.

Just like earlier when it had granted her father's wish, the staff reacted instantly. A golden glow shone from the majestic artefact and the red gem lit up as it replied to her.

"Your wish is granted." it softly said to Emerald.

Emerald sighed with relief. Tony was still alive! She was sure the staff was going to tell her that the wish was denied because he was dead. She stood still for a moment as the staff glowed brightly and Tony's body lit up with a heavenly aura. Marcus stepped back as if afraid he'd ruin the spell if he interrupted. A warm, healing glow spread all throughout Tony's body. Emerald imagined it was healing all the damage that had been done to him by his disease and everything was being restored to normal. She could see already that the colour was returning to his face. The process lasted about a minute until eventually, the glowing stopped and Tony was returned to normal. He lay still for a second. Then suddenly, he groaned and his eyes slowly opened up again. He coughed and then sat up. He looked genuinely amazed to still be alive right now. He ran a hand over his chest.

"I'm...I'm alive? And...I feel great!" Tony exclaimed, "Better than I've felt in ages!"

Marcus pulled his son into a hug, his face drenched with tears. Caroline emerged from her hiding place so that she could hug Tony as well. She'd seen the whole thing and was overwhelmed with joy. The Summers family embraced each other tightly, safe with the knowledge that this wouldn't be their last.

"Oh my special little boy! You're all cured at last!" Caroline wailed happily, "This is just the miracle we've been looking for!"

"We're so thrilled! You're going to live!" Marcus exclaimed, "How do you feel Tony?"

"Incredible!" the brunette boy replied gleefully, "It's like I've been given new life! Now I don't have to worry about dying ever again!"

His parents then let him go so Emerald could have her turn. The brunette girl wrapped her arms tight around her best friend. Tony hugged her back. The two were thrilled beyond compare that they wouldn't have to say goodbye to each other in the end.

"I'm so happy Tony! You're all cured, and it's all thanks to the Staff of Wishes!" Emerald screeched, "I only wish that you made the wish yourself, but I had to do it for you in the end." she said, sounding guilty for taking what should've been Tony's.

"I don't care who made the wish just as long as it got made anyway." Tony said jovially, "You're the hero of the day little gem! Finding the staff was your idea in the first place and now thanks to you, I'm cured!"

"You sure are!" Emerald cried happily, "But you could still die out here anyway. We're still in the middle of a fight here, so you and your parents best get back to your hiding place." she insisted.

"We will." Marcus declared, "We'll take the staff too so that woman doesn't try to take it from you."

Emerald nodded. She was about to hand the staff over to Marcus, but a gunshot blasted from nowhere and made Emerald jump back in fright. Alice had scrambled back out of the water and she was pointing her gun at Emerald. She was completely drenched and shivering from the cold, but she tried her best to ignore it. The anger welling up within her was at least providing her some warmth.

"Wonderful, you managed to make your wish and save that boy." Alice said sarcastically, "Now hand over that staff you little brat or else I'll kill you and this family!"

Emerald swallowed nervously. Tony, Marcus and Caroline were equally as petrified with fear. They didn't know what to do. If they tried to run now, Alice would shoot the three of them dead and Emerald wouldn't be able to protect them all with her barriers in time. If Emerald refused to hand over the staff, then Alice would simply use the Summers family as bargaining chips. It was the worst kind scenario where no matter what Emerald decided, it would be the wrong choice. She couldn't let the Summers family die, but she couldn't let Alice have the staff either. What could she do?

Meanwhile, the fight with the Cyber Dragon and Draven wasn't going too well. Some of the Rimor agents had been killed trying to stop the machine and any attacks the kids threw at the Cyber Dragon barely even scratched it. As it was a machine built to capture or kill supernatural creatures, it was naturally going to be very resilient and hard to destroy. Its powerful laser blasts also meant everyone had to dive out of the way just to avoid being hit. Ruby, Sapphire and Karim had dived into a nearby bush and were hiding away from the Cyber Dragon for a moment so they could rethink their strategy.

"We can't take it down by force." Ruby acknowledged, "It's just too tough. Even when you redirect its laser blasts, it just takes the hits like they're nothing!"

"If only we could get into its head somehow!" Karim muttered, "I'd love to simply rip its circuits apart and put the damn thing down for good!"

It was at that moment when he got a brilliant idea.

"Hey...what if I use my psychic powers to break its innards?" Karim suggested, "That should stop it!"

"You sure you're strong enough to do that?" Sapphire asked doubtfully, "We haven't trained in the more advanced stuff yet. You might not have the powers to pull it off."

"We don't know unless we try!" Karim said bravely, "Let's give it a shot!"

Karim leapt out of the bushes and ran up to the Cyber Dragon just as it was shooting at more Rimor agents. He noticed that Paul had joined up with the others to shoot back at the machine. Judy was with the civilians to give her side a rest. Karim looked back to the Cyber Dragon. He could only pray that this would work. He held out his hands and put all his concentration onto the Cyber Dragon's head. Maybe he could get something in its head to break and that would stop the machine. If anything, it would be worth a try to see if he could at least break its laser cannon. Karim fixed his eyes hard on the Cyber Dragon's head and pointed his hands in its direction. Then, focusing all his psychic energy on the robot, he clenched his fists. Karim hoped he didn't have to be in close range for this to work as that only made things riskier. To his relief, it seemed he had made some kind of impact on the machine. After clenching his fists, the Cyber Dragon flinched and he was sure he'd heard something crack. But unfortunately, it didn't have the effect he'd been hoping for. Instead of stopping the machine, the Cyber Dragon suddenly flailed around wildly and began blasting at everything around it. It was completely out of control, flailing and blasting in a frenzied state. It looked as if it might be having a seizure. Draven watched with horror as his machine flew around crazily. Now he had to duck for cover as well. Karim put his hands to his face in horror.

"Oops!" he exclaimed feebly, "That didn't turn out quite how I'd hoped!"

"Never mind that, get down!" Ruby shrieked, tugging on his coat and yanking him back.

She was just in time as the Cyber Dragon blasted at the two. It missed them by centimetres. In its frenzied state, it forced even Alice, Emerald and the Summers family to duck down and run for cover. One laser blast hit the ground behind Emerald and she was thrown off her feet. The staff fell from her hands and it crashed down onto the ground. It bounced back up a little, and then another random shot from the damaged Cyber Dragon hit the magical staff. It was instantly obliterated by the blast. The Staff of Wishes was reduced to nothing more than a smouldering pile of broken metal. Emerald cried out in shock while Alice saw the broken staff and screeched in anger.

"NO!!!" she roared furiously, "Our only chance of getting rid of magic and abnormal creatures, it's gone!"

She turned on Emerald, her teeth clenched so hard that they nearly cracked.

"This is all your fault!" Alice screamed, "If you'd just given me the staff, then this wouldn't have happened!"

She advanced on the young girl, her gun in hand and ready to kill. As that was happening, Draven was trying to stop the Cyber Dragon's uncontrollable rampage. He had a remote control in his hand and he was stabbing furiously at the button to switch the machine off. But it wasn't working. Karim had damaged it so much that it didn't even respond to its controls. The Cyber Dragon couldn't be stopped. It crashed against the mountainside, causing rocks to crumble away and roll down to the bottom. Then it suddenly blasted its laser again, and the shot was heading towards Draven. His tough armour would provide no protection against the Cyber Dragon's laser. If it hit, he would be obliterated. Ruby saw this and she charged towards him.

"No! Not again, I won't let it happen again!" she shrieked frantically.

She stood in front of Draven and took the shot for him. Just as expected, Ruby survived the blast as her protection spell kicked in and saved her life once again. Her hair glowed brightly, the magic energy radiating from it causing her hair-dye to dissolve away, restoring her hair to its natural silver colour. Draven was incredulous. Ruby had just saved his life! But why? He didn't have time to ask her for Ruby suddenly turned around and looked at him.

"Launch me at the robot!" she ordered.

Draven nodded, understanding what Ruby's plan was. Her spell would make her strong enough to stop the Cyber Dragon. He didn't like letting Ruby destroy his creation, but it was necessary to make sure he and Alice didn't get killed. Draven picked Ruby up and launched her into the air as if he was performing the javelin throw. With his enhanced strength courtesy of his armour, the throw was enough for Ruby to reach the Cyber Dragon. Ruby landed on the dragon's head. The machine flailed around, still caught in its mad crazy dance. Ruby held on tight, desperate not to fall off. Her spell wouldn't last forever, so she had to make this quick. She climbed on top of the Cyber Dragon's head and then plunged her fist down through its cranium. Her protection spell made it so she was strong enough to tear through its armour as if it were tinfoil. Once its head was opened up, Ruby grabbed whatever bits of circuitry she could and ripped it clean out. She knew she didn't have to be delicate. The Cyber Dragon let out a metallic screech as it was torn apart. Eventually, Ruby ripped out one last piece of machinery and that finally caused the machine to switch off. The Cyber Dragon's optics went blank and the black and gold robot collapsed to the ground. It crashed down heavily in a heap of metal. The noise of the draconian machine crashing down was incredible. Ruby stood atop the wreckage, completely unharmed. Her hair stopped glowing now there was no threat to her life anymore. She jumped off the robot and panted heavily, feeling a little drained from the fight and her spell activating. She wiped her forehead.

"Whew...thank goodness that's over." Ruby puffed, "That could've been disastrous."

She gasped as all of a sudden, she found herself staring face-to-face with Draven as the cyborg came up to her. Ruby felt frightened. Would he try and kill her? Her spell might activate again, but it wouldn't save her for long now it had activated once already. But Draven didn't seem like he wanted to hurt her. If anything, he looked curious as if he was faced with a particularly puzzling specimen he wanted to figure out.

"Why did you do it?" the leader of the hunters asked.

"D-do what, D-Draven?" Ruby asked nervously.

"You saved my life. That Cyber Dragon nearly blasted me to bits, but you stopped it. Why did you do it?" Draven asked curiously, **"You're the last person who should ever want to save my life when I've constantly been trying to take yours."**

Ruby held her hands together and coughed anxiously.

"When I thought I'd killed you two months ago, it tore me apart." Ruby explained, "I was having nightmares about the whole thing and it just destroyed me, thinking that I was responsible for killing someone! The fact I didn't actually kill you in the end was a great relief to me. So as you can imagine, I just didn't want to stand back and let you die, not when I had the chance to save you. I don't care how cruel and horrible you are Draven, murder is still murder regardless! I couldn't just do nothing! I can't go through all that trauma again!" she added, cringing in disgust as bad memories came back to her.

"And this may shock you," she continued, "But I don't hate you, even after everything you've done. I don't wish death on you or anything like that, because I'm not evil like you are. I don't want either of us to kill each other, rather I want us to come to some kind of compromise. If we can figure out a way to work side-by-side instead of being enemies, then there's no need to kill one another!"

She held out her hand.

"So that's why I saved your life. I...I guess things will be different between us from now on?" Ruby asked hopefully.

She was certain that saving Draven's life would finally get him to leave her alone. Surely even someone like him had a sense of gratitude? Draven looked at Ruby's hand for a minute, contemplating how to respond to such a gesture. He wasn't sure how to feel. He wasn't going to make peace with someone who was practicing witchcraft and protecting alien creatures from his men, not in a million years! This girl had nearly killed him, and she expected him to just bury the hatchet just like that? But she did save his life and thanks to her, nobody else got killed by the Cyber Dragon. He hated to admit it, but it was thanks to magic the situation had been solved in the end. He also thought back to the very question that had him in doubts a while back: am I a good man? If Draven truly was a good man, then he would accept this truce. A good man wouldn't show ingratitude for having their life saved. A part of him also liked Ruby's idea of a compromise. If they could learn to live together, then they wouldn't be fighting and getting in each other's way all the time. And just maybe, that would get him closer to his goal to keeping mankind safe. He reached out, ready to take Ruby's hand.

"N-no! P-please! D-don't kill me!"

Ruby and Draven turned around to see what was happening. The silver-haired girl's eyes widened with horror as she saw Alice Daniels standing over Emerald, her gun in hand and ready to blow her brains out. Emerald was lying on her back with her eyes fixed on the gun that was aimed straight for her head. At this distance, Alice couldn't possibly miss and Emerald would never be fast enough to create a barrier to protect herself. The Summers family were helpless to do anything. If they tried to help now, they'd be too late. Alice would kill Emerald before they'd taken two steps, and then she'd probably kill them too.

"EMERALD!" Ruby shrieked.

Alice heard Ruby's voice and she glanced in her direction for a second. Her bright red lips curled up in a smirk of sadistic glee.

"Oh good, you're here." she sneered, "Now you'll get the "pleasure" of watching me kill your sister. You nearly killed father, so I'm returning the favour..."

"NO, DON'T!" Ruby screeched frantically.

"Too late!" Alice crowed.

She turned back to Emerald. The brunette girl whimpered. She was sure she was about to die at this very moment. She wanted to beg for her life, plead with Alice to spare her. But what good would it do? Emerald could see it in Alice's eyes that the evil woman was beyond reproach. There would be no mercy from her. Alice's finger tightened on the trigger just as Ruby tried to run towards Alice and stop her. Emerald clasped her hands over her eyes, unwilling to witness her own demise. Ruby ran desperately towards Alice in spite of how obvious it was that she'd never stop her in time. There was a loud gunshot and Emerald flinched...but felt no pain. She lay still on the ground, shaking and whimpering feebly. It took her a few seconds to suddenly realize something incredible: she was still alive! But how? She uncovered her eyes. She definitely hadn't been killed. She sat up and saw that it was Alice who had been shot instead. But who had fired? It was Ruby who pieced everything together. She turned and saw that to her amazement, Draven was standing there with a stun gun of his own in hand. He had fired the shot. Alice lay on her back, her eyes closed and her chest slowly rising and falling as she breathed. That told Ruby and Emerald that Draven hadn't killed her, only knocked her out. Draven put the gun away.

"A life for a life. My debt is repaid..." he muttered to himself.

He strode up to his unconscious daughter and shook his head disapprovingly. He was going to have serious words with Alice the minute he got back to headquarters. He ignored her for now as he looked to Emerald. The young girl was still shaking from how close she'd come to death. She looked up at Draven, her eyes full of fright and her hands clutching her chest as if to stop her heart from escaping.

"Are you alright Emerald?" Draven asked kindly. He sounded genuinely concerned for the girl's wellbeing.

Emerald was too frightened to speak. She could only shake her head in response. Draven nodded in response.

"I'm so sorry for my daughter's behaviour." he said apologetically, **"I made it very clear to her this wasn't about revenge, but she did it anyway. I also made it clear that you weren't to be killed. You did save Rodriguez's life after all. Mark my words, Alice will be punished."**

Emerald eventually found her voice again.

"Oh th-thank y-you! Th-thank you so m-much!" she whispered, her voice strained and hoarse from how frightened she'd been.

"We can't thank you enough for saving her life." Ruby said gratefully, "But why did you?"

Draven shrugged.

"You saved my life, so I saved her's." he said casually, **"Consider us even."**

"It was very kind of you, sir." Tony said graciously, kneeling down beside Emerald and hugging her for comfort, "Thank you ever so much for saving my friend."

Draven didn't answer him.

"So where's the Staff of Wishes?" he asked, addressing Emerald.

Emerald just pointed to the remains. Draven pieced together what had happened without her needing to explain anything. It was just unfortunate his Cyber Dragon had to destroy it before he could use it.

"That's...disappointing." the cyborg muttered, **"Now nobody will be able to wish our supernatural problem away."**

Nobody was more disappointed than Ruby herself. She had planned to use the staff to wish all the otherworldly creatures of the world back to their home dimensions and for the dimensional barriers to close. Now Rimor and the Coopers were stuck having to do things the hard way. She looked back to Draven.

"So...what now?" Ruby asked.

Draven picked Alice up and draped the unconscious woman over his shoulder.

"The hunt is off." he announced, **"As gratitude for saving my life today Ruby, we will no longer be hunting you down. But don't think this makes us allies."** he warned, **"Let me make this perfectly clear: I'm only letting you go out of gratitude for what you've done. But if you step one foot out of line, if you or any of your friends and family become a threat to mankind with your magic powers, then I won't be so generous. If you so much as kill one single person, then we'll be after you again, and I WON'T let you go the next time. Am I, in anyway, unclear?"**

"Not at all Draven." Ruby insisted, "If any of us become a danger to mankind, then by all means, do what you want with us. I know I'd rather be put down than be a threat to anyone. But let me make one small request: can you and the hunters at least dial it back on the killing? As a compromise, how about you let us and Rimor investigate any new creatures that get found and you let us send them home before you do anything? You and the hunters can only come in if sending them home doesn't work and they're too dangerous to leave alive. Is that acceptable?" she asked.

Draven thought for a moment.

"I'll...consider it." he murmured, **"But I make no promises. Overall, it will be best for both of us if our paths do not cross again. I hope you, your sisters and your friends will use those powers of yours to become protectors of mankind. You used magic to save my life today, so I think it's fair I give you all the chance to do it again."**

"That's so nice of you." Emerald said brightly, "I guess you're not such a bad guy after all."

Draven looked to Emerald. Deep down, he appreciated hearing that from her. It made him feel as if he truly was a good man after all.

"Farewell, Ruby Silverlock." Draven said grimly, **"Whatever you do, don't make me have to resume the hunt for you..."**

He walked away, carrying Alice with him. With his Cyber Dragon completely destroyed, he had to call the other hunters to send another Cyber Dragon to pick him up and take him back. Ruby, Emerald and Tony watched him go. Once he was gone, everyone breathed a sigh of relief. It was all over. At least for now, Draven was off their backs and would leave them alone. Sapphire, Karim, Annie, Michael, Caroline, Marcus, Paul, Judy and the remaining Rimor agents all gathered together around Ruby, Emerald and Tony.

"That's that I guess, we're off Draven's kill list for now." Ruby said half-jokingly.

"What a relief!" Emerald exclaimed, putting a hand to her heart, "Now we don't have to worry about him anymore!"

"I'm so glad he's letting us go." Tony said happily, "It's lucky for us that he has a good side."

"I'd more call it an honourable side myself." Ruby suggested, "Still, it's a pity the staff had to be destroyed. We could've solved everything with it." she lamented.

"I'm sorry!" Emerald whimpered, "It was my fault! I dropped the staff and the Cyber Dragon shot it!"

"No, it was my fault." Karim muttered, "I caused the Cyber Dragon to malfunction and go crazy. If I hadn't been so bad at using my powers, I wouldn't have caused this to happen."

"Alright children, let's not play the blame game." Annie said softly, "There's no need for that. All that matters is we're all alive and the hunters will let us be. Now that's over, we can just relax and enjoy the rest of our holiday."

"I second that." Caroline agreed.

"So what now mum?" Sapphire asked, "We've pretty much seen the glacier now."

"We'll have to get back before the place opens up for the tourists." Paul noted, "We'll be in for some tricky explanations if we're all still here by then."

The group quickly left the glacier and made their way back to the car park so they could catch the bus back to the docks. After all that, the Silverlock and Summers families wanted nothing more than to just relax and chill out back on the *MS Nova*. They'd seen the glacier, so they wouldn't need a day out in Olden. They could spend the rest of the day on the ship and be ready for tomorrow when they would visit Haugseund. That was sure to be less action packed than this whole fight at the foot of Briksdal glacier! As everyone headed back, Tony walked beside Emerald and took her hand into his. Emerald looked to Tony in surprise. Tony smiled warmly at her.

"Thank you little gem, for everything." he whispered.

Then, with one last token of gratitude, he leaned forward and planted a kiss of thanks on her cheek. Emerald gasped and put a hand over her mouth. She blushed bright pink. Ruby and Sapphire giggled mischievously. They knew this would happen eventually, and here they were.

"Oh...um...y-y-you're w-welcome!" Emerald replied shyly.

She was just happy that Tony wasn't going to die now. His disease was gone and he could live happy and healthy again. This holiday was going to have a much more pleasant ending than it had initially seemed...

Chapter 16: The End of the Holiday

It took Alice a couple of hours before she finally woke up. In that time, Draven had arrived back at his submarine, given the order to return to base and taken Alice into his private cabin so the two could talk once she woke up. This was the one room on the submarine that nobody was allowed in except for Draven himself or Alice. It was the perfect place for the two to talk privately in the huge, dark vessel. The submarine sank back down into the water and sailed away out of the fjords, heading back to the ocean. It would be a long trip back to England, which meant Draven and Alice had all the time in the world to talk. For Alice, it wasn't going to be a pleasant one. The second-in-command groaned as she stirred back into consciousness. She found that she was lying on a bed in a dark room with dim, red lighting. Alice sat up and massaged her temples. Why did waking up from being knocked out by a stun blast always come with the mother of all headaches? She opened her eyes and saw that Draven was standing there, his arms folded and his cold, blue optics gazing back at her. Alice could sense straight away that something was wrong.

"Father?" she asked in bewilderment, "W-w-what's going on? Wh-where are we?"

"Back in the submarine, heading back home." Draven said coldly, **"And it's going to be a long trip, so make yourself comfortable. You and I are going to have a little chat, and it's not about anything good…"**

Alice gulped. Her lips quivered in fright.

"Wh-wh-what's this a-all about then? Why are you s-speaking t-to me as if I'm in trouble?" the tall woman stammered.

"Because you are, my dear." Draven snapped as if the answer as obvious, **"Would you care to tell me what that was all about back there?"**

Alice's head spun. What was he talking about? She cursed herself mentally. She knew exactly what Draven was referring to.

"This is all about me trying to kill Emerald, isn't it?" Alice answered, "Now father, if you just let me explain…"

"Explain what? That you deliberately disobeyed me and tried to enact your vengeful tendencies?" Draven said coldly, **"I made it EXPLICITY clear that this mission wasn't about us getting revenge on Ruby! And don't deny it, I heard you saying as clear as crystal to Ruby that you were "returning the favour" for what she nearly did to me! In your desire to get revenge, you attempted to murder an innocent girl, who has done nothing wrong, out of spite!"**

"Ruby nearly killed you father! She must pay for her crimes!" Alice protested, "Why are you defending her like this? You want her dead too, don't you?"

"Not for the reasons you want her dead!" Draven retorted, **"Revenge is a worthless cause and we do not kill out of revenge! We're protectors of mankind, not mercenaries carrying out acts of vengeance! And why did you try to kill Emerald in the first place? You know full well that only Ruby was the target, we weren't here to kill anybody else! She saved the life of an agent that YOU nearly killed, so she was especially off-limits!"**

"She was interfering with our mission father!" Alice snapped, "Thanks to her, the Staff of Wishes got destroyed! I was merely paying her back for jeopardizing our mission!"

"And then what? Killing her wouldn't have fixed the staff, would it?" Draven growled, **"Just like killing that vampire didn't bring your mother back! Your desire for revenge would've resulted in the needless murders of innocent civilians and compromised our position as protectors of mankind! Do you have ANY idea how serious the repercussions would be if it was found out we were killing innocent people? I told you already**

how the government would shut us down in a heartbeat! Do you want us to be shut down, Alice Daniels?!" he snarled.

"Of course I don't father! Don't suggest ridiculous things like that!" Alice screeched angrily.

"THEN DON'T DISOBEY DIRECT ORDERS!" Draven thundered, **"In this organization, I am in charge and when I give orders, I expect them to be obeyed to the letter! When I say someone is off-limits, they're off-limits and they're not to be killed!"**

"So you're perfectly fine with letting Ruby and her friends live despite the fact they all have magic powers now?" Alice scoffed, "Did you not pay attention when Ruby's sisters and Karim also displayed magic powers too? Are you OK with letting them become a threat to mankind despite wanting Ruby dead?"

"I'll confess, I didn't consider them at the time. I was hyper-focused on Ruby and then later the Staff of Wishes." Draven admitted, **"But with the Staff of Wishes, I would've at least removed their magic without needing to kill them. My wish may not have been granted, but maybe there was some loophole I could've exploited to get it granted. As is, Ruby used her powers to save my life, so in gratitude; we're calling off the hunt for her and giving her a chance to continue using her powers for good."**

Alice stared at Draven in shock and disgust. She felt as if he'd slapped her across the face. She couldn't believe what she was hearing.

"WHAT?! You let her go?! You're just going to let the little brat live in spite of what she's done?!" Alice shrieked in disbelief.

"Yes, she did nearly kill me, but she made it clear to me that she regretted her part in that, and it was that which drove her to saving me from being killed by the Cyber Dragon after it went haywire." Draven replied, **"You should be grateful to her since it's thanks to Ruby and her powers that the Cyber Dragon didn't kill**

us all and destroy the glacier. Since she proved herself heroic and willing to save lives despite us being on opposing sides, I think it's fair we give her a chance and continue to prove that she's not a threat to mankind, but a protector. She may even be able to prove to us all that the supernatural can be a force for good after all..." he said thoughtfully.

Alice was speechless. She felt as if she was going crazy. Was she sure she wasn't still unconscious and this whole thing was some crazy dream she was having?

"What's happened to you father?!" the second-in-command asked, her voice full of shame and disappointment, "This isn't like you at all! That girl must've messed with your head or something! I bet she's pulling some kind of witchcraft on you and is making you crazy!"

Draven grabbed Alice by the collar of her coat and yanked her off the bed. He brought her right up close to her face, so close that Alice had to close her eyes because his optics were too bright to look at. Her heart began to race with terror. Her breath caught in her throat. Draven had never gotten physical with her in this way before.

"I am perfectly fine Alice. There's no witchcraft at play here." Draven growled softly, **"I've merely had my eyes opened to possibilities that I'd never considered before. Emerald used magic to save a life, Ruby also used magic to save a life, hence we should let them have the chance to save more lives with their magic. If we want to be mankind's protectors, then we have to give people like them a chance to do so too. If magic can be used as a means to save mankind from threats, then we should let it."**

He dropped Alice back on the bed. Alice gasped loudly and panted furiously, her nerves still shaking from the shock of what had happened. Draven gave her a minute to recover before he spoke again.

"**Rest assured dear daughter, I'm not letting Ruby or her friends and family off the hook entirely.**" Draven said, speaking more softly and gently, "**I've made it clear to Ruby that if she steps out of line, then we will come for her again. I have a feeling she'll take it very much to heart.**"

"I'd rather we kill her now before she even has a chance to become a threat..." Alice growled viciously.

"**Do you? Or would you rather we killed her now just so you can have the satisfaction of seeing her dead in order to satisfy your meaningless need for revenge?**" Draven asked coldly.

Alice fell silent. She didn't want to openly admit it, but Draven had her all figured out. Even now, she couldn't dare bring herself to lie to her father. Her silence was the only answer Draven needed. He shook his head in disappointment.

"**I thought I'd raised you better than this. It's clear that I was wrong.**" the cyborg muttered, "**Your actions both today and back in Stavanger leave me with no choice...Alice Daniels, you are confined to headquarters. Permanently. You will under no circumstances ever be allowed out on the field again. I only wish I didn't have to take such an extreme measure, but if it keeps you on a tight leash and prevents you from potentially jeopardizing all future missions, then so be it.**"

His voice was heavy and full of despair, evident signs that he meant what he said about wishing it didn't have to come to this. If Alice could see Draven's face, she'd see he was dismayed and full of shame. Not that she cared how he felt at the moment. All she could think about right now was the rising anger boiling in her blood as she began to see red. She shot up from the bed and glared directly into her father's optics. Draven didn't flinch.

"WHAT?!" Alice screamed, her face a mask of uncontrollable rage, "After everything I've done for this organization, after serving you loyally for many years, after saving your life after Ruby came so close to killing you, THIS IS THE THANKS THAT I GET?!?!"

"This is the thanks you deserve." Draven snapped, **"Disobedient children need to be punished. Talk to me in that way again, and I'll have you relieved of duty in my organization. Do you understand?"**

Alice gritted her teeth and clenched her fists. She was shaking with nerves. She had so many things she wanted to say, but none of which would win favour with her father. It was best for her own sake that she didn't dig herself an even deeper grave to throw herself into. Sighing heavily, Alice slumped back down on the bed and looked down at the floor. She couldn't even look at her father anymore. Draven nodded, taking that as her answer. He turned around and headed on out of the cabin.

"I'll leave you here to come to terms with your punishment." Draven said solemnly, **"I only hope you've learned a valuable lesson here today..."**

At this point, he sounded completely drained and tired. He no longer had any other feelings in him, only a hollow feeling in his chest that things had had to go so sour with him and his daughter. He left the cabin, closing the door behind him. Alice waited until she could no longer hear his footsteps as he walked away. The moment she was sure she was completely alone and nobody could hear her, she stood up from the bed again. Then she threw her head back and a primal scream of rage, despair and anguish erupted from her throat. She'd wanted so much to please her father, and instead she'd only disappointed him. And it was all Ruby Silverlock's fault! If that wretched girl had never gotten involved in their affairs in the first place, none of this would've happened. Alice crashed her fists against the wall and screamed angrily again. Tears of anger trickled down her face. She pounded the wall again, imagining that she was smashing Ruby's face into a bloody mess with her fists. She panted heavily and dug her nails into her palms. Her eyes had narrowed into pinpricks of fury.

"I'll get you Ruby Silverlock, you mark my words! Father may be willing to let you go, but I'm not! I'll be coming for you, and I WILL kill you, you see if I don't!" Alice roared, "Damn what my father says, Ruby Silverlock will pay for this if it's the last thing I do!"

Once the hunters were back at headquarters, she would begin formulating a plan to get her hands on the insolent girl. Next time she and Ruby met, it wasn't going to end well for the silver-haired teen...

After the Silverlock and Summers families had gotten back to the ship, they both went into their cabins to have a much needed rest. They were worn out from the climb up to the glacier and the big battle with Draven and also the fact they'd gotten up really early. They settled down to sleep for the rest of the morning, not waking up again until lunch time. After they'd had something to eat, both families returned to their cabins again and the Silverlock sisters thought now would be a good time to call the Cooper family and let them know about the Staff of Wishes. They'd told the whole story from Emerald going into the glacier to get it to the battle and how it had ended with the staff destroyed and Draven in Ruby's debt for saving his life. The trio had been intrigued by the story and were naturally thrilled to hear the staff was real. All these years of believing it to be a story, it turned out to actually exist. They had also been shocked to hear that Draven wasn't dead. At first, Selina had been enraged, but she also came to see it as a good thing since it meant Ruby didn't have to feel guilty over his death anymore, which meant she was much happier knowing she wasn't a murderer.

"While it sucks the Staff of Wishes was destroyed before we could use it to fix everything, at least we were able to save Tony's life and we've convinced Draven to leave me alone for now." Ruby concluded, "Needless to see, our little holiday became a big adventure like we weren't expecting!"

"Yeah. Emphasis on BIG." Selina Cooper muttered bluntly as if Ruby had told her the most boring story of all time.

"I appreciate that you were able to confirm to us that the staff was real at all." Betty said graciously, "I only wish, no pun intended, that we could've seen it ourselves..."

"It was for the best it got destroyed." Howard said matter-of-factly, "Now we won't have to worry about the staff falling into the wrong hands."

"Too right." Ruby agreed, "God, I'd hate to think what would've happened if the hunters tried to use it..."

"It was lucky for us it refused to grant Draven's wish!" Emerald cut in, "We'd all have lost our magic powers if he got what he wanted! Thank goodness Gideon Trammell put restrictions on what wishes the staff could grant or we'd have had a lot of dead bodies and no magic left in the world."

The Coopers nodded. Nobody was more grateful than they that Draven's wish couldn't have been granted in the end. Their family had used magic for generations, it was unthinkable to imagine the next generation of Coopers growing up without it.

"So how about Draven? Do you think he'll keep his word?" Selina asked curiously, "You really think he'll back off now you've saved his life?"

"I think he will." Ruby said with an air of certainty, "He seemed genuinely grateful to me for saving him. He also saved Emerald from getting killed. He didn't have to do it, but he did it anyway. It seems we've pegged him wrong this whole time."

"Yeah, it seems even a monster like him has an honourable side." Sapphire agreed, "Though we must remember that he will come back for us if we're seen as a threat, so we have to continue to prove to him that we're no danger to anyone."

"That'll be easy! We're good girls, we'll use our magic for good!" Emerald piped excitedly, "Draven will easily see we're not dangerous!"

"We tried to convince him of that years ago and it fell on deaf ears." Selina said bitterly, "I'm frankly surprised it took you saving him from being blasted to bits to finally convince him that magic doesn't equal bad."

"I guess somebody had to do it eventually." Ruby said with a shrug, "I only hope he'll take my suggestion to heart and let us handle supernatural creatures before he goes around killing them. Though I'm convinced he'll dismiss that idea completely..." she said grimly.

"Yeah, don't be surprised." Selina said bluntly.

Ruby was about to bring the conversation to a close until suddenly, Emerald remembered something and she quickly whipped her phone out.

"Hold on a second, I just remembered!" she said quickly, "I forgot to mention this, but I saw some kind of cave drawing when found the Staff of Wishes. I don't know what it's about, but I think you might know."

She put her phone screen to Ruby's so the Cooper family could see it. The Coopers stared at the photo of the cave drawing that Emerald had taken. Ruby and Sapphire stared at the photo as well, they too were intrigued at the picture.

"What is that?" Ruby murmured.

"We have no idea." Betty said solemnly, "I wish we could tell you what it is dear, but all I can guess is that it's a drawing of an old battle from centuries past. Looks like a duel between a wizard and a demon of some kind."

"Could it be Lord Hallows?" Sapphire suggested, "Maybe that's the demon in the picture and he's fighting against Gideon Trammell for the staff?"

"No, that's not Gideon in the picture." Howard confirmed, "He doesn't look anything like that man."

The sisters gasped in astonishment.

"Then...who is he?" Ruby blurted in confusion.

"Beats me." Selina said with a nonchalant shrug, "Just like how we've never heard of Lord Hallows, we don't know who that guy is. Maybe he's Hallows's arch-enemy for all we know."

"Well then, I guess me and my sisters better investigate this." Ruby declared, "As supernatural explorers, we'll see if we can solve the mystery of who that wizard is and who he's fighting! Gosh, just wait til we show this to Karim, he'll get his dad and all of Rimor looking into this in a flash!" she chuckled.

"We should show him once we're done here." Sapphire decided, "Once our holiday's over, we have ourselves quite a mystery to delve into."

"We'd be happy to look into that too." Betty said eagerly, "If he has any descendants still alive to this day, we could potentially find ourselves a new magical family to make friends with. Maybe we're not the only family of sorcerers left in Galarsfield after all..." she said thoughtfully.

"Whatever we find out, I'm sure it'll be an incredible discovery." Ruby said optimistically, "We'll see you all later when we come home in a couple of days."

"You too, darlings. Enjoy the rest of your cruise." Betty said sweetly.

After the conversation had finished, the Silverlock sisters met up with Karim and Tony and told the boys all about Emerald's cave drawing discovery. As expected, Karim was instantly fascinated and wanted to tell Idris about it.

"Talk about finding more than what we came for!" he said excitedly, "We came for the Staff of Wishes and also find out there's a cave drawing of some mystery wizard fighting a monster! Hoo boy, dad's going to flip when he hears this!"

"We knew you'd be excited to see this!" Emerald giggled.

"I have to admit, my curiosity is piqued as well." Tony said with fascination, "Who was that wizard and who, or what, was he fighting? I'm sure you and your friends at Rimor will find that out." he said supportively.

"If anyone will find out, it'll be us supernatural explorers!" Ruby said enthusiastically, "Now I think about it, I wonder if this wizard has something to do with my protection spell..." she murmured curiously.

"I doubt it." Karim said dismissively, "The guy will be dead by now if that drawing's anything to go by. He'd have to be immortal to put a spell on you."

"Who's to say he isn't?" Sapphire retorted, "I'm sure magic can grant immortality. And besides, it doesn't have to be that wizard specifically who did it, his descendants, if he has any, could've done it."

"I guess." Karim said uncertainly, "Only way we'll find out is by investigating it! We should get right to it the moment our holiday's over."

"If I may ask, would it be OK if I could join you all in your adventures?" Tony asked.

He'd put his hand up shyly, like a student in a classroom wanting permission to speak to the teacher. Ruby, Emerald, Sapphire and Karim looked at Tony in surprise. They hadn't expected him to suddenly ask a question like that.

"You want to join us?" Karim asked, "I'm all for anyone joining us, mate, but where's this coming from?"

"Well, it's mostly out of gratitude for Emerald saving my life with that staff." Tony admitted, "And it's also down to how I wanted to help you all in that battle, but I wasn't able to do anything. I was powerless. You were all able to do incredible things like throwing fire, shooting ice, throwing rocks with your mind and making shields to protect yourself, and I wasn't able to help. So, if you'll let me join you and learn magic as you all have, would that be alright? Or is that a really tall order?" he concluded, smiling queasily.

He didn't have to wait long for a response for Emerald threw her arms around him and hugged him tight. She looked as if Tony had just told her he'd won the lottery and wanted to share the money with her.

"Of course we'll take you in! We'd love to have you on the team!" Emerald shrieked happily.

"I think she actually means SHE'D love to have you on the team." Sapphire said cheekily.

"In any case, I don't think the Cooper family will object to teaching someone else magic." Karim said casually, "We'll be sure to ask them about it. And I'm sure my dad will be happy to train you as he's been training me and the girls."

"Oh that would be splendid." Tony said brightly, "Though much like my little gem here, I think I'd rather be a healer than a fighter."

"Two healers on one team? That'd be pretty handy actually." Ruby said approvingly, "Though you will still need to learn some combat skills Tony, even Emerald's had to learn how to fight as well."

"By all means, I'll do it, just as long as I don't have to hurt anyone too badly." Tony said meekly.

"I think you'll do great, just as I have." Emerald said brightly, "I may still get scared easily, but I've become a lot braver since training with Rimor and the Coopers. I think you will too. It's going to be so great having you on the team as well Tony!"

Tony only laughed in response.

"Likewise little gem." he said smoothly, "Though I'll need to convince mum and dad to let me go through with this..." he added nervously.

"I'm sure they'll let you." Ruby said reassuringly, "We can talk with them about it when the holiday's over. For now, we should just focus on enjoying the rest of it while we still can. We only have tomorrow and the day after before we return to England."

"Then let's have some fun together before it's over!" Emerald said eagerly, "And now you're not sick anymore Tony, you'll be able to join in with us."

"Oh I certainly will." Tony said happily, "In fact, how's about a dip in the pool together? I'm itching for a swim now I'm all cured."

It didn't surprise the girls at all that that was the first thing on Tony's to-do-list. They imagined that swimming was the one thing he'd missed the most since being diagnosed with his disease and having to miss out because of it. Later on, all five teens decided to go in the ship's pool together. After their experiences that morning, they were due for something more fun and laid back. Annie, Michael, Caroline and Marcus accompanied the kids to the pool and sat in the deck chairs nearby to watch over them as they went in. Paul and Judy were watching too. The pair were quietly pleased to see the teens just able to kick back and have fun for the rest of the holiday, no longer needing to worry about the hunters anymore. They'd have to make the most of it, for once they got back to England, it'd be back to training all over again and they'd be making all of them work extra hard. The battle against Draven had only proven that the girls and Karim had a long way to go before they were anywhere near their level. They'd had Draven outnumbered and he still handled them with ease. But for now, they could just stand back and let the children enjoy themselves. The five friends spent a wonderful, fun-filled hour or two in the pool together swimming around, splashing each other, creeping up and making one another jump in surprise and playing games with a beach ball. In that moment, everything from this morning was forgotten about. It was as if the hunters had never showed up on this holiday. For now, any and all problems they'd had were gone and they were just there in the moment having a good time. It made Emerald feel good inside to see Tony looking so fit again and playing about without a care in the world. The Staff of Wishes had more than done its job. Her best friend was back to his old self again, his health no longer under threat. She couldn't wait for him to join the team and get magic powers too. It was going to be even more enjoyable having him around to join her and her sisters on their adventures.

Once this cruise was over, whole new adventures would be waiting for Emerald, her sisters and their friends. They had no idea what their adventures would entail, but they would be ready to tackle them as a team, and with Rimor teaching them how to fight and the Coopers teaching them how to use magic, no threat would be too great for them to handle...

Author's Notes

Alright, you made it to the end of the book again...glad you did!

I hope you enjoyed reading the second title of *The Silverlock Sisters* series and found it a worthy sequel to the first. I know I had a good time writing it and I hope you had a good time reading it.

When I conjured up *The Silverlock Sisters*, I planned it right from the start for it to be a series, and you no doubt realized that with how *Supernatural Explorer* ended with so many plot-threads hanging and left unanswered. I thought with the series starring three protagonists that it only made sense that the first two sequels would focus on the other sisters. Ruby was the star of the first book, so Emerald and Sapphire are the stars of the second and third books. You'll see Sapphire get her starring role in the next title, which is titled *Sapphire Silverlock: The Curse of the Dragon Tattoo* and I intend to release that one at about the end of the year. What's that story going to be about? You'll find out in due time.

For now, let's talk about this book. *Emerald Silverlock: A Cruise To Adventure* is a story actually inspired by life experiences. Like the girls did in this story, I actually did go on a holiday cruise around Norway back in 2023. We sailed with P&O Cruises on the *MS Iona* and as you might've already guessed, we visited the exact same locations that the girls have done here. We started in Stavanger, then went to Ålesund, then Olden and finished in Haugseund. A lot of the things they see and do are also things I saw and did when visiting there, including dinner at their local pizza chain, visiting the all year round Christmas shop and taking troll cars up to see the glacier. Though I guarantee I didn't go in any caves to find any magical staffs when we went...or did I? (grins mischievously) Jokes aside, Norway is an absolutely beautiful country and I knew I had to write a story involving a Norwegian cruise, which this series provided the perfect excuse for. When mapping out the story, I felt that the Briksdal glacier Olden would be the perfect setting for the climax. It seemed like a logical place for a magical item to be hidden away, and also the large, spacious scenery and beautiful glacial lake provided a lot of opportunities for the final fight to be exciting and action-packed.

Ruby's struggles with trauma and having to acknowledge she needed help were also another life experience thing. While I haven't actually suffered trauma in my life, I did have a period of anxiety where I'd frequently have panic attacks over changes in my life, weird feelings in my body and it got to the point where I actually considered ending my life. Instead, my parents would seek help and eventually, we found ways for me to cope with my anxieties and nowadays, I don't panic over little things anymore. Although I still struggle sometimes with larger issues/changes, I know it's OK and will pass. Ruby's struggles are considerably greater than mine of course since she had to deal with the fact she believed that she'd killed a man. Like me, she was in denial of needing help for a time and only after several talks with her family did she come to accept she needed it in the end. I hope from myself and Ruby that you can take away the important lesson that it's OK to seek help if you're suffering and struggling in life. Don't be afraid to reach out and talk to others, there's ALWAYS someone out there who will listen and help you out.

If you're curious on what behind-the-scenes trivia I may have, I do have some titbits to share. I originally planned to end this story with another Lord Hallows scene at the end in where he laments over the loss of the Staff of Wishes but croons how his plans won't be impeded by it in any way. In the end, I decided not to put the scene in. It might diminish Hallows's mysterious nature if he just appears in every book and monologues to himself. Instead, having him cameo via a cave drawing gave him a presence to show that his shadow very much hangs over our characters but without forcing in a scene of him talking to himself like last time.

And it may interest you to know that the couple standing near Judy and watching the view on Page 145 are actually cameos of myself and my girlfriend. I actually suggested putting us in there as passengers on the ship and she was naturally all for it. If you're reading this my love, just know that I love you lots and thank you for reading. XXX

Also, Draven originally didn't have that deep worry about whether he was a good man or not. That idea was a suggestion from my friend, R.M. Walls (author of *The Solitale Vampires* and *Misty Beetle*) after I sent him the first chapter as a preview. He felt Draven should be troubled by the angel statue considering his men impure and what that means to him, and I was happy to include that. It added more layers to Draven's character for the readers to peel away and I feel it's helped to make him a more three-dimensional character. He's not just a one-note villain as you can see here.

Also, when concepting the plot, I once considered making it so the Silverlock sisters meet an actual troll. It just seemed fitting a plot point for a story set in Norway. But I thought making up my own creature would be more creative and also avoid me unintentionally offending anyone by getting cultures wrong and all. Hence the troll was dropped and I made up a creature I called a Hydrogriff. It's a horse-like creature made of water and was based on the Nokk from Norwegian mythology. It very nearly got included in the story, but I came to realize that including the Hydrogriff, Ruby's trauma, the cruise to Norway, the Staff of Wishes and Tony's illness made the story feel too cramped full of stuff and so the Hydrogriff had to be dropped as it was the least important of all the plot-points I had here. Making it just about the Staff of Wishes made the story more straight forward and coherent to follow and it was for the best I did so. The Hydrogriff might appear in another book, but we'll see on that for now...

As is, I thank everyone who purchased and read *Ruby Silverlock: Supernatural Explorer* and also left reviews for it on Amazon, and I thank you all again for purchasing and reading this one. If you want to stay updated on all future books from me, follow me on Instagram (username themediamanblog) and Facebook (username Scott Tatt) or visit my website, www.themediamanblog.com[1], and also follow my Author Page on Amazon. I'll see you all again when *Sapphire Silverlock: The Curse of the Dragon Tattoo* is completed. Happy reading everyone and I hope to see you again in the next book!

---

1. http://www.themediamanblog.com

www.ingramcontent.com/pod-product-compliance
Lightning Source LLC
Chambersburg PA
CBHW061430150726
47987CB00001B/162